Praise for *South Beach*

"From the old Jewish retirees and Cuban refugees to Miami's greedy developers and international super celebs. Wild and scary sex scenes, but also tender love and redemption. Brian Antoni is the unofficial mayor of South Beach. This tour of America's most decadent, nauseatingly hip time and place is hilarious, moving, extremely readable, and picture perfect. You might just recognize some boldface names and their bold doings, I did." —Patrick McMullan, author of *S08Os* and *Glamour Girls*

"Brian Antoni brilliantly captures that fleeting moment when South Beach was young and wild, where New Yorkers, the international fashion crowd, and Miami's choice specimens of beauty created the cultural combustion that defined America's newest decadent/sensual destination. Antoni lived among these pioneers, social mavericks, artists, image elitists, and real-estate predators who inspired this memorable novel."
—Glenn Albin, editor in chief of *Ocean Drive Magazine*

"In his book, *South Beach: The Novel*, Brian Antoni perfectly captures the essence of this wild, crazy, surreal, pharmaceutically and alcohol fueled place. He writes about people and events here with a connoisseur's discerning eye, which should not be surprising, considering he's had a front row seat to it all for years." —Carolina Garcia-Aguilera, author of *One Hot Summer*

SOUTH BEACH

The Novel

Also by Brian Antoni

Paradise Overdose

SOUTH BEACH

The Novel

Brian Antoni

Black Cat
New York
a paperback original imprint of Grove/Atlantic, Inc.

Published simultaneously in Canada
Printed in the United States of America

FIRST EDITION

ISBN-10: 0-8021-7043-9
ISBN-13: 978-0-8021-7043-9

Black Cat
a paperback original imprint of Grove/Atlantic, Inc.
841 Broadway
New York, NY 10003

Distributed by Publishers Group West

www.groveatlantic.com

08 09 10 11 12   10 9 8 7 6 5 4 3 2 1

To my parents,
Lynette Tucker-Antoni and Dr. Robert Antoni

SOUTH BEACH

The Novel

SUNSTROKER

by Skip Bowling

What's happening on South Beach, aka God's Waiting Room, Mausoleum In the Sun, the Elephants' Graveyard, Varicose Beach, the Place Where Neon Goes to Die?

It all started when **Christo** wrapped beer can islands in Biscayne Bay and turned the eyes of the world not only on the flamingo pink crowns but on this lost in time deco land. It all started when *Miami Vice* realized that sherbet-colored decay would make a perfect backdrop promoting not only unstructured linen jackets and "three-day bender" facial stubble but South Beach itself. It all started when New York Anglo boys discovered Miami Cuban boys. It all started when the first fashion photographers, after a night at a "let us worship the erection" party, noticed the perfect light on their way home and realized South Beach was the perfect place to shoot not only their loads but their photos.

This led to a migration of tender young models who became little more than expensive chum, exotic garnish, for the straight moneyed and powered. Well-to-do dogs descended, accompanied by an entourage of sleazy crooks, visionary hustlers and hangers-on, and they all needed a place to screw! Real estate, the true Miami art form. Rehab it and they will cum. Sloppy seconds for all. Redo cheap hotel

rooms while using each other like cheap hotel rooms. Forget
about the beautiful old Jews that have lived here for the
greater part of this century. They are an eyesore. Chic
buildings don't go with shabby people. Glamour and geezer
clash.

I checked out celebrity, local bad boy, actor-pugilist
Mickey Rourke's bar—**Mickey's Place** (aka Mickey's Rats
by locals because of the seedy-boxing-club-meets-mafia décor,
a Cosa Nostra **Friday's**). There was the odd tourist trying to
get a glimpse of the star of *9½ Weeks.* But, Mr. Rourke was
nowhere to be found after his arrest last night for resisting
arrest after an impromptu fight outside his club. I ran across
Lord Michael Caruso, New York's hot club promoter (**Tunnel,
Limelight**), who was in town scouting a space. He introduced
me to his hunky-in-a-Guido-way partner, **Chris Paciello,** who
showed me his lower-abs tattoo of a masked gangster,
complete with a smoking gun, stolen cash and the legend
"Easy Money."

Our eclectic island home has been christened by the magic
word, "HIP." And God help us when fairy dust is spread from
Lincoln Road Mall to **Joe's Stone Crab.** Where will this
slippery slope of lust, this designer food chain, this fab
Darwinian hand job lead us? Heaven or hell. Sometimes I
think they are the same place.

Gabriel Gets the Letter

Gabriel Tucker's head was overflowing with a gobbledy-gook of been-there, done-that, bought-the-T-shirt. He was a twenty-nine-year-old rolling stone that collected a lot of moss. He kept telling himself that he'd know when to stop, kind of like you're supposed to know when you've found true love. Then he got the letter.

Gabriel could sniff out the sleaziest part of a place, could smell the edge. That's where he felt the best. He tried to live as cheaply as possible even though at the time he was worth millions. Gabriel checked into a hotel, called the Bee's Knees, in the Shinjuku neighborhood of Tokyo. Shinjuku was all covered in neon. He loved neon the way other people loved nature.

The Bee's Knees was for men only. Instead of rooms, there were fiberglass capsules, piled on top of each other, floor to ceiling. Each had a TV and an alarm clock embedded in the shell. It was like being in an incubator or a coffin. Gabriel liked it because he felt isolated and connected at the same time.

That afternoon, Gabriel went to the American Express office to pick up his mail and to get his monthly stipend from the trust fund that his grandfather Alvin had set up for him.

He had been traveling for over a decade now. The longer he stayed away, the fewer letters he received. People were forgetting him. The only mail he received were trust statements from his uncle Ian. He would use the back of these pages to write his travel journal.

Gabriel would mail these pages to an apartment in a building he owned in Miami Beach called the Venus de Milo Arms, which his grandfather left to him in his will.

The key Gabriel had to the door of his apartment in the Venus, his official residence, was made of solid gold and had a diamond at the top. His grandfather left the key to him in his will also. When people asked Gabriel where he came from, he would stroke the diamond-studded, golden key and answer, "The Venus de Milo Arms." If there was any anchor in Gabriel's life, then it must have been the old, elusive "Venus," which his grandfather had never stopped talking about. It seemed like the only thing his grandfather missed about America since his forced tax exile to numerous tax havens right before Gabriel was born. Gabriel felt no connection to anywhere because they were always moving to stay one step ahead of extradition. He was sure his grandfather would have taken him to see the Venus if he wouldn't have been arrested for tax evasion the second he entered the United States.

Gabriel smiled to himself thinking that his one anchor was a building he had never seen, in a city he had never visited. But even rolling stones had to have a home, and for Gabriel, the old Venus would serve.

There was a letter from his uncle Ian waiting for him at the AmEx office in Tokyo:

Dear Gabriel,

I regret to inform you that when you get this letter, I'll be dead and you'll be broke. I lost all your money and my money in the market. Your trust is empty. You still have the Venus de Milo Arms because, as you know, Alvin's will stipulated that only you could sell it. I suggest you do because it's falling down. I am now going to jump off the roof of your Venus. I would rather be dead than broke.

No hard feelings,
Love,
Uncle Ian

Jesus Gets a Stop Sign

Jesus Mas Canosa shut his eyes and saw red—the red color of a stop sign. He lay naked on the overly stuffed, flattened-with-age, goose down bed of Señora Helena Ruth. He had absolute black hair, huge dreamy dark eyes and succulent overripe lips. He was a Cuban Billy Budd.

Señora Helena Ruth shivered with anticipation as she stared at Jesus' hard, twenty-one-year-old body. The only other man who'd ever made her feel this way before was Fidel Castro.

Helena was nude except for a new blue, faux-fur stole that she'd bought with black market U.S. dollars at the Hotel National. The sales clerk had told her it was the height of fashion in Miami, not knowing that it was the height of fashion not to wear, but to put on the floor around your toilet.

Helena lightly stroked the toilet rug that hung around her neck, as she reached her other hand between her long legs. She still had beautiful legs even though she was sixty years old, but the rest of her had surrendered to gravity.

Jesus stared out past Señora Helena Ruth, out past the billowing curtains of yellowed crochet, out past the leaking red barrel-tiled rooftops of what was once Havana's most exclusive neighborhood and even out over the indigo sea. He kept staring until he saw all the way to Miami. This was the last time, he told himself, the last time he would be a whore.

"*Muy* sexy," Jesus cooed. In truth, he didn't see Helena as she was, a fat elderly woman complete with brittle, black-rooted, peroxide hair and a garishly made up face. Instead, he saw a painting by Botero, one of the Three Graces, Mother Earth, an ancient fertility goddess. That was why he was such a good whore. He was always able to find something beautiful in everyone. But he was not only a whore with a heart of gold; he also had a dick of gold.

Jesus half-smiled at Helena, his pearly teeth glinting. All he had was beauty, which he knew he needed to trade on before it tarnished. That is why he had to get to Miami.

"Bad *niño*," Helena pronounced as if she were scolding a child.

"*Lo siento!*" he apologized in a little boy voice. "I'm sorry."

"I want that you must stay a boy," she ordered.

Jesus spread his legs shamelessly. He knew this script by heart. He just wanted to get to the last act.

"What this?" Helena asked, pointing at his sparse patch of blue-black pubic hair. Other than this and his underarms, his body was hairless and smooth and the color of molten copper.

"It just grew," he answered, feigning embarrassment. He was a gifted actor.

"You becoming a man."

"No," he protested.

"What do men do?" she asked.

Jesus shook his head.

"Men hurt women, men hurt women, men hurt women," she repeated over and over like a mantra, removing her toilet rug and gingerly folding it and placing it on a hanger, then covering it in the plastic bag in which it had come wrapped marked "Bed, Bath & Beyond."

"So what we must do?" she asked, grabbing a tweezers from her bedside table.

"We must stop that I becoming a man," Jesus replied.

Helena's hands shivered. She plucked one of his pubic hairs out with the tweezers, dropped it into her shoebox marked "Payless."

"He loves me," Helena chanted. She touched herself with her other hand, took a deep breath. "He loves me not," she gasped.

Jesus distracted himself by practicing English in his head. He knew if he was going to succeed in America, he must speak English. *Peter Piper picked a peck of pickled peppers,* he practiced. *Helena Ruth picks a pound of pubic hairs.*

Each pluck felt like a mosquito bite. Each pluck was a U.S. penny. Each pluck took him closer to Miami. He needed one dollar to buy the stop sign. She was sweating and giving off the sweet smell of Agua de Florida.

"This hurt me more than it hurt you," Helena announced, and Jesus knew this was a sign that she was about to orgasm. Her head rolled back. She was at number ninety-six.

"He loves me. He loves me not." She breathed heavy, ninety-seven. A black mascara tear escaped from her left eye.

"He love me! He love me not!" The stained tear trailed a snail path.

"He loved me!" she exhaled between gritted teeth. She came at exactly one hundred, as the seam of the mattress ripped, exhaling a cloud of fluffy feathers which hung unnaturally long in the sun-touched air before fluttering earthward.

Jesus thought it was a sign from God that he wanted him to go to Miami. She dropped the tweezers. He looked down, his eyes following falling feathers. He had no pubic hair left. He was totally smooth.

"How much, boy?" Helena asked, curtly. She refused to look at him, turned into a different person.

"One hundred cents," Jesus answered.

"As always, you cheat me," she scolded, taking a folded U.S. dollar bill from her purse and dropping it onto the wet spot of her bed.

Jesus grabbed the buck and dressed. He knew he wasn't supposed to say anything afterward. Those were her rules, but he couldn't help himself.

"Adios," he whispered.

Helena looked up angrily.

"I go forever."

"There is no place to go. I keep you a boy forever."

"No," Jesus declared. "I will be a man!"

"To where do you think you are to go?"

"Miami!" he announced, and it was like he'd said a magic word.

"And I go to the moon," she snickered.

Jesus fixed his eyes on her. She stopped laughing, instantly. She pushed a Polar beer and a brown paper bag into his hands.

"Gracias," Jesus answered, and walked out and sat down on the steps in front of her apartment building, El Edificio de las Cajas de Muertos. He opened the brown bag. There was a sandwich inside. He took a bite. It was sweet and salty at the same time. It tasted of turkey and cranberry jelly on soft white bread. It was the best thing he had ever eaten. He felt like he was eating America.

Gabriel Gets a Job

at the Lucky Hole

Back in Japan, Gabriel Tucker sat in his capsule in the Bee's Knees Hotel, rereading the letter from his uncle Ian. He felt like he had also jumped off the roof of the Venus de Milo Arms, though it bothered him that he could not picture the details: the stairs, the roof, the ground below. His anchor was a name and a key and not a real-life building. And his greatest fear had come true. He was broke.

He walked across the street to the *sento*, the public baths. He craved water, as if he could wash away what had happened. He sat on a dwarfish white plastic stool, wet himself, scrubbed his body hard with soft soap.

Japanese men stared at him as he gazed in the mirror. No matter how unhealthy a life he led, he continued to be six feet three inches of hard body.

As he washed off the suds, a gang of Kazuki, gangster pimps, sauntered into the baths. They stopped and stared at him.

Gabriel met their stare, thinking of Brutus from Popeye, their muscled, inked bodies reminding him of comic books. The biggest, toughest-looking guy's dick had a tattoo of a snake coiled around it.

Snake said something to him in Japanese. Gabriel didn't understand. The whole gang laughed. Then, Snake grabbed his hand and pulled him into the hottest tub. Gabriel's feet, his legs, burned up to his knees. Gabriel refused to feel, refused to show pain. He grinned instead.

Steam rose out of the tub like out of a pot of rapidly boiling water. Snake slowly submerged himself up to his neck, gritting his teeth. Everyone was watching. Gabriel took the challenge. He dunked his whole body and then his head completely underwater. He stayed submerged, holding his breath and boiling. He told himself he would hold his breath until he was dead. Being broke was as good as being dead.

The next thing he knew, hands were grabbing him. He heard Japanese voices grow more agitated as the water dripped from his ears. Gabriel opened his eyes right when Snake was about to give him mouth-to-mouth. Gabriel cringed, spat up water and wiped his mouth, and then he took a deep breath and air never tasted so sweet.

Everyone clapped. Gabriel stood up, bowed stiffly, very Japanese-like.

After they dressed, Snake led him through the Shinjuku Nii-Chome neighborhood, past the noodle dens, the twenty-four-hour love hotels, the *okonomiaki* stalls, the fetish mix boxes, the gay pride boutiques, the karaoke bars, the pachinko parlors. From street to sky, a carnival of neon signs repulsed and attracted him: "Transistor Glamour," "Glan's Freak," "Morning Tissue," "G. Shower," "Hotel Nuts" and simply "Cunt." Finally, they entered a club called Lucky Hole. It was mucous membrane–colored. A round bed sat on a circular stage, surrounded by mirrors on three sides. The other side had rows of velvet theater seats.

Snake stuffed a wad of yen into Gabriel's pocket. "Money, money for fucky, fucky, pretty pretty girl," he said. "You exit clothes."

Gabriel stripped, thinking, I'm broke now. I need the money, so why not? He lay down naked on the bed and propped himself on a pink lip-shaped pillow. He shut his eyes as the audience was led to their seats.

Then the show started. Bruce Springsteen's "Born in the U.S.A.," played as the round bed started spinning slowly. Gabriel saw himself in multiple reflections on the mirrored walls and ceiling, spinning around and around, getting smaller and smaller, spinning away from himself into nothingness.

He felt like a celebrity, like an animal in a zoo, like a whore. People stared at him in Japan even when he had his clothes on, even when he was not on stage. They stared at his golden blond hair and steely blue eyes and deep dimples. They called him Brado Pitto.

Then a girl came out wearing some kind of geisha mask and a flowing silk kimono. The music changed to something Japanese. She did some kind of traditional dance that was graceful and robotic and looked like it was in slow motion. Then she took off her robe and she was totally nude, and alabaster and womanly and creamy and totally shaved, and he couldn't help but get excited and for an instant he forgot he was part of the show.

She danced over to the spinning bed and bowed formally to Gabriel. The expressionless cartoon mask mocked him. He focused on the dark eyes behind the mask.

She crawled on top of him, and he slipped into her and then she was pumping, pumping, silently, and a picture of that little naked girl running, running, after the bomb dropped on Hiroshima or was it some place in Vietnam flashed into his head. And he couldn't. It didn't. It got soft. Mocked him. The harder he tried, the softer it got. It just flopped around and bent in half as the half-cartoon girl tried to stuff it back inside. He couldn't believe it. His dick was the only thing he could count on in his life besides his trust fund and his Venus key.

The audience started to laugh behind their hands. Show's over.

"You shame me," Snake yelled as he took back the wad of yen and then the gang dragged him out the back door and threw him and his clothes into a Dumpster in the alley.

A flyer stuck to Gabriel's face. It was an advertisement for a restaurant called Fuku Fuku where:

"You are delicious cheaply and can eat a lot of blowfish dishes."

He walked to the restaurant and ordered a plate of blowfish sashimi because he had heard that it could kill you. He ate the fugu and waited to die, but the only thing that happened was a tingling in his mouth.

Then he went to the airport and bought a one-way ticket to Miami. He took a deep breath as they checked his platinum AmEx. He found out that even though he was broke and impotent, at least he still had credit. For now.

Jesus Becomes a *Balsero*

Jesus sauntered past Havana's decaying downtown buildings as he hugged the stop sign that he had bought with the U.S. dollar Helena Ruth gave him in payment for his pubic hair. He carried the sign in the brown paper that Helena had also given him lest anyone ask him why he was carrying a stop sign through the streets of Havana.

A skinny girl in denim daisy dukes and a tube top called a *baja y chupa*, "lower and suck," in Cuba, whistled at him. She was so young and had on such heavy makeup that she looked like a little girl dressed up like a whore for Halloween. She dug into her pocket. "*Mira*," she said. A miniature bar of hotel soap rested on her dirty palm. It was marked, "Dove."

"I screw a Soviet *puerco* for it," she bragged. "To get clean."

"Great," Jesus said, and he felt sorry for her, felt sorry for Cuba, knew he had to get away from a country that forced you to fuck someone just to get clean.

"We can take a bath together?"

"Maybe some other time," he answered. She kissed him hard on the lips and hugged him tightly and he felt a tingling in his groin.

"Adios," she whispered into his ear. "Good luck on your trip."

"Adios," he replied, pushing away from her, shocked, realizing that she knew he was leaving, which made him nervous because if she knew, others probably knew. In Cuba, the walls had eyes and ears. In the port, there was a cemetery of confiscated boats.

Jesus arrived at his house. He knocked the secret knock and Chino, his best friend, opened the door. The house looked normal on the outside but inside there was the raft and nothing else. Jesus and Chino had sold everything they owned to build the raft. When they'd had nothing left to sell, they'd sold their bodies. The raft was made from a wooden frame with a platform of stop signs, which were screwed to sheets of polystyrene. There were no sides, so that the sea could wash over it. They made a sail from old sheets. The raft looked like a pile of scrap tied together, but to Jesus it looked magnificent.

Jesus took the stop sign from the brown paper and Chino started to clap. Jesus smiled, bowed. They screwed the stop sign to the last naked spot on the frame of the raft.

Now, they were ready. Jesus and Chino smashed out a window and part of a wall and shoved the raft through. They hauled it across the road toward the bay.

The shore was crowded with people. It was like a party, like a day at the regatta. A woman gave Jesus an umbrella, saying, "To protect you from the sun, *bonito*." Another gave Chino a ripe navel orange.

A feeble old man, on a truck inner tube covered in netting, tried to paddle out with a homemade oar as Jesus and Chino shoved their raft into the water. A few people applauded nervously, looking around to see if any authorities were watching. Then a shrill siren screamed in the distance.

"The police!" someone shouted. It had been only a matter of time: When a crowd gathered in Castro's Cuba, the police were sure to follow. The squealing of the siren grew louder, closer.

Jesus and Chino pushed their raft into the bay as fast as they could, gasping for breath. The water felt cool climbing up their bodies.

Jesus looked over his shoulder as the police car, an old Soviet Volga sedan, screeched to a stop. His heart skipped a beat.

A tired-looking, overweight cop jumped out as fast as his beer-fed gut allowed. He was followed by a younger skinny-looking cop with a handlebar mustache, who was talking into a bulky old walkie-talkie.

"Stop!" the fat officer ordered, as he drew his gun. "You are committing a crime against the state!" he shouted, glowering, waving the gun menacingly.

Jesus and Chino kept pushing the raft. Just when they reached the spot where they could no longer stand, a shot blasted. The back of the head of the old man on the inner tube next to them exploded, red blood gushing as he fell back into the water.

Chino froze. The crowd scattered in all directions, screaming. Jesus held his hands in the air and turned around slowly. He could not believe this was happening. He would be killed or sent back to jail. He would never leave Cuba.

Then Jesus saw a woman approaching the police officers. He thought he was seeing things. It was Helena Ruth. The blue toilet rug was around her neck. She walked up to the two policemen, reached into a bag marked "GUM," grabbed a wad of American bills and threw them up into the air.

"Go! Now! Jesus," Helena Ruth screamed. This was the first time she had ever called him by his name and not "Boy."

The money seemed to take flight in a gust of wind—a flock of green. The two police scrambled, grasping for the bills: jumping into the air, diving into the sand, on their hands and knees. Then they grabbed the same bill, the last bill. It was a twenty-dollar bill. It ripped in half. Fists started flying.

Jesus and Chino jumped on the raft and started to row and row and row. Jesus felt the water give way, felt the sweat form on his body, felt his heart beating hard in his chest. He felt the current catch hold of the raft. He prayed that no Cuban Coast Guard boats would arrive as he yelled, as loud as he could, "Miami! Miami! Miami!"

The Prodigal Son Returns

Gabriel Tucker rode in a cab from Miami International Airport to the Venus de Milo Arms. He hadn't slept a wink on the endless flight from Tokyo. His mind fought the jet lag, trying to figure out what he was going to do now that he was broke. He absentmindedly stroked the gold key around his neck, wondering what home it might unlock and whether it would ever be all right again.

The Florida heat hit him like a slap, like Calcutta in August. They arrived in South Beach and drove along the ocean on the aptly named Ocean Drive, past buildings that looked like rotting cakes, streamlined boxes, great beached steamships decorated with glass blocks, Vitrolite, chrome and stainless steel. Old people sat on vinyl-strapped aluminum chairs, like rows of crows, on the front porches, staring out past undulating palms and golden sand to the horizon where blue sea met blue sky.

Then the cab pulled in front of a once fabulous building that looked like a grounded luxury ocean liner, like the SS *Normandie*. It was some sort of decomposing nautical fantasy, five stories of flaking navy blue and white paint, wave-shaped friezes, porthole windows, ship railings and a fake smokestack. Air conditioners hung precariously from some of the windows, their drains trailing tails of rust stains on the white walls. Involuntarily, Gabriel looked up to try to imagine where his uncle had jumped from. Anger flashed briefly, then pain.

Over the front door of the building was a larger-than-life, gold-leafed, plaster relief of the Venus de Milo. Someone had painted stubby hands where her arms should have been, so it looked like the Venus de Thalidomide. Someone had also spray-painted the word "arms" after the Venus de Milo sign so it read:

The Venus De Milo ARMS

Gabriel entered his building thinking, *This is all I have left in the world. This is home?* He remembered his grandfather and felt sad and lonely. He missed him. Gabriel had left on his trip ten years ago, right after his funeral. He felt the molding on the front door and ran his hands over the stylized art deco door handle, like trying to make friends with a new pet. Or brother. Or mom. But he had no one. His mother and father died in a plane crash when he was a baby and his grandmother died before he was born and he never had any siblings. The only family he had left was this building, this Venus de Milo Arms. He thought how hard his grandfather had worked to build his empire, and all that was left was this rotting building. He blamed himself.

Gabriel glided along geometric-patterned icy white-and-blue terrazzo lobby floors, until he was stopped in his tracks by a beautiful light-skinned, black woman. She sat regally on a chair that looked like a Disney Spanish throne. Her complexion was flawless. Her hair was an intricate pattern of braids and curls. Her legs went on forever, with beautiful smooth calves. Her eyes were shut. She was listening to music through earphones, mouthing the words, writhing seductively, unconsciously in her seat. A fan placed a few feet from her softly blew her wispy white cotton dress, wafting her sweet gardenia scent toward him.

Gabriel breathed it in as she opened her eyes. They were big and brown and for an instant he saw shock and then she smiled.

"I'm Gabriel. I'm moving in here, I guess," he said. He didn't say, but wondered if he should say, "This is my home."

The woman said nothing.

"Do you know where thirteen is, apartment thirteen?" he asked.

She removed her earphones.

"Do you know where apartment thirteen is?" he repeated.

The woman just smiled, searched through her bag, pulled out a tape and stuck it into her boom box. She raised one eyebrow and then pressed "Play." Music blared. She stood up. Her body began to sway with the music:

"I should have changed that silly lock, I should have thrown away that key."

She lip-synched perfectly. The words seemed to be coming from her.

"Go! Walk though that door, I'm not that helpless little person, not in love with you anymore."

She motioned for Gabriel to follow with long black fingers, her long nails painted white. He couldn't help but stare at her ripe honeydew ass defeating gravity, as she boogied from the lobby out past a dry pool built above ground and punctuated with portholes. She led him up some stairs with aluminum railings stylized like cascading waves to a door labeled, APT. #13, LANDLORD.

The song ended and she stopped dancing and left without saying a word.

Gabriel shook his head, thinking, *That chick is psycho but totally hot.* He yawned and took out the golden key with the diamond on it that his grandfather had left him, pushed it into the lock, turned the key and the door swung open. *Home sweet home,* he thought as he entered, half jokingly, half as a test.

He smelled mildew, headed toward the dusty beams of light streaming through the cracks in the Venetian blinds. He pulled them open and was hit by a tsunami of bright.

His apartment had streamlined deco furniture, green Vitrolite-covered walls, translucent glass brick and columns of cotton candy pink keystone patterned with millions of fossils. He imagined Fred Astaire and Ginger Rogers waltzing around the room.

Then, he noticed that the travel journal letters he had written to himself during his endless trip were neatly piled on the dining room table. There was another larger pile of envelopes marked:

To Alvin Tucker
From: Mera Levy

Gabriel opened his dead grandfather's mail. The first envelope had two hundred-dollar bills inside and a Hallmark "Happy Birthday" card. It said: Rent-January 1936-Apt 10A- with love, Mera. He opened another envelope and it also contained two hundred dollar bills and another Hallmark card that said, "Home Is Where the Heart Is, Welcome Home." It said: Rent-August 1959-Apt 10A. He opened another envelope. They all contained money and cards.

Gabriel wondered who this Mera Levy was as he opened all the envelopes and pulled out the cash from the cards and started making thousand-dollar stacks. The more money, the more excited he got. He had hit a jackpot of $120,200. He was in shock. He was no longer broke. He looked for a place to hide the money. He opened the closet in the bedroom. It was filled with clothes. He hid the money inside a black top hat.

Then he heard a noise. A flyer was slid underneath his front door.

TUESDAY, AUGUST 20
THE ARTS ASYLUM
MONTHLY EVENT

MARINA PRESENTS
POETRY OF THE SKIN

THE AQUARIUM
VENUS DE MILO ARMS
10:00 p.m.

On the bottom of the page:

> *Dear Mr. Landlord,*
> *Please Come!*
> *Welcome to the Venus de Milo Arms, the Love*
> *Boat on XTC.*
>
> *MARINA*

Gabriel was so tired, he couldn't think straight.

Jesus Drinks a Flying Fish

The Gulf Stream's currents dragged Jesus and Chino's raft somewhere between Cuba and Florida. They had been floating for twenty days. Their world had turned a monotonous blue: sky and sea wedged together. Jesus tasted salt, felt like a block of salt. Everything burned. The sun scorched.

There was no more fresh water. They had rationed the ten gallons by the thimbleful, in super-slow motion. Water, the most delicious nectar. Hours stretched out between drops they'd come to live for. They could no longer piss.

Jesus searched the cloudless sky, the endless horizon for birds, for planes, for boats, for any sign of land. He gave up and stared at a flying fish; its tail treaded water, and then its fin-wings spread as it flew toward him and crash-landed on the raft. Jesus grabbed it, wiggling and wet, like liquid silver in the sharp sunlight. He bent the fish in half till it broke—the sound of cracking knuckles. It leaked red. He sucked the metallic-tasting wetness from the flesh.

Then, Jesus held the broken flying fish to Chino's parched lips, but he only laughed hysterically, clenching his mouth shut. In desperation, Chino had started drinking saltwater. It had made him crazy. Jesus had tied him to the raft to keep him from jumping overboard.

Jesus chewed the fish meticulously in order to draw out every bit of nourishment.

Shadows circled the raft, dark ghosts with fins like knives. Jesus shut his eyes and fell asleep. He dreamed of rainwater. The sky turned gray and then the sun was gulped up by the Gulf Stream.

Later, Jesus woke up to pitch black: no moon, no stars. Waves, like undulating hills, picked the raft up and dropped it down. The wind whistled. Then suddenly, the raft reached the top of a swell and Jesus saw something flicker in the darkness. He rubbed his eyes. He was sure now. It was not a mirage. There was a city in the distance, getting closer — a moving island of multicolored lights.

Then, he realized that it was an enormous cruise ship that was heading straight for them. He lit his flashlight, a pinprick of light in the bleak black.

"Help!" he shouted, as loud as he could, screaming until he had no voice. The ship came so close, he thought he could reach out and touch it. Through the portholes, he saw people dancing. Jesus was sure the ship was stopping, that it had seen him. Thank God, he thought but then it started moving away. Slowly. Jesus read its name on the stern.

Ecstasy

He hugged his knees, folded himself into the fetal position. He tried to cry but there was no moisture for tears. Then, the storm hit. He was covered in a blanket of whitecap. Thunder boomed. Lightning flashed. Bubbles hissed. He held on tightly, his nails digging into the mast, as waves poured over him, as water tried to pull him overboard. Sheets of rain stung like pellets. There was no longer sky or sea, only storm. For the first time, Jesus wanted to die.

"Miami!" Chino screamed as he jumped overboard, a toothy smile on his face.

Then the raft sunk. The mast banged Jesus on the head. Everything went black.

Gabriel Sees Poetry

Back in Miami, at the Venus de Milo Arms, Gabriel awoke in a jet-lagged stupor and peered out the window. It was dark except for a sliver of moon and a bright cruise ship, *The Ecstasy*, on the horizon. He looked at his watch: ten-fifteen. Then he remembered the flyer slipped under his door and figured that Marina's Skin Poetry show would just be starting. He had to do something. This was a beginning. He flipped on the light and opened the bedroom closet. He checked to make sure the top hat full of money was still there, to make sure he hadn't dreamed it up. Then he tried on a 1940s candy-striped shirt and white linen short pants. They fit him perfectly. He went in search of The Aquarium.

He heard muted noises coming from inside the aboveground pool in the courtyard. Six portholes on the side of the dry pool glowed like sextuplet moons. He peered into one of them. People, mostly young or very old, sat in clumsy rows on the bottom of the pool aiming flashlights at a woman sitting on a beach chair in the deep end.

Gabriel climbed a flight of stairs to the deck and then down more steps into the pool. The audience went silent, shifting their flashlights onto him. He froze in the glare.

"Welcome," Marina said, leaning forward in her beach chair. "You're just in time for poetry." She had an aphrodisiac voice, bottomless and smooth.

"Thanks," Gabriel replied, and he looked at her, her red-red lips and big-big eyes, the blue color of the Caribbean, and her glossy black hair, like she had too much for her head, as she pushed back escaping strands cascading-contrasting across her creamy face. She looked vintage to him, a colorized 3-D black-and-white starlet with Betty Page glam, Jackie O sophistication.

Then, Pandora, the lip-synching black woman who had showed him to his apartment, grabbed his hand and pulled him down next to her. She handed him a flashlight.

Gabriel lit his flashlight and joined in with the multiple beams from the other people's flashlights bathing Marina in light. Gabriel stared at Marina and subconsciously licked his lips. Then she stood up and took off her generic white T-shirt, revealing graceful shoulders and unrestrained breasts. Gabriel stared. Her breasts seemed to stare right back at him as he imagined cupping them from below. She seemed to Gabriel exotic and ghostly and erotic all at once.

Marina pulled off her faded Levi's, undressing casually, without shame. Now, she was wearing only plain white cotton panties with "Sunday" printed across the band. It was Wednesday.

Marina smiled casually and took them off. The audience shuffled.

First, Gabriel felt shock, and then he connected with her vulnerability. After that, he removed himself and his eyes grazed her body, resting on the nape of her swan neck, her elegant long arms and legs, her wrists and ankles, and her incredibly smooth white skin and her belly button, half innie, half outie, like a little eye, and then down to her silk triangle, and her cool beauty awed him. He had to look away, like she was glare.

Marina opened a Burdines shopping bag and pulled out a metal printing plate and placed it on the floor of the pool. Then she turned the bag over and out poured letters of the alphabet, raised old-fashioned typesetting letters. She knelt down on the pool bottom and picked up the letters and then manipulated them into the metal plate. She was spelling out something, making words, phrases from the letters. Gabriel thought of alphabet soup and Scrabble and strip poker.

When Marina finished arranging the letters she stood back up and said, "I need some volunteers."

Nobody moved. People stirred and whispered.

"There's nothing to be afraid of," she announced, smiling briefly.

Then Skip, an anorexic-looking young man with a Mickey Mouse ears cap, stood up. A notepad and pens jutted out from the ink-stained front pocket of his untucked dress shirt. The tail hung down, almost covering his corduroy cutoffs. He was the only volunteer.

"I need one more victim," Marina announced. Then her eyes were drawn to Gabriel's disheveled blond hair, which shone golden in the moonlight—half mop, half sparkler. Gabriel looked away, felt embarrassed, thinking, *Why am I embarrassed?* She is the naked one.

Then Skip bent over and tapped Gabriel on his shoulder. He slid his wire-rimmed glasses nostril-ward, squinted over the frames. "Come with me," he demanded.

"Please," Marina implored, as a few isolated claps echoed around them.

Gabriel rose reluctantly to more applause. The jet lag made him feel like he was sleepwalking. He followed Skip to Marina and her letters, felt the eyes of the audience on him. He felt like he was back on the round bed in Japan going around and around in circles— impotent.

"OK," Marina whispered.

Gabriel forced himself to stop checking out her nude body. Marina pushed a stray wisp of black hair from her face. "I'm going to lie on this printing plate and I want you both to sit on me. I'll tell you when to get up."

"What?" Gabriel asked, taken aback.

"Sit on me," she insisted.

"I don't want to hurt you."

"Please," Marina said, and her expression turned businesslike as her tone altered, as she demanded dominatrix-like. "Now!"

She lay on the pool bottom, placing her stomach on the letter-press, on the prearranged words-phrases. She spread her arms out, crucifixion-like.

"There's pleasure in pain," Skip whispered to Gabriel, and then he crouched down and sat on Marina's back, facing backward. Then

Gabriel sat facing Skip, as gently as possible, lowering his weight onto her ass.

Skip whispered, "You only hurt the ones you love."

Gabriel shut his eyes, thinking, *This guy is another weirdo. How the hell did I get into this?* Then slowly, sitting on Marina's naked body made him feel trusted in some very strange way. He concentrated on the feeling of his body on her body. He felt her breathing, like an ebbing tide, and something from her seemed to be seeping into him, a feeling of intimacy. He breathed with her. He felt himself get hard. She had cured his impotence. A cell phone rang in the audience, startling Gabriel.

"OK, you guys can get up now," Marina announced.

First Skip stood up and then Gabriel and then Marina. She looked like she was waking from a trance.

"Please come and see," Marina told the audience.

People stood up and began walking toward them, forming a line behind Gabriel. Marina had converted the dry pool into a church and it was like they were waiting for Holy Communion.

Skip shined his flashlight at Marina's creamy stomach. A halo of white light surrounded the letters, the words, the phrases which had engraved her flawless skin. They looked like they had been carved in blood, like the letters had slit her.

"Thank you," Marina said to Skip as he read her stomach.

"Now I have to go and figure out where that quote came from," Skip said.

"Primo Levi meets Larry Kramer. But feel it, don't intellectualize it," Marina replied.

"You know I have no feelings," Skip said, leaving.

Marina smiled as Gabriel took his place.

"Thanks for your pounds, Mr. Landlord," Marina said.

"How did you know who I was?" Gabriel asked, forcing himself to calm down. He didn't know why he was nervous. The flashlight trembled in his hand.

"The Venus de Milo Arms is a small world. Everyone knows everything about everybody. And everyone's really strange but me," she said, rolling her eyes.

"That's reassuring." Then he looked down and read her flat stomach:

We must love each other or die.
If not now, when?

He felt the words, deep down in his own gut. He realized they were just words, hippy-dippy words at that, but for some reason they affected him. For the first time in an extremely long time, he got an intense urge to write.

"My name's Marina," she said, pulling him out of himself.

"My name's Gabriel," he replied, dragging his eyes from her stomach, wanting to shake her hand or hug her or kiss her or something. He felt like they had experienced something personal together. Instead he left.

He went back to his room and grabbed a paper and pen and walked up Washington Avenue on broken red concrete sidewalk. He passed Soak Up the Sun Letter Press Inc. In the window of the empty shop, a hand-lettered sign said, "All contents for sale." Outside the door was a garbage can full of old-fashioned typesetting letters like Marina had used to carve the words into her skin. Gabriel took a "G" and an "M" and put them in his pocket. He walked across Collins Avenue to the beach and climbed into a retro-futuristic lifeguard tower that made him think of ray guns, rocketeers, blimps and floating cities. It was painted pink and yellow and had a stylized fifties antenna with a red ball on top. He sat down and leaned against the NO LIFEGUARD ON DUTY sign, stared up at the impossibly beautiful bloated moon over Miami and the twinkling ships at sea and thought of the Jetsons, Buck Rogers and Flash Gordon, thought of a time of optimistic futurism.

He glanced out over the hissing black ocean and opened his pad and started writing and the words flowed. He had been in South Beach for only a little while and he was no longer broke, impotent or suffering from writer's block. Was it the Venus or Marina or maybe both?

SUNSTROKER

by Skip Bowling

Another night in South Beach, world of the weird, where in the dry pool of the **Venus de Milo Arms,** a gathering of the elite and not so elite were treated to an eyeful of stomach poetry by our own artist in residence, the stunning **Marina Russell.**

Reading words from **Primo Levi** and **Larry Kramer** carved on Marina's stomach were the new tribe of artists joining the homeless, drug attics, criminals, crazies and male, female and trans prostitutes on **Lincoln Road Mall,** which used to be the **Fifth Avenue** of the South, where white-gloved ladies who lunched would browse at **Bonwit Teller, Saks Fifth Avenue, Van Clef & Arpels** and **Elizabeth Arden,** where Ingrid Bergman held the premiere of *Arch of Triumph.* Now the artists are taking over the abandoned storefronts on Lincoln Road between the schlock and dollar stores, the mental health center and the social security office, breathing new life into the remnants of this once beautiful street.

Seeing stomach words were designer **Pat Field** and girlfriend **Rebecca, Kitty Meow, Louis Canales,** the **Skull Sisters** and **Son,** the **Bone Boyz, Varla,** and new South Beach resident and eighties art legend **Kenny Scharf,** who said, "I

love South Beach; it's just like the East Village on a beach,"
and **Mitch Kaplan,** another Lincoln Road victim-pioneer who
complained about a guy who keeps coming into his store,
Books and Books, to masturbate on **James Joyce's**
Finnegans Wake. At least there's one person left in the world
who appreciates Literature.

As I took my turn gazing at Marina's graffitied stomach, I
thought, whether performance art or performance perver-
sion, she seemed to strip the nudity from her nude body,
making me think of where I came from and where I'm going,
about where South Beach came from and where it's going,
about the Holocaust and AIDS, how different yet how very
similar they are. She made me think about the thirty South
Beach hotels that were raided this week that provided room
and board in exchange for social security checks. Elderly
Jews were found locked in rooms with overflowing portable
toilets, living on dog food, bedridden, forgotten. She made me
think about the painfully skeletal young man who was sitting
in front of **Torpedo** with a crude sign that said "aids," his
begging jar completely empty. She made me think how these
people were all abandoned. She made me think about love and
how we never seem to learn how to love. We must love each
other or die, if not now when?

At the performance, I met a piece of eye candy with an
edge that reeked of T.F.B. (trust fund baby). He turned out to
be my long-lost slumlord, **Gabriel Tucker**—lucky sperm. He is
grandson and heir to the throne of **Alvin Tucker,** who
developed much of South Beach and then ran away, owing
Uncle Sam millions in taxes.

Opening later that same night in the old **Mickey's** space on
Washington Ave. near the **Strand** was **Chris Paciello** and
Lord Michael's club **Risk,** door king **Gilbert Stafford**
carefully controlling the outside pandemonium. Near-naked
neon-painted bimbo babes boogied on the bar, zebra print and
smoke machines ran amuck, liquor and pharmaceuticals for
all, the packed omnisexual crowd getting heated on the floor

and then cooling off in the showers in the back. Then I fell into the opium / VIP room, seeking silk pillows to rest my tired ass on. The handsome Mr. Paciello himself, cock of the walk, random women just walking over and grinding themselves on him like dogs in heat, has had a complete makeover—Guido to glamour, head to toe **Armani, Versace** and **Gucci.** Rumors flying from club royalty as they sucked down comp drinks that Mr. Paciello was mafia and that the mob was taking over South Beach nightlife. But as one club kid said, "Who cares if he's mafia? He's beautiful and throws a great party!"

Gabriel Sees and Turns into a Ghost

Gabriel heard a scream. His eyes snapped open. He jerked awake. He looked around, confused. He was in his apartment in the Venus de Milo Arms. An old woman stood at the foot of his bed. She shook, staring at him, her mouth agape. The sunlight, piercing through the slits between the Venetian blinds, lit up her transparent white hair hanging just below a knitted orange cap with a green pom-pom on the top. She had on matching oversized orange-framed sunglasses and a matching checked orange and green pantsuit. She was half clown, half glamour gal.

Gabriel froze. He was naked. He pulled the sheet over himself, covering up.

"Alvin?" the old woman asked.

"What?" Gabriel asked, wiping the sleep from his eyes as Marina, the coolly beautiful performance artist from last night, burst into his bedroom. Marina grabbed the old lady and hugged her.

"What did you do?" Marina asked Gabriel. Her big blue eyes sparked. The old woman seemed to be recovering from a trance. Then, the lip-syncher walked in and glared at Gabriel.

"I don't know . . . ," Gabriel answered, sitting up, wondering why all these strange people were in his room, thinking this Venus de Milo Arms was a crazy house.

"I, I, I just woke up. She was here," Gabriel stuttered. "She screamed."

"Alvin?" Miss Levy questioned, pointing at Gabriel. "He looks exactly like Alvin, like when we met," the old woman muttered, calming down. "He even has the same dimples."

Gabriel shook his head, now understanding. "Alvin Tucker was my grandfather."

The old woman smiled sadly. "You lay in his bed looking like a carbon copy of him," she said. She cleared her throat. "This was his home. His clothes," she said, pointing to the open closet.

Then, Miss Levy reached out an age-spotted hand to Gabriel and her fingertips brushed the golden key with the diamond hanging from the golden chain around his neck. She couldn't believe it. Tears started to flow from her eyes, trailing down her wrinkled skin.

"Alvin made this one for me," she said, pulling the chain from beneath her blouse. Hanging from the chain was an identical key with an identical diamond. I would always say to him, "A *goldener shlisl efente ale tirn.* . . . A golden key opens all doors." Her voice cracked. "Alvin said it was the key to the door of his heart." She pointed at Gabriel's key. "And then I made that copy for him."

Miss Levy suddenly had a flashback of the train to Auschwitz. The train door slid open. Precious light and fresh air floated in, carrying strains of Mozart's *Magic Flute.* Her mother ripped the hem of her dress, pulled out the two diamonds. She handed one to her and one to her twin sister. "Swallow them," her mother insisted, in a tone that begged and demanded at the same time.

"How is Alvin?" Miss Levy asked, shaking her head to stop the memories.

"He passed," Gabriel answered softly, and she gazed at him with such abject longing that he had to look away. "He left me the golden key with the diamond in his will," Gabriel said. "And the Venus de Milo Arms. It's all I have, and I never even saw it until yesterday."

Miss Levy started to cry again, and hugged Gabriel. She smelled of hair spray and Vicks. She felt soft and bony at the same time. Then Gabriel realized that Miss Levy was the person who left all the money and Hallmark cards on the table in the apartment. She was the reason he was no longer broke.

She let go of him. She stared at the twin diamonds that her mother had made her and her sister swallow. One was now set on Gabriel's key and the other was set on her key. She dried her eyes.

The lip-syncher took a tape from her purse, slipped it into her omnipresent boom box:

> *I'll be loving you always*
> *With a love that's true always*
> *When the things you've planned*
> *Need a helping hand,*
> *I will understand always.*

> *Always.*

> *Days may not be fair always,*
> *That's when I'll be there always.*
> *Not for just an hour,*
> *Not for just a day,*
> *Not for just a year,*
> *But always.*

The words seemed to be flowing from her mouth.

Miss Levy shut her eyes. Marina held her hand. Pandora finished the song, dancing around the room and then out the door.

"'Always' was Miss Levy and your grandfather's song," Marina said as she led Miss Levy out of the apartment.

Gabriel shut his eyes and tried to picture his grandfather Alvin and Miss Levy as young lovers. Here in this very room. The Venus de Milo Arms seemed determined to capture his heart as well as his soul.

Who Is Art Deco?

Gabriel lay on the beach in front of the Venus de Milo Arms, smelled a mixture of Coppertone, salt and Ben-Gay. He watched the elderly couple across from him. The woman had on a skirted bathing suit and a ruffled pink cotton candy–like bathing cap. She caressed the numbers tattooed on the wrist of the old man sitting next to her. He had on a green golf cap and a white napkin under the bridge of his wraparound sunglasses. Then a woman emerged from the sea wearing only the tiniest G-string. She had perfect breasts. The sunlight made her look golden. Two men with shaved heads in matching black G-strings walked toward her holding hands, and their bodies were so built and hairless, they looked like huge erections. They simultaneously kissed the golden woman on both cheeks, and Gabriel felt a jolt in his groin, craving someone to kiss. He imagined kissing Marina, imagined her lips.

"Before, I could never get my Israel here to come to the beach. But now that he can see bare boobies." The old lady shook her head. "I just ignore him; that's how I could stay with him for sixty years. We were married before any of these buildings were here. Now they're trying to make this area historic, save the old buildings."

"Why do they want to destroy these buildings?" Gabriel asked her. He looked up and down the beach at a line of improbable deco buildings that seemed somehow just perfect for the sun and mood of the place.

"To build high-rises," she said. "Filing cabinets for people. They want us senior citizens to go away."

"I'm not going anywhere. See this," Israel declared, speaking for the first time, pointing to the numbers tattooed on his wrist. "Anyone with this, you don't force to go nowhere. Never again!"

"There's a protest today, in front of the New Yorker Hotel at three o'clock. You should go," the woman said.

"I will," Gabriel replied, curious, getting up. "Where can I get something good to eat?"

"Puerto Sagua, on Collins, a few blocks up," she answered.

Gabriel walked up Ocean Drive, passed the Victor, the Colony, the Clevelander, the Crescent, the Breakwater, the Park Central, appreciating the dormant beauty of the buildings: all beat up, decaying, yet so magical, so playful, so full of optimism. He stared at the old people sitting on the front porch of the Century Hotel. The wrinkled women with gray hair in puffy do's and bright sundresses and men with bald heads and Bermuda shorts, all sitting on chained-together, vinyl-strapped golden aluminum lawn chairs, their walkers and canes sitting next to them. They were talking and laughing, some sleeping, some reading the *Jewish Daily Forward*. He cut over to Washington Avenue, headed past Friedman's Kosher Bakery #1, windows piled high with sweet spongy round *babkas*, flaky *rugelach*, crispy nutty *mandlebread*, cheesecakes, macaroons, hamantaschen and challah.

A flamboyant, middle-aged red-haired man sat in front of the bakery sketching.

"Do you see?" he asked Gabriel.

"What?"

"The building? Friedman's Bakery? I'm trying to make them see it," the man declared.

"Who?"

"The people who want to knock it down."

"I don't understand."

"These buildings have been here so long, they've become invisible. I have to make them up like a face. Brain, be a color wheel," he said as if talking to himself. "Pastels are the answer, subtle, not garish. Who am I? It's not historically accurate. I think I must. Yes, I will!" The man turned to Gabriel, held out his hand. "Leonard Horowitz is the name."

"Gabriel Tucker. Nice to meet you," Gabriel shook his hand.

"Can I dare?" he asked. "Dip them in pastels?"

"Go for it," Gabriel answered, trying to imagine the colors in his head as he looked at Leonard Horowitz's drawing of the bakery. It looked like a cake with pink and periwinkle and mint and sage icing, instead of the way it was, a drab vanilla color with brown trim. "It looks beautiful," Gabriel said, but the man was no longer listening. He was staring at the bakery as if in a trance.

Gabriel continued walking up Washington Avenue. "Do you know where Puerto Sagua is?" Gabriel asked a tiny old man wearing very white sneakers and a very white captain's hat and carrying a very green iguana.

"I'll escort you there, *mi* amigo," he answered.

"Can I buy you and your iguana lunch?" Gabriel asked.

"*Muchas gracias*," the man replied. Gabriel followed him into Puerto Sagua, where time seemed to have stopped in the fifties: stainless steel panels, boomerang-patterned Formica, minijukeboxes in every booth.

"My name Amadeo Odillo Medina-Jonas," the man said, putting the iguana on the seat next to him at the lunch counter, taking off his cap and holding out his hand. "And this here is my amigo, Crocodillo."

"My name is Gabriel Tucker." They shook hands.

Gabriel ordered a matzoh ball soup and brisket and Amadeo ordered a Helena Ruth sandwich, and lox for the iguana.

"What is a Helena Ruth sandwich?" Gabriel asked.

"It turkey on white bread *con* cranberry sauce. It name after the most beautiful Cuban woman who ever live. They say Fidel steal her money to pay for his revolution and leave her at the altar."

Gabriel looked around Puerto Sagua. Sitting across the counter from them were two models, who without makeup looked like they were on their way to cheerleading practice. They were decked out in vintage chic, much the same as the two old women sitting next to them and wearing their old clothes. Beside them was a scary-looking man with a scar across his cheek. Two cute Goth boys were making out next to him. And Gabriel realized why he felt like he belonged in South Beach: It was a place that knew no outsiders.

Gabriel went to the bathroom, entered a stall, sat down on the toilet. A man in the next stall prattled on his cell phone.

"I have to move," the man said in a German accent. "There is already talk about a historic district. Saving these old buildings. They are built out of concrete that was mixed with beach sand. They're rusting from the inside out."

Gabriel looked at the man as they walked out of the bathroom. He was about sixty, with a masklike handsome face which looked like someone had erased all the wrinkles. He had a built, young man's body with wrinkly old-man hands.

Gabriel went back to the counter. The food had arrived. Amadeo tied a paper napkin, biblike, around his neck. Gabriel took a sip of his soup.

"How long have you lived in Miami?" Gabriel asked.

"I come in 1959. I thought I would go home in a couple years." He ate pieces of his sandwich with a knife and fork. Between each bite, he dabbed his mouth with his napkin. "Castro dump all his criminals and crazies on Miami Beach."

"What?"

"During the Mariel boat lift. He send them here to molest the poor old people who come here to take some sun in their golden years before they die," Amadeo said. "But something is happening. New, young people are coming. Like you. It is up to you."

"To do what?" Gabriel asked, finishing his soup.

"To save it, *mi hijo*," Amadeo answered, wrapping half of his sandwich in a paper napkin. Gabriel paid the check and Amadeo insisted on leaving a dollar tip.

Gabriel walked up Collins Avenue past abandoned buildings, which seemed to him like walking through an American Pompeii, only without the ash. He squinted up at the New Yorker Hotel, studied its streamlined beauty, stared at the overgrown needle at the top, which seemed to pierce the cloudy sky. A spray-painted sign on a piece of plywood was nailed over the dead neon sign: "All Contents for Sale." Two groups of people marched in front of the building as workers hauled old toilets, refrigerators, air conditioners to a Dumpster. One group carried homemade signs:

Art? Deco Is Ugly
Time to Clean Up Miami Beach
Scrap Junk

Dreco Schmeco

Separated from this group by a policeman wearing shorts with muscular, tanned shaved legs was another group with signs:

Save the New Yorker
Say No to Greed
These Buildings Are Our Heritage

Marching with this group were Marina and the lip-syncher. One fey-looking man in short-shorts and a Miami Dolphins T-shirt walked from group to group, as if he didn't know where he belonged. He carried a cross:

GOD IS LOVE

was written on one side and

It's Adam and Eve and Not Adam and Steve

on the other.

About fifty people stood around watching the protest as if it were a show. "Who's Art?" the old man next to Gabriel asked. "I don't understand. Does Art own the building?"

A man who looked to be in his seventies—bald, tanned-lined face, polyester brown pants and striped brown tie that hung well past his waist—started to speak through a megaphone. "I'm Abe

Rosenbaum; I own this building" he announced. "I've been a slave under the Nazis and Russians. I didn't have any rights. Now I'm in the land of the free and if you own something, it's yours."

Skip walked up to Gabriel. "That mule would destroy the *Mona Lisa* if he could make a buck," he said, writing in his little pad.

A stretch black limo pulled up and parked on the side of the road. A black-tinted window rolled down. The German man Gabriel had overheard in the bathroom of Puerto Sagua watched from the limo.

"The New Yorker is full of rats," Abe announced. "It's my land and I want to build a parking lot. This is the land of the free."

Pandora, the lip-syncher, walked up to Abe and grabbed the megaphone and planted a kiss firmly on his lips. Abe's arms flayed backward as if he were trying to go in reverse. Pandora flipped on her boom box.

> *They paved paradise and put up a parking lot,*
> *With a pink hotel, a boutique and a swinging hot spot,*
> *Don't it always seem to go, that you don't know what you've*
> *got till it's gone.*
> *They paved paradise and put up a parking lot.*

The German sat in his limo and shook his head. "Dummkopf! People always want to stop progress," he said, shaking his head. Then the tinted window rolled up and he pulled away.

Marina cleared her throat. "It is a miracle that these buildings survived," she proclaimed. "There's nowhere else in the world where they have such a concentration of this type of building. They are called art deco. They want to knock them all down to put up high-rises. We must save our beach." She smiled at the people. "Save the New Yorker."

"Save the New Yorker. Save the New Yorker," people chanted with her.

Gabriel Gets Blown

The Warsaw Ballroom loomed above the crowd, like a massive gray wedding cake. A solid blob of people thronged the entrance. They screamed and shoved. A rank of bouncers, dressed in black, stood guard at the door. Their steroided muscles strained behind red velvet ropes, holding back the crowd.

"There's no way we're getting in," Gabriel said to Skip.

"I'm the most fabulous person here and because you're with me, you're the second." He wedged himself into the crowd. Gabriel followed, oozed through the maze of muscles and tits and hips and asses. Then, they were thrust to one side.

Four overgrown bodyguards plowed the crowd so the German man from the bathroom of Puerto Sagua, who was dressed in a black silk leisure suit that looked like it was designed by the gestapo, and his dates, three busty blonde hooker-looking triplets, could get through.

"Pick me up," Skip demanded. "So the doormen can see me."

Gabriel grabbed Skip by the waist, held him up above the crowd. He was painfully thin.

"Hood," Skip yelled, saluting the head doorman. He was dressed differently than the others—B-movie gangster style from the thrift shops. Then, two of the bouncers parted the sea of people, shoving them aside.

"Skip! Skip! Skip!" people cried. The red ropes parted.

"Fabulous!" Skip exclaimed, aglow.

"You some kind of masochist?" Gabriel asked him above the racket.

"Yeah, baby—hurt me, hurt me."

Then the door swung open and the leisure suited German man stamped out.

"Please, Mr. Lerman. Please, Mr. Lerman, don't leave," George Nuñez, the Warsaw's owner, begged.

"There is no table, so I don't stay. No table. No respect."

"The club just lost five thousand dollars when Mr. Heinz Lerman walked out. That's what he spends a night in booze," Skip said.

Then they entered the Warsaw Ballroom, and the whole club pulsed, like a hunk of just-killed flesh. It beat against them. House music, tribal-techno-electronic beats blared, forced their way into Gabriel's ears, shook his body. As he breathed, he sucked it down his throat—smoke, air-conditioned, sweet sweat smell. Darkness was sliced by green lasers, spotlights spun red-blue-yellow from the high vaulted ceilings. Wheels of light. The writhing sea of bodies rose in tiers, level upon level. The dance floor was in the center—a sweating black hole of ecstasy.

Gabriel followed Skip as he made his way through the crowd, semi-dissolving in front of him into the smoke and darkness.

"Where are you going?" Gabriel yelled.

"To the VIP room."

They climbed staircase after staircase until they couldn't ascend any farther, and then they arrived at more red velvet ropes, guarded by a three-hundred-pound hairy man dressed only in a pink tutu.

"You look lovely, Miss Piggy," Skip complimented.

"So do you, Skippy," Miss Piggy declared as she opened the velvet ropes.

They entered the VIP room. Gabriel felt like he was in an airport control tower as he looked through the sweating glass down at the pulsating dance floor four flights below.

"Who are these people?" Gabriel asked Skip, scanning the VIP room.

"Beach trash, hustlers, whores, drug dealers, scumbag developers, corrupt city officials, Eurotrash. People who are fabulous because they can snare drink tickets. South Beach is a separate country and drink tickets are its currency. It's a sunny place for shady people," Skip answered.

Then a gang of models followed them into the room.

"Wow," Gabriel exclaimed, staring at them, wanting them.

"I see the parsley has arrived," Skip said.

"What?" Gabriel asked.

"Models. Garnish. Six-footers."

"Introduce me," Gabriel said, involuntarily.

"Open your mouth and close your eyes," Skip said, ignoring him. "Skippy scored you a little surprise."

"What?" Gabriel asked.

"Just do it!" he urged.

Gabriel opened his mouth. Skip put a bitter pill on his tongue. Gabriel swallowed.

"What did I just take?" Gabriel asked.

"E. Ecstasy. You just swallowed love."

Then, Skip froze dead in his tracks. "Salvatore Fabrizio!" he gasped.

"Who?"

"The designer."

"Who?" Gabriel asked again, looking at the handsome older man: kindly eyes, silver hair perfectly coiffed, salt-and-pepper beard, exquisite suit.

"So suffice it to say we're not the most fabulous people here anymore. Fabrizio practically invented over-the-top Italian style. Think Botticelli meets Batman!" Skip said, rushing over to him.

"I'm Skip Bowling, reporter for *Wire*," Skip said to Fabrizio, pulling his pen and pad from his shirt pocket. "So, what are you doing in Miami?" he asked, yelling over the music. "Is it true you're buying a building, opening a Fabrizio store?"

Fabrizio smiled at Skip. "Miami, to me, is like a lover!" he pronounced, staring at Gabriel, from the tip of his spiked blond hair to the pronounced bulge in his Levi's. "I can't get enough of South Beach. It's so fun, superficial. The attitude. I adore."

"If I could be hanging out on the Italian Riviera or Lake Como, I wouldn't spend another second in God's Waiting Room."

"Miami, beauty, beauty, Miami," Fabrizio chanted dreamily.

"What beauty?" Skip asked.

"Twelfth street—the boys," Fabrizio declared, his hands sweeping in the direction of the beach.

Skip rolled his eyes at Gabriel.

"In Miami, I have finally find the center of my circle," he said as his attention shifted totally to an angelic A&F-looking boy, dressed only in combat boots, who started dancing on a small, raised stage, obscuring what looked to be a foot-long hard-on with an American flag. He had a thin, adolescent build with an overripe, gravity-defeating bubble butt. It was like his midsection was exaggerated all around—front and back.

Fabrizio walked directly up to the boy, stared up at him, took out his wallet, peeled off a bill, waved it. There was a flash of diamond-studded golden ring on his middle finger as he tried to get the boy's attention. The boy refused to look. Salvatore Fabrizio threw hundred-dollar bills, one after another, at the dancer as if they were pieces of confetti. The boy just danced on them. Fabrizio looked crushed. He fumbled with his wallet. No money left. So he started to throw his credit cards.

The boy turned around, dropped the flag, bent down and picked up the cash and cards. He was thrilled but refused to show it. He had just made his month's rent and drug money in minutes.

Fabrizio bent forward toward the boy, his neck stretched and his lips puckered, and kissed the boy's ass. The boy took a step back and shoved his white butt into Fabrizio's face, and Fabrizio stuck his tongue out and flicked one lick as if the boy's ass was made of vanilla ice cream.

"That twink's ass made the richest, most famous designer in the universe into an ass," Skip said.

"I need water," Gabriel said. He felt incredible thirst.

Skip went to the bar and the half-naked bartender, who had pecs like sweet-sixteen tits, gave him a comp bottle of water and a lollipop shaped like a baby's pacifier.

"That's the ecstasy kicking in. Drink this and then suck this," Skip ordered.

At once, the music stopped—frozen silence, freeze frame and pregnant pause—the lights turned off and there was total darkness. Sensory depravation. Gabriel sucked down the water. Then there was an explosion, like simultaneous lightning and thunder. Firecrackers flashed and popped as bright spots flicked back fractured light from the opening sequined curtain. A carnival band flooded the stage, and Gabriel felt so happy, like the crowd had become one solid hunk of happiness and he didn't know why and he didn't care why. He gulped water. The band danced down onto the floor— horns honked, drums beat and bells rang.

Everyone went wild and started dancing and Gabriel was dancing without even knowing it, thinking, *I love this beach with all my heart. After all that searching around the world, I finally found the place where I belong.* He lost Skip in the crowd as a girl grabbed him, pulled him into an endless Congo line, and then she moved his hands from her hips to her breasts as another girl behind grabbed his ass, as the club went dark again. Dead silence and pitch black again. Gabriel felt so connected. He felt all touchy-feely, wanted to touch and be touched, feel and be felt.

Then the spotlights illuminated the tops of little stages all over the club, lit up totally nude dancers painted gold, boys and girls, and they were faux-fuck-dancing to the beat, in all combinations, as a giant cartoon stiff dick and hanging balls were lowered from the ceiling. From the tip of the dick, white stuff ejaculated out. It was foam, and it started squirting all over the club, and people screamed and ran toward it, ran away from it, took off their clothes and covered themselves in it. Gabriel felt like he was taking an endless bubble bath with the world, being bathed as a child. Mr. Bubble after mud pies. More and more and more foam squirted out, filling up the dance floor. It climbed higher and higher till it covered his waist. It pounded to the beat of the music, and Gabriel couldn't control himself, couldn't stop moving, body on automatic, brain turning more and more on as he shut off. He was in the foam, being covered up in foam, and it was like a baptism of pleasure. Foam, the color of pearls. He pulled off his shirt, tied it around his waist. He felt every molecule of his body. Bubbles glistened, popped. Sweat dripped. And the lights were spinning and blinking and lasers were swigging and it was like being caught in an electrical sexual wave, an orgy-filled blender. Then in the foam, right next to him, three of the models were going at it, so much silky hair and skin, a perfect pink nipple, prominent cheekbones, green cat eyes that seemed to be staring at him as he felt his mouth watering and he felt something, felt a woman grab his crotch, and he didn't care who it was, just wanted that feeling as blood rushed. That feeling that he wasn't alone and he didn't want to look at her, afraid to lose it, and it felt so good. The hand pulled down his zipper, took him out and it stood up, pulsating, proud, and then his pants were down by his knees, balls dangling in the foam — then heat and wetness surrounding him and he had to look, and she was down on her knees almost covered in foam, and she was a goddess and he knew he should be down on his knees to anyone who could make him feel this good. The woman's head, above the foam now. Then he recognized her, the lip-syncher from the Venus and the song

> *I'm every woman, it's all I am,*
> *I'm every woman, it's all I am,*

filled the air at the exact moment he felt that feeling, felt it rush from his head down, reached the point of no return, he saw a hard big black uncircumcised dick pulsating in the pulsating white foam and it was sticking out from under the lip-syncher's miniskirt and he exploded, pumped into her mouth. She swallowed. He cringed! He had just been blown by a woman with a bigger dick than him.

What the Tide Dragged In

Gabriel yanked up his pants. He walked straight out of the Warsaw Ballroom and continued up Espanola Way for a block and a half until he reached the beach, and then dropped onto the sand. He looked up at the rising sun—the darkness dissolving into light, puffs of white and streaks of orange. He saw a strange raft floating on the horizon. Then he heard a noise and turned around and watched a stretch black limo with tinted black windows pull up and park on Ocean Drive.

A chauffer opened the limo door and the fabulous Fabrizio and the hot go-go boy stepped out. Fabrizio clutched the hand of the boy, who was now dressed in a gaudy Fabrizio silk fruit–patterned shirt marked, MIAMI, FLORIDA, USA and a skintight pair of white Fabrizio jeans, cut low at the waist. They stopped, looked at Gabriel for a moment and then continued a little way up the beach.

Gabriel squinted at the raft as it drifted closer to shore. It looked like something Huck Finn would have built. Then the chauffeur walked over. "Mr. Fabrizio would like to invite you to join him for breakfast," he said with a half British–half Brooklyn accent. Gabriel stood up. He craved water.

"Your name, sir?" the chauffer asked, bowing formally.

"Gabriel Tucker," he answered, following the chauffeur past a bag lady bathing fully clothed in the beach shower.

"Mr. Gabriel Tucker, I'd like to present to you Mr. Salvatore Fabrizio and Mr. Butch," the chauffer announced.

Fabrizio flashed Gabriel a phony-looking Chicklet smile. Butch rolled his eyes at Gabriel. He wanted to get his surfboard and catch a wave, wanted to go home and watch *The Simpsons*. He wanted to be anywhere but on this beach with this old dude. He had just given up his construction job. He had quit every real job he ever had. He kept being pulled into the gay-for-pay way of life.

"You looked so delicious sitting over there, so Thinker, so all-American, so how you say, so hobo-chic," Fabrizio said to Gabriel with an Italian accent. "Coffee, Pellegrino, or you want my man to fix you one of those American orange-champagne, how you call them, minusas?" Salvatore asked.

"Mimosas," Gabriel corrected. "You have any regular tap water? That Italian designer water gives me the runs." Butch cracked a smile.

Fabrizio laughed. "How delicious you are—so crass, so American. You want?" Fabrizio asked, as the chauffeur brought out a shining silver doily-covered tray with tiny pastries that looked like jewels. Gabriel grabbed a miniature éclair.

"You got any Pop-Tarts?" Butch asked. He was hungry, but not for this fancy food. He had a craving for Kraft macaroni and Miracle Whip.

"So you like Butch?" Fabrizio asked Gabriel, flicking his hand toward the boy. "He is delicious, no? So like a big steak, very rare, so U.S. prime. You want to, how you say, fuck with him? While I, how you say, watch?"

"No thanks," Gabriel answered, shocked. He looked at Butch for some sort of reaction but there was none.

"What's that thing?" Butch asked, pointing at the raft. "Is someone on it?"

"I think so," Gabriel answered, stripping off his grandfather's shirt and pants.

"Me, too," Butch said, stripping off his Fabrizio clothes down to his American flag thong, looking all of a sudden older.

Gabriel ran to the surf and dove into the ocean and Butch followed. They swam to the raft and climbed aboard. Lying on a bed of red stop signs in the fetal position was Jesus. His eyes were closed. Gabriel put his ear to Jesus' chest and heard his heartbeat.

"We have to get him to land before the police come," Gabriel said to Butch. "Dry-feet policy. If we get his feet on land, he's an American. I just read about this in the *Herald* yesterday."

Gabriel scanned the shore, and there was no one except for Fabrizio, the chauffeur and an old lady with blue hair, wearing a polka-dotted nightgown, who was searching the beach with a metal detector.

Butch lifted Jesus off the raft and into his arms, and together they looked like some sort of twisted *Pietà*. Gabriel helped Butch pull him to shore, where the muscle-bound chauffeur scooped him up. Fabrizio yanked the silk sheet from underneath the picnic, like a magician's tabletop trick. He wrapped it around Jesus, who looked like a mannequin wrapped in the world-famous lion's head, the designer's logo.

A police car pulled up behind them. The chauffeur threw Jesus onto the backseat and they pulled away down Twelfth Street onto Collins Avenue, the police car trailing them. Fabrizio took out a bottle of Pellegrino from the bar and poured some on his handkerchief and wiped Jesus' sunburned face and neck. Then, he wet the handkerchief again and held it to Jesus' lips, and he started to suck, like a baby. Gabriel couldn't help but smile, thinking the most famous Italian designer in the world was suckling this rafter with Italian designer water.

"Neptuno, a god," Fabrizio exclaimed. Then Jesus coughed. The police car's siren began to scream and blue lights flashed.

"Want me to lose the pig?" the chauffeur asked.

"Per favore!" Fabrizio said, and tires screeched as the car sped away. The buildings rushed by in a blur as car horns blared and Fabrizio clapped and Butch yelled, "Far out" and "Rad" and "Cool."

"What fun! It's so *Scarface*," Fabrizio screamed.

Gabriel shut his eyes as they jolted to a complete stop and hid in an alley behind the Strand. The police car zoomed past.

"We need to take him somewhere," the chauffeur said to Fabrizio. "They probably called in the limo and will trace it to you."

"We can go to my house," Gabriel said. "The Venus de Milo Arms, 1666 Ocean Drive."

"Yes, away we go," Fabrizio demanded.

"Who owns this magnificent building?" Fabrizio asked as they pulled up to the Venus. "It's so *Titanic*. It is my favorite."

Butch and the chauffeur carried Jesus up to Gabriel's apartment. They put him on a couch in the living room. Fabrizio and Butch undressed him, took off his transparent wet white shirt, and his torso was perfect and copper-colored and his muscles looked as if they had been etched onto his body with an X-Acto knife. Then Fabrizio pulled off his pants. His hands and feet were sunburned red, as if he were wearing gloves and socks. Fabrizio took a deep breath and removed his underwear. He expected him to have no genitals, expected him to be smooth, like an angel, but he certainly wasn't.

"Wow," Butch said. "He's gonna be one popular guy on this beach."

Fabrizio covered Jesus with a blanket, tucked him in and just stared at him as if in a trance. "This South Beach. It is magic. It send me this Neptuno. This god of a boy. To give me inspiration. This season, Salvatore Fabrizio presents: Cuban Rafter Chic!"

Sleeping Beauty Wakes

Miss Levy worked on her sewing machine, making a skirt out of an olive and baby blue beach towel she had bought on sale at Woolworth's on Lincoln Road. She didn't understand what it was about clearance racks, how gravity would just pull her toward them. Her entire apartment was painted purple and filled with her hand-made clothes and rows of shoes, and stuck to all the walls, floor to ceiling like invading pods, were her homemade hats, covered in plastic bags. She had shelves full of matching sunglasses; she'd painted the frames herself. She had her matching jewelry, all color coordinated like a rainbow, spread across her golden cherub–based glass coffee table. She watched Jesus through her open bedroom door. He was asleep on her big round bed, covered in red satin sheets. The quilted headboard was upholstered in red velvet.

Jesus stirred. Miss Levy felt his forehead and then rearranged the sheets. Gabriel had moved Jesus to Miss Levy's apartment so she could take care of him. She couldn't stop fussing over him. She was so happy to be needed. All her old friends had died or moved away from South Beach. She remembered when she would gather every day with over fifty friends in Lummus Park at their friendship circle and little orchestras would form. Someone would play the mandolin and someone else the guitar and they would all sing old Yiddish ballads together. She remembered the Cinema Theater on Washington Avenue, how it was like the Borscht Belt South and for ninety-nine cents you could watch a movie and a show. She remembered seeing the Feder Sisters, Charlotte Cooper, Howie Pepper.

Miss Levy heard a knock on her door, pulling her from her daydream, and she opened it and it was Gabriel. It was his turn to relieve Miss Levy. He, Skip, Pandora and Marina took turns watching Jesus when Miss Levy couldn't. Even though Miss Levy was unusual, Gabriel liked her. The way she cared for Jesus made him like her. And not only had she given him all that money but more important, she was a link to his past. She made him feel like he was not alone in the world, like he was not the only one left in his family.

"I love your outfit," Gabriel said, checking her out. She was dressed in a Valentine red cap, candy cane striped blouse and slacks and shoes and bag with matching white piping. "Why don't you paint your nails to match?"

"Oh, no, that would be ostentatious," she replied.

"How's our rafter doing?" Gabriel asked, following Miss Levy into her bedroom. Jesus looked like some kind of flawless mannequin asleep on Miss Levy's bed. His beauty was otherworldly.

"He wakes up and just smiles and falls back asleep," Miss Levy answered as she rubbed aloe gel onto Jesus' burnt red hands. "Never says anything. But the doctor says he's almost better."

Then the phone rang. Miss Levy answered it. She went over to her desk, pulled out a bunch of racing forms. She searched through them until she found Gulfstream Park. She grabbed her pad and starting writing. "So, Saul, that's Gulfstream, Captain of My Soul to win, five hundred dollars, race five at four o'clock." She looked at her watch. "Your number is three, eight, two, three." She stopped writing. "You have a nice day, Saul. I'll see you at the shuffleboard courts at Flamingo Park, usual time." She hung up the phone and stood and fluffed Jesus' pillows.

"I have to make some money now," Miss Levy said. "My job as part-time secretary. Wait for me in the living room. And shut the door please, dear."

"OK," Gabriel answered, wondering what kind of job she had, getting the feeling he should not ask about it as he closed her bedroom door.

Then, there was a knock on her front door. Gabriel answered it.

"I heard my muse was here. The rafter angel," Fabrizio said to Gabriel as he entered Miss Levy's apartment.

Fabrizio froze. His eyes moved all over the room. "This is fantastic. So top over. It is artwork. I love South Beach. Everywhere treasure."

Then Miss Levy walked out of her bedroom, shutting the door.

"Oh, it is you, you live here! I should figure," Fabrizio said. "I see you afar on Lincoln Road. You are fabulous. Are you a designer?"

"Yes, but I do it for my own pleasure, not like you," she said, recognizing Fabrizio from her fashion magazines. "I work as a secretary."

"So much talent and you are a secretary. A crime!"

"I taught myself. I never use a pattern, like Elsa Schiaparelli. I work by instinct. I can't help myself. My creations are taking over my apartment like a fungus. I am the custodian of over four hundred outfits. Soon I will have to rent another apartment from Gabriel and come back here to visit them."

"You are a genius," Fabrizio said, thinking, *This South Beach is so surprising.* This old woman knows about Schiaparelli. He walked over to her sewing machine and stroked a piece of chartreuse faux-fur fabric. "I must know where you get this material. It is too beautiful, so Miami Beach."

Miss Levy smiled. "I found it in the bathroom accessory department of Woolworth's." She grabbed a matching furry cap, held it up. "I made this out of the commode cover."

"You are pulling me, my·leg, funning with me," Fabrizio said, laughing.

"No, I'm serious," she said, opening the door to her bedroom. "I have to go now. You take good care of the rafter," she said to Gabriel.

Then Fabrizio saw Jesus on the bed, and he couldn't contain himself. He got so excited, he pushed past Miss Levy, entered her bedroom, pulled out a little camera and started snapping pictures of Jesus.

"Stop!" Miss Levy barked as the camera flashed. She could not believe how rude this man was, wondered if it was because he was so rich and famous.

Jesus opened his eyes, as if the flash of the camera had snapped him awake. He stretched and started to mumble something in Spanish. The only word they recognized was "Mama." He could talk!

Jesus was confused, didn't know if he was dead or alive.

Miss Levy grabbed Jesus' hand and told him, "You're safe in Miami."

Jesus' face clenched. Sharp lines of sweat formed on his forehead.

"Miami?" Jesus asked, confused, throat burning. He tasted salt, felt dry and stiff, exhausted. He craved water. The word "Miami" had cut through the fog in his head. He searched the room, trying to figure out if he was really here or if he was just dreaming. Everything was blurred, coming in and out of focus in waves, as if the moving ocean had got into his eyeballs.

Then Fabrizio began to snap more pictures.

"Are you crazy?" Miss Levy yelled, shoving herself in front of the lens. "Get out," she ordered. "The boy needs rest!" Her voice trembled.

Fabrizio grabbed Gabriel and pulled him through the door with him. "Please," he begged. "I must have three things. I need them. Some yards of that toilet fabric, that boy for my campaign and this Venus without arms. Help me. Please."

"I'll have them wrapped and delivered!" Gabriel said, laughing, and he turned around and shut the door.

Why Pandora Lip-Synchs

In her apartment at the Venus de Milo Arms, Pandora stepped out of the shower. She stood naked in front of her full-length mirror, wiped off the fog and stared at herself. Water dripped down her body as she touched her beautiful auburn, shoulder-length hair. Her mother used to always say she got her "pretty white-people hair from her good-for-nothing father." Pandora's mother met her father when he was a guest and she was a maid at the Grand Bahama Holiday Inn. He was visiting for spring break. Her father gave her mother an address in New York City. When she wrote him there nine months later, the letter was returned, stamped "Address Unknown."

Pandora searched for the only picture she had of her father. He was with her mother, who was dressed in a crisp white maid's uniform with a cap. She wore a name tag:

Hello, My Name Is Gwendolyn

She was only fifteen. Her father was wearing a Yale T-shirt with the sleeves cut off and a Speedo. There was something noble in his bearing.

Pandora stared at her face in the mirror. She saw her father's face. They had the same features, only Pandora's were softer, more feminine—her lips were fatter, lush, more like her mother's. She touched her neck, felt for her Adam's apple. It didn't stick out like a man's.

Pandora's big brown eyes followed the dripping water down her smooth body, past her narrow shoulders to her chest, to breasts that were getting fuller, now that she was getting estrogen shots.

Pandora looked down at her hips, and they were the slightest bit slender. She turned, looked at her ass in the mirror, and it was pure woman, rose up proudly, defeating gravity.

Then she winced and forced herself to look down there, between her legs, to look at it. That's what she called it. Her *it*. It didn't belong.

She grabbed *it*, grabbed her genitals and yanked—until they hurt. She shoved *it* up and back between her legs, squeezed her legs together as she imagined they were a guillotine and she was slicing *it* off. Then, she dried off and pulled on her gaff, shoving her *it* back inside the crack of her ass.

It was just a matter of time before she would earn the money for the sexual reassignment surgery. She wanted to get it done right, to get the best doctor. Her friend Tammy had cut off her own genitals with gardening shears. She thought that the doctors would finish it off for her at the hospital and turn her into a woman. But they just sewed her up. Now she was like a doll, neuter, no genitals at all but a pink hole, like a baby's anus.

Pandora got dressed. She grabbed her boom box and went downstairs and sat on the throne chair in the lobby of the Venus de Milo Arms. She switched on the stereo, put on her earphones and mouthed the words along with Judy as she sang "Over the Rainbow."

Then Gabriel walked into the lobby. He froze, smelling Pandora's sweet gardenia smell before he even saw her. Ever since their night in the Warsaw, he'd avoided her.

Pandora pulled the earphones from her ears and marched up to Gabriel, blocking him. She tried to smile. She was nervous. She had to let him know she was sorry. She had told herself she wouldn't do this anymore, not fool any more men, but there was something about Gabriel. She couldn't help herself.

Pandora blocked Gabriel, not knowing what to do. Then, she realized why she was so attracted to him. He looked like the man in the picture, like her father. Gabriel tried to get around her. But she reached forward and grabbed him by the shoulders. He yanked her hands away.

Pandora flinched, jumped back as if Gabriel was going to hit her. Then she started to tremble. Pandora remembered the buttons flying, the handsome man, the beating, the rape and then waking up in the Rand Memorial Hospital in the Bahamas. Miss Levy was there in one of her matching ensembles. They used to have lunch every week when she came from Miami to Freeport to pick up cash at the El Casino for her boss. Pandora thought she was the most glamorous person she had ever met. She remembered Miss Levy back in the hospital room wiping the tears from her eyes and saying, "As soon as I can get you out of this hospital, you are coming back with me to Miami Beach where I can take care of you and keep you safe."

Gabriel saw such fear and sadness on Pandora's face that his anger dissolved and he felt pity. She covered her eyes.

"Don't be afraid," Gabriel blurted. "I wouldn't hurt you. I'm sorry," he apologized. She just stood there crying silently.

"Please," he begged. "Say something."

Pandora's lips quivered. She couldn't. He didn't know. She hugged herself. She couldn't take it anymore. She couldn't stand her own forced silence.

"Talk to me!" Gabriel demanded. The silence screamed. "Say something, please!" Then Gabriel heard a noise behind him. He turned around.

"What's wrong with you, asshole?" Marina screamed. "She can't talk."

Pandora ran out of the room. Marina rushed after her.

Gabriel stood there alone, feeling shocked and really stupid. He realized he had never heard Pandora speak. She had always talked through the songs.

Gabriel shook his head. He was about to leave when Miss Levy walked into the lobby. She was wearing baby blue pants and a pink blouse with a matching pink and baby blue checked cap. She was pulling a big matching bag that had wheels at the bottom.

"I've been looking all over for you. I have something to show you."

Gabriel shook his head, tried to forget what had just happened with Marina and Pandora. He followed Miss Levy to the back of the lobby and then down a staircase that led to a parking garage and a car covered in a canvas tarp.

"It's yours," she smiled. "It was your grandfather Alvin's and now it's yours."

Gabriel yanked back the tarp. Sunlit dust floated through the air. He coughed. It was a gorgeous, perfectly preserved, vintage baby blue Cadillac Coupe De Ville.

She pulled out the car keys from her bag on wheels and handed them to Gabriel. "Your grandfather called this bag my Cadillac. I made it to match his car. The bottom is a skateboard. I made this before they had bags on wheels." She looked deep into his eyes, a faraway smile on her face as if she was seeing his grandfather and not him. "I am so happy Alvin sent you here," she said.

"Thank you," he said. "For the car. For the rent money."

"Me. What have I done? Nothing! Those things were always yours."

Gabriel smiled, and he saw something in her eyes. He saw love. It had been so long since he'd felt that anyone really cared about him.

"So you can't give the old lady who sweat her kishkas out taking care of your things a hug?"

Gabriel hugged her.

"My beautiful boy," she whispered into his ear, and he softened in her arms.

I Will Not Be a Whore

Jesus beamed as he gazed around his tiny studio apartment in the Venus de Milo Arms. It had a galley kitchen and a bathroom checked with pink and black tiles. There was one round porthole window that looked out toward the sea. As the day progressed, sunlight swam through the round window, spotlighting different parts of the apartment, making Jesus feel like he lived on a stage.

Jesus had only a bed, a desk and the folding beach chair that he was sitting on, but he felt like the richest man in America. *God bless America*, he thought.

He stared at the sparkling sea and said a prayer of thanks to Our Lady of Charity. Then he heard a knock on the door.

"Jesus Mas Canosa?" a gruff voice called out.

He didn't recognize the voice. He panicked. He'd learned to fear strangers in Cuba.

"Apartment five-A? We have a delivery for a Mr. Jesus Mas Canosa."

Tentatively, Jesus cracked open the door. The deliverymen were carrying a sumptuous-looking love seat upholstered in Byzantine patterned silk.

"Where do you want it, guy?" the burly man asked. His paunch fell over a leather weight lifter's belt.

"For me? No?" he asked, confused.

"You are Mr. Mas Canosa? Right? This is five-A? Venus de Milo Arms?"

"Yes," Jesus answered.

"Well, it's for you, bud," the deliveryman confirmed.

Jesus stepped aside. The men carried in the love seat, followed by an electric-baroque chair. Then huge cushions with mismatched, brilliantly colored Grecian, Medieval and Renaissance patterns; a pantry full of Fabrizio china with seashell and coral patterns; Fabrizio towel sets in black with golden palm tree appliqués; and a Fabrizio cloisonné vase. Then they carried in a dining table and chairs made with gilded silver and inlaid wood, and a gleaming crystal lamp. The stuff all looked rich and tacky at the same time—like Vegas meeting Versailles in a deco time capsule. But to Jesus it was unimaginable elegance. He was thrilled and scared.

Then they rolled in a complete wardrobe of Fabrizio clothes on racks, totally filling what little space remained in the apartment. Finally, the deliveryman brought a single, pink, perfect rose with dewdrops speckling the petals. The attached card said:

My Dearest Muse,
Just a few things to make your new life in
Miami more comfortable,
Fabrizio

P.S. Get much sleep. I need you fresh for the
shoot this week.

Then the men left and Jesus sat on his new couch and it was like sitting on a golden cloud. Now he was really petrified. He realized that this guy Fabrizio wanted him. Nobody would give him all this stuff for free, not even in America. He had to keep it professional. I will not be a whore, he told himself.

Jesus took off his T-shirt and replaced it with a Fabrizio tank top made from metal mesh. It felt cool against his skin. He had never seen anything like it. He took off his shorts and put on low-waisted, tight pants made from rubber, with raised pleated seams that clung to and accentuated his butt and groin, seeming to thrust them both out, one forward, one back. He looked in the mirror and liked what he saw. He winked at himself, slapped some sweet-smelling stuff called "RISK by Fabrizio," on his face. Then, he went out into the night.

As Jesus walked the streets of South Beach, both men and women looked at him. Some stopped and stared, while others stole glances out of the corner of their eye. He saw the desire. He felt his power. Miami Beach and Jesus were a perfect match. They both reeked of sex. Florida was a gigantic dick that hung off the continent of North America, and Miami was its head and South Beach its tip, ready to explode.

Cruising in a Vintage Cadillac

In the garage of the Venus de Milo Arms, Jesus slid from under the hood of Gabriel's Cadillac. He was wearing Fabrizio designer white overalls without a shirt, and looked like a blue-collar wet dream.

"In Cuba," Jesus explained, "this is a *nuevo* car. After Castro, no more cars. So we have to make them to work. How you say in English? Necessity is the mother of infection."

"Invention. To invent." Gabriel said, laughing. "'Infection' means to make sick."

Jesus grabbed a pair of pliers and slid back under the hood.

"One more try and then we go to a real mechanic, to Shorty's and Fred's garage on Alton," Gabriel said.

"Quiet!" Jesus yelled from under the hood.

Gabriel thought about how even though Jesus had just washed up on South Beach, he was the most normal person in the Venus.

Jesus slid back out from under the car. "Start it," he said, wiping sweat and an oil blotch from his face.

Gabriel turned the key. Jesus made the sign of the cross. The engine ground.

"*Gasolina!*" Jesus cried, fiddling with something under the hood.

Gabriel pushed the gas pedal. The car convulsed and started. Gas fumes filled the air and then dissipated.

Gabriel held up his hands and Jesus high-fived him and then jumped in the car. Jesus was deliriously happy to have helped Gabriel after all he had done for him.

Gabriel pulled out of the garage and cruised north up Ocean Drive. The sun was setting. They passed beach on one side and decaying deco buildings on the other. A sexy babe blew them a kiss at the same time as a muscle god whistled. Gabriel and Jesus looked good together. One Nordic beauty and one Latin beauty. One steel blue–eyed and golden and the other dark brown–eyed and bronzed. They kept cruising, not really heading anywhere.

"Can I ask you a question?" Gabriel asked Jesus.

"Sure."

"And you won't make fun of me?"

"Me?" he smirked.

"Did you know that Pandora had a dick?"

"Yes. I know she was a travesty."

"A transvestite," Gabriel corrected. "A pre-op transvestite."

"What pre-op means?"

"Before the operation, to make her a woman."

"They make them into woman here. America is *fantástico*," Jesus said, shaking his head in amazement.

"I didn't know," Gabriel said. "Did you know she couldn't speak?"

"Of course. She never say nothing." Jesus laughed.

"You said you wouldn't laugh at me."

Then they drove past two buildings, the Marlin and the Waldorf Towers, that sat gutless on Collins Avenue. Windows and roofs had been removed; there was nothing left but walls. They looked like deco houses of cards. Most of the paint had been sandblasted off the buildings, leaving them with blotches of color in weird patterns, like peeling tourists, revealing a faint old sign, like a ghost from prejudice past, that said, "Always a View, Never a Jew."

"Pandora blew me and I didn't know and then I found out she had a dick. I freaked and then I tried to talk to her and she couldn't and I yelled at her."

Jesus laughed again. "I'm sorry," Jesus said, putting his hand on Gabriel's shoulder.

"Go to hell!" Gabriel said.

"When I was a whore in Cuba, a travesty pay me to eat her balls."

Gabriel couldn't help but smile. Every time he got mad at Jesus, he would tell a ridiculous story and then Gabriel would stop being angry at him.

"She would make *albóndigas*—balls of meat."

"Meatballs."

"Then she cut a hole in a plate of paper and stick her *pinga* through and place two meatballs on either side. She would pay me to eat them. They was the best balls of meat I ever eat."

"Listen, I was telling you something serious and you start bull-shitting me."

"No bull was shitting on what I tell you. It true."

"I hurt Pandora."

"Listen, amigo, you don't mean to. She frighten you. I know. A dick on a chica can be a scary thing. She should have tell you."

Gabriel turned up Washington Avenue and passed empty store-fronts, windows filled to the brink with tchotchkes, thrift shops, open-air Cuban *frutarias*, a kosher supermarket, a shop that adver-tised, "Dentures While You Wait." A woman at the bus stop kept yelling: "Florida—the sunshine state—shit-rainbow-asshole-roses-cunt-puppies-dick-wish I had an Oscar Mayer wiener-son-of-a-bitch-shithead-asswipe-Miami-the magic city," as if it were all one word. Then, they passed a sprinkling of ultrahip stores that had popped up overnight to supply outfits to the new club kids: Meet Me in Miami, House of Flesh, Bomba, Sin. They kept driving through the hood where Goya met Manischewitz met Tomorrowland, where Geritol met G. They watched the passing people parade: Hasidic Jews in fur hats and long black coats, starving models on Roller-blades, Cuban *papis* smoking cigars, overbuilt muscle boys cruis-ing. An amazing palette.

"The worst thing was Marina showed up when I yelled at Pandora to speak. She called me an asshole."

"You like her?" Jesus asked as they passed Torah Treasures, Tutti Plein and then Jessie's Doll House.

"I guess."

"Just tell her you don't mean it. That you not know," Jesus said. "It is sure, you are a nice man and a smart man. Just talk with them."

"OK," Gabriel said, looking in a window of a store called Vanity Novelty Garden that had a sign marked, "Everything Cheap!"

"I need tell you *gracias*," Jesus said, pushing back the strand of impossibly thick blue-black hair that had blown across his sparkling brown eyes. They drove past Botanica Caridad, a Santeria store in which you could buy statues of saints, love potions and live roosters to sacrifice.

"For what?"

"For giving me the apartment before I could pay," Jesus said. "For lend me the money. For show me Miami."

"You're welcome," Gabriel said.

"Fabrizio will pay me much money to model," Jesus said. "I will pay you back soon."

"Don't worry."

Jesus couldn't believe he was going to be one of those people he used to see in the smuggled American glossy magazines in Cuba. He had stared at the pictures and imagined he was inserting himself into them and now it was really happening.

Gabriel drove, felt the warm air on his face. He wondered what it was about this place. Even though he had been in South Beach for only three months, he had started to feel like a part of it, a part of the community. This was a new feeling. Then he tried to figure out what to say to Marina, went over it in his head. He wanted her badly. This was also a new feeling.

SUNSTROKER

by Skip Bowling

The virus that is South Beach continues to spread. **The Warsaw Ballroom** has become world famous after a few months. Twinks and muscle daddies, like bugs to bug lights, come to worship the new god (aka HARD-ON) at the altar known as the Warsaw. From the ghost of the kosher **Hoffman's Cafeteria,** which used to host a monthly raffle where the prize was removal of a concentration camp tattoo, the Warsaw has risen into the gayest/hippest happening club of the megasecond in the galaxy. The boys sell their toys and life insurance policies and they come to South Beach for the Masque of the Red Death. Dance as if there is no tomorrow because there could be none. Flip side of the party is the funeral. *Après moi, le deluge.* AIDS and no safe sex to be found. Might as well die with a tan! Last person alive in South Beach, turn off the disco ball!

Fey girly-boys with suitcases stuffed with three-and-a-half-inch stilettos, depilatories and dreams keep getting off the Greyhounds. Our town has become Drag Hollywood, a place where boys can be girls. Drag queens were performing on top of the **Warsaw** speakers, a multi-ring circus. **Adora** performed as **Edith Piaf,** along with the **Adorettes—Marvella, Taffy Lyn, Mother Kibble, Placida, Brigit Buttercup** and **Gidget. Damian Dee-vine** started stabbing a raw piece of meat and accidentally cut herself and blood spurted all over but she never stopped her act. Always a professional. Spotted shirtless **Rupert Everett** and boyfriend **Martin** in a dark corner. Baseball player **Billy Bean** also seen. Is he or isn't he? Don't be ridiculous; no one in professional sports could be homo. Gays can't throw balls, only play with them. Italian fashion designer, **Salvatore Fabrizio** spotted throwing mucho money at tasty postpubescent **Butch,** the most genitally gifted go-go boy, who was a real patriot, hiding his ten-inch flagpole with an American flag. **Fabrizio** and Butch were seen leaving together at sunrise. Maybe Fabrizio was going to help Butch with his algebra homework. Septuagenarian **Miss Henrietta Robinson,** South Beach's original Queen, telling yours truly that they used to throw you in jail for impersonating a woman. Once she got arrested for wearing women's clothes—shirts with ruffled sleeves and hip-huggers—but she had bought them at the **Slack Shack,** a men's store on **Lincoln Road Mall,** and she had a receipt to prove it. The judge dismissed the case.

Then to add some yin to the yang, from fake girls to real girls, off to the super-hetero battleground **Rebar** (located in the old **Stein's Hardware** store), where pussy rules. A bevy of **Barbarella**-looking go-go girls gyrated, hot pants slipping up barely covered boxes.

Then off to **Chris Paciello**'s club of the moment, **RISK.** There were models galore, everywhere. Fashion photographer **Bruce Weber,** here shooting a pseudopornographic **Obsession** ad with a bevy of nude greased models on the roof of the **Breakwater,** caused a massive traffic jam on **Ocean Drive.** Photographic genius **Helmut Newton,** in South Beach shooting senior citizen, ex-porno star **Vanessa del Rio** for a **Taschen** ad at writer **Brian Antoni's** over-the-top home. **Gianni Versace** with sister **Donatella,** here shooting a book, rumored to be called *South Beach Stories* (Latin hunks in kitsch Florida-inspired silk shirts draped all over South

Beach). Met model mogul **Irene Marie,** who introduced me to a beauty she discovered on the beach that day named **Niki Taylor.** A dozen modeling agencies, including **Ford, Elite** and **Michelle Pommier,** have all opened on our magic sandbar.

Then saw lovely, local-born "It" girl, **Ingrid Casares,** in tailored Chanel suit, in lip-lock with luscious-lipped comedian **Sandra Bernhard. Chris Paciello** fawned all over the couple as every **Malibu Barbie** in the room fawned over him. The Gals of South Beach sure like their guys with a little thug in them!

Gabriel and Marina
Get Buck Naked

Gabriel stared through a porthole into the empty pool of
the Venus de Milo Arms. He pictured Marina lying on the pool's
bottom, his weight piercing the words into her skin.

We must love each other or die.
If not now when?

And then he felt a delicate tap on his shoulder and turned around.
Marina, in the flesh. Their eyes met. He took a deep breath. She
looked down, shifted her weight from one foot to the other. The
sun stuck to strands of her long black hair. "I'm sorry," she said,
sheepishly.

"For what?" Gabriel asked, forcing a smile to cut the tension.

"I'm sorry for calling you an asshole," she said. "I didn't know, um,
that you didn't know that Pandora couldn't speak." She paced. "I
didn't know that you didn't know she had a . . . you know, that. . . ."
She paused. "A penis." She exhaled.

"I was shocked," Gabriel explained.

"Pandora shouldn't do that."

"I'm so sorry I hurt her."

"She's saving money to get sexual reassignment surgery."

"I feel so bad for her."

Marina paused, looked at him for a second, and then she leaned forward and kissed him. Gabriel felt her lips and his lips, soft against soft, and before he could focus on the feeling, she pulled away. He exhaled, taken aback.

"What was that for?"

"'Cause you feel sorry for Pandora. 'Cause you apologized to her," she said, "'cause you are not some macho asshole."

Gabriel tried to kiss her again. She turned her head. His lips grazed cheek.

"Let's go somewhere," she uttered, nervously.

"Where?" he asked, frowning.

"Swimming—let's go swimming," she said. "I'll take you to my favorite beach."

She grabbed his hand and they walked hand in hand to her pickup truck. Marina drove without paying very close attention to the road, looking at Gabriel as she talked. They drove up Alton Road, passed an incredible deco Firestone tire store. Then they passed a three-story-tall green arm with an open hand jutting out from the ground, surrounded by a black pool.

"What's that?" Gabriel asked.

"The Holocaust Memorial," she answered as they pulled into the Publix supermarket with the neon sign, "Where Shopping Is a Pleasure." The building had a two-story winged central pylon that looked like the gigantic fins of a fifties Cadillac. They walked inside, from the sweltering heat of the parking lot into the frigid air-conditioning.

"What do you like to eat?" Gabriel asked, pushing the cart down the aisle.

"Vegetables, fruit," she said. "I don't eat anything with a face."

She threw carrots, celery and peanut butter into the cart. Gabriel added mangoes, bananas and grapes. He grabbed a bottle of wine, a bottle of water, a bag of ice and some Brie.

Then they drove north out of South Beach, up A1A through cookie-cutter condo canyons and then the tiny town of Surfside,

until they crossed a bridge and drove through Haulover. They
parked and walked through a grove of sea grapes onto the beach.
There was a sign that said:

Warning, you may encounter nude people beyond this point.

The beach was crowded, golden sand covered in naked skin,
thousands of breasts and balls, asses—everything swinging, palm
fronds blowing, the smell of suntan oil, competing radios, cloudless blue sky and choppy blue sea.

They strolled down to the hard sand, walked through the in-out
of the waves, passed the family section, passed the gay section, passed
the naked volleyball, until it got less crowded. The sun burned
down. Gabriel felt sweat.

Marina stopped. "Here," she said, "the perfect spot." She spread
her smiley-face towels, pulled off her clothes. Gabriel bit his lip,
looking but trying not to stare at her creamy skin, the arc of her hips,
at her taut stomach, her smooth thighs and between.

"That feels better," she said, "I love being naked."

Gabriel pulled off his own shirt, his bathing suit, sat down on
the blanket, unclenched his abs and took a deep breath. Even though
he usually felt totally comfortable nude, he felt nervous.

"You have a beautiful body," Marina told him, studying him as
if she were looking at a sculpture. She blinked.

"So do you," Gabriel said, relieved.

"Thanks. I want to sketch you sometime," she said, jumping up.
"Let's go swimming." Then she ran and dove into the sea. Gabriel
followed her, the cool water climbing up his naked body, higher
and higher, hot skin sizzling cool.

She swam out and then back and then they lay in the surf, letting the waves break over their bodies, staying in until their skin
started to shrivel. Then they walked to their towels and sat down,
water drying on their skin, cool turning to hot. They started to eat
the fruit and cheese and bread and passed the bottle of wine between them. They watched a woman with huge bubble breasts

blow soap bubbles for her hot dog–shaped dog, which would jump up and bite them into nothing.

"Rub some on me," she said, handing him a bottle of Coppertone.

Gabriel spread lotion on his hands and as he touched her back, the current went from her skin straight to his groin. Then, he handed her the bottle and flopped onto his stomach.

She massaged the oil onto Gabriel's neck and then his shoulders. Jimmy Buffet's "Margaritaville" played on someone's radio. Her fingers touched the small of his back, then descended to the top of his ass and didn't stop, going lower and lower.

Edge Play

Gabriel sat in the office of Miami Beach Property Inc., the company that managed the Venus de Milo Arms. He tried to listen to Brandy, the woman in charge, but the painted mole on her papery-looking cheek distracted him. It looked just like a fly. He wanted to slap it.

"Honey doll," Brandy explained in a smoky, Florida-cracker accent. "Between maintenance and electricity costs, along with water, gas, garbage, insurance, licenses, taxes and our management fees, you are losing a couple thousand and change a month."

"Great," Gabriel said.

"Oh, sweetheart." She sighed. "Everyone knows you inherited more money than God." She fluttered thickly blue–eye shadowed eyelids and stuck out her breasts, her cleavage like the crack of a baby's ass. She licked the point of her pencil and said, "You owe about one hundred thousand dollars and change."

Gabriel hung his head. If he paid that off, he would be broke again.

"You should let me dispose of the Venus for you," she said, flipping her card at him:

Brandy Byrd, Licensed Real Estate Agent
Service with much more than a smile

"I can get you one and change for the Venus," she said. "One cool million, sugar. It's a teardown. That's property value. South Beach is hot. I have clients assembling beachfront parcels to build condos."

"What about fixing it up?"

"Fixing that albatross is like pouring money down the drain. Your uncle Ian, God rest his soul, ran your building into the ground."

"I'll think about it." Gabriel stood up.

"One of my clients would go hard for your dump."

"Hard?"

"Cash," she leered.

"Thanks," Gabriel said, nodding.

"No, thank *you*," she replied, standing up, her hands on her hips. "My home phone is on the back of the card, sexy." She winked obscenely.

Gabriel walked to Skip's apartment to get his advice. He knocked. No answer. He heard a strange noise, like a moan for help. Gabriel turned the knob. The door was locked.

The creepy gagging sound got louder. Gabriel stuck his diamond-studded golden key into Skip's lock. This key seemed to open every lock in the Venus. The latch on Skip's door clicked and then unlocked. He smelled stale cigarettes. It was dark.

"Skip," he mumbled, stumbling toward the sound. He tripped, caught his balance and then fumblingly, opened the Venetian blinds. Setting sunlight streamed, highlighting the books and yellow pads and magazines almost completely papering the floor. Ashtrays full of cigarette butts and empty cans of Diet Coke littered the room. The only furniture was a beat-up metal desk, a tartan La-Z-Boy chair with duct-taped rips and a rusted iron bed. Gabriel rubbed his eyes, squinted.

A naked man was tied to the iron bed with red velvet ropes. His sweaty body was adolescent-looking — bony and awkward. His head was completely covered with a leather hood. Gabriel opened his zippered mouth carefully, afraid to catch the man's lip. It looked so alien, surrounded in silver zipper and black leather. Cigarette-stained teeth outlined a slippery tongue. The man choked and then took deep breaths and spoke, and Gabriel realized it was Skip.

"Untie me," Skip demanded.

Gabriel untied the ropes as gently as possible. Then Skip yanked the hood and it slowly stretched off, revealing his head, like a baby being born. His face was red and covered in sweat, his hair all matted and messed.

Skip got up and checked his wallet. "Shit!" he yelled, throwing it against the wall. "Butch took all my money." Then he pulled on a pair of pickle-patterned Joe Boxers, lit a cigarette, got a Diet Coke from the fridge and swallowed it down in a few gulps. He burped and, sitting on the La-Z-Boy, kicking up the footrest said, "You should have seen him."

"Who?" Gabriel asked, sitting across from him on his old-fashioned wooden rolling desk chair.

"Butch," he said. "The trick. Has an A&F face, an adolescent body, a porn star cock."

"This Butch guy dance at Warsaw? I know him. He helped me rescue Jesus."

"Yeah, he's so hot. Super straight! I think I'm in love."

"You're in love with the asshole who tied you up and robbed you? You shouldn't do this shit. You could get hurt."

"I like getting hurt."

"That's messed up."

"It turns me on. My body was never my friend—I want to get back at it."

"Why?"

"Why anything?" Skip asked, and his look shifted. He lit another cigarette, inhaled deeply and glanced at Gabriel. "OK, I'll try." He sighed. "I was just like you. I was rich, an heir."

"I'm not rich. My uncle stole all my money. All I have left is the Venus, and it's in debt."

"Well, we both lost fortunes," Skip said. "I lived in a mansion in Indian River, Florida. Redneck central. My grandfather was king of citrus; shipped Honeybells all over the world. When he found out I was gay, he told my dad that if I didn't change my last name, he would disinherit him. Family values. Didn't want anyone carrying the family name to be gay. My dad made me do it. I signed the papers and then told him to fuck off and ran away to Maimi Beach. I was fifteen. Haven't seen anyone in my family since."

"How did you survive?"

"I met the love of my life the day I got to Miami. In Wolfies. Dennis was his name. He was the first guy who ever fucked me," he said softly, combing his hair with his hand. "I knew I should have used a rubber. But Dennis was a doctor. Forty years old. I trusted him. He told me it would feel much better without one. He told me he loved me. He told me he would never do anything to hurt me. After Dennis fucked me, he told me he had AIDS." Skip took a deep breath. "I wanted everything he had. He was the only person that ever loved me. I kept letting him screw me bareback. I was young and stupid. I stayed with him till he died of AIDS. He left me some money. I used it to go to U of M."

Gabriel wanted to console Skip but didn't know how.

"In a couple months, I'll be thirty. That will be a decade and a half I've spent with the virus. I've had full-blown AIDS for six years now."

"But you don't look sick."

"That's the joke. All these muscle boys moving into town are full of virus. They're on steroids, to prevent their bodies from wasting. They're turning their life insurance into steroids and ecstasy. That's why they dance all night. South Beach is becoming a giant coffin disguised as a club."

Gabriel thought how South Beach had now really become God's waiting room. All the old retirees and now the AIDS retirees. The old and wrinkled and the young and beautiful living side by side in the same deco apartments. The young people were even dressing like the old people, buying their clothes in thrift shops. Both groups dropping dead.

"Sometimes I can't sleep, I'm so afraid of dying," Skip said. "Other times, I imagine myself in a coffin and I fall fast asleep."

"You need to get help," Gabriel said. "Go to a shrink."

"I go to hustlers instead of shrinks."

"They might kill you."

"The first real sign of AIDS, I'm going to kill *myself*," he said. "I'll control it. It won't control me. Death is like coming—the same chemicals are released. I'll die when I want to, on my terms."

"They'll find a cure. You'll be fine," Gabriel said because he didn't know what else to say.

"Yeah, and we'll all live happily ever after," Skip said with a shrug.

Not for Sale, Maybe?

Gabriel sat on his terrace at the Venus de Milo Arms. He wore sunglasses, suntan lotion and nothing else. His skin was oiled and glistening gold and his sun-bleached hair was slicked up with sweat. He looked half punk, half surfer. Sweat zigzagged past abs, pooling into his belly button and then overflowing onto the Venus financial papers, blurring the ink. As it was, the numbers already blurred before his eyes, mainly because they reminded him that he didn't know how he was going to pay the money that he owed on the building.

Gabriel had realized that the first cut he could make was to fire Brandy and Miami Beach Property Inc. and take over the management himself, and had done this earlier that day.

Suddenly he heard a knock on the door. He wrapped a beach towel around his waist and answered it.

Fabrizio was dressed in a white linen suit and carried a Louis Vuitton suitcase. His eyes rested an instant on Gabriel's crotch. Then, he kissed him on both cheeks and sat down on the couch, putting the suitcase next to him.

"I no have much time. The limo, she is waiting. I must meet Elton at the airport. I need you to sell me this Venus Without Arms. I am prepared to give you," Fabrizio said, taking out a small leather-covered pad and golden Montblanc pen from his pocket. He wrote something on a piece of paper, ripped it from the pad, folded it and slid it over to Gabriel.

Gabriel opened it. Written daintily on the sheet of paper was "$1,500,000.00 dollars U.S.A." Gabriel took a deep breath, his brain going into overdrive, thinking this could be the answer to all his problems and that he could squeeze Fabrizio for more money. In fact, he didn't want to sell at any price, but there was the problem of paying off the taxes, and future income.

Fabrizio smiled at him weakly, waiting for an answer. "I want to make this Venus With No Arms into my *casa*, a showplace of Fabrizio style."

"I don't know" was the only answer Gabriel could muster.

"The limo. She is waiting," Fabrizio said, practically licking his chops. He placed the suitcase flat on the coffee table and dramatically flipped open the top with a click. "Me, I like-a the cash!"

Bundles of green, perfectly stacked — the suitcase was crammed full of them. Gabriel looked closer and saw that they were all crisp one-hundred-dollar bills. He had never seen so much money at one time before. Fabrizio pulled out a contract, handed it to Gabriel.

"My lawyer, he draws this up. There is one hundred thousand in the case. You sign, you get the rest."

Gabriel froze, thinking, *The money is freedom.* Sweat formed under his armpits.

"Sign it," Fabrizio urged.

Gabriel drew a breath. "How about two million?"

"That is not a problem," Fabrizio answered without a pause, changing the selling price on the contract and initialing it. "We have a deal." He smiled, holding the golden pen out to Gabriel.

Gabriel grabbed it, tried to sign the contract, but the pen turned into a slippery snake. "I want you to always keep the Venus in the family," he heard his grandfather say in his head. It would be like selling his history, his only connection to his family. *It is only brick and mortar,* he told himself, but in fact he thought of the building as flesh, as a living thing. The pen dropped out of his hand.

"I need time," Gabriel said.

"Let me know soon, because there is another building I can buy instead," Fabrizio said firmly, snapping the case full of money shut. He picked it up and walked toward the door. Then, he stopped and turned. "Come to Jesus' photo shoot the day following tomorrow. It will be much fun. I must to know by then."

"OK," Gabriel said, and fought the urge to yank the caseful of money out of Fabrizio's hand as he left. He felt like he was losing a lifeline.

The Kiss

Gabriel walked along Ocean Drive. Pelicans, Frisbees, wild parrots, seagulls, kites, the Goodyear blimp, clouds and an airplane pulling a banner of Marky Mark wearing only his Calvins floated by in the sky. White breakers broke from blue water. Sun burned. Ocean breezes caressed. Palm fronds rustled.

Gabriel plucked a butter yellow double hibiscus from a bush by the sidewalk. "Sell the Venus, don't sell the Venus," he chanted, tearing the petals from the flower.

A blaring ambulance with blinking red lights pulled in front of the Victor Hotel. Gabriel made the sign of the cross. He wondered if it was an old retiree or a young AIDS retiree. He kept walking, passed an alley next to the Cardozo Hotel, newly rehabbed by Gloria Estefan. Next to some putrid garbage cans were two whores dressed in identical chartreuse Lycra hot pants, a junkie smoking crack— and Marina. Cats surrounded her.

"Marina, what the hell are you doing?" Gabriel asked.

"What does it look like?" she replied, kissing him on the cheek. Her face was hot and slick. She smelled of coconut.

"You're either a whore or you're doing research for your audition for *Cats.*"

"I'm feeding the strays," she said, laughing. She grabbed his hand, pulled him across Ocean Drive onto the beach and then into the cool water. Gabriel followed her as she swam farther and farther into the ocean.

"Look," she said, pointing toward the shore. "South Beach is most beautiful from here."

Gabriel wiped his eyes and stared. He saw a carpet of blue water, an outline of golden beach and then the deco buildings rising up against the sky: the Surfcomber, the Ritz Plaza, the Sands, the Delano, the Shore Club, the Tides, the Venus de Milo Arms. He followed the pattern of line, plane, angle and curve of the buildings and they looked like gigantic Cubist sculptures — yet somehow so human and simple, as if made by a gigantic child playing with gigantic blocks. Gabriel shook his head.

"What's wrong?" Marina asked.

"I don't know what to do," Gabriel said, and then they swam in until they could stand.

"About what?" Marina asked, taking off her wet T-shirt, marked, "Whitney Biennial." Her tanned breasts bobbed in the water.

Gabriel took off his shirt, imagined his nipples up against her nipples.

"About the Venus," he said. "Fabrizio wants to buy it for a lot of money."

"To knock it down?"

"To turn it into his home. A house of Fabrizio style."

"Fabrizio style?" she repeated, shaking her head. "That's an oxymoron."

"I owe a lot of back taxes. If I pay them off, I'll be broke."

"It's the beginning of the end," she said. "Gays and artist—urban pioneers create their own extinction, are pushed out by their own good taste. You can't stop the tide."

"What should I do?" Gabriel asked. "I don't want to sell," he said, thinking, *I want to stay here with you.*

"Well, then we have to fix up all the empty apartments, rent them out, make the Venus turn a profit," she said. "I'll help you. Maybe we can stop the tide."

"Maybe," he said, the thought of bringing the Venus back already exciting him. It would make his grandfather proud.

"I rehabbed my loft in Soho," she said. "I know all about construction."

"You lived in Soho?"

"For ten years."

"Why'd you leave?"

"It changed. Galleries to boutiques. Artists to millionaires. I put everything I owned in a big pile in Deitch Projects Gallery. I let people take what they wanted. Then I got in my car and started driving. When I got to South Beach," she said, scratching her head, "I stayed. I don't know why."

"I feel the same way. South Beach has seduced me," he said, thinking, *And so have you.* Then he made up his mind. "Fuck Fabrizio!" he yelled. "He can't buy me. I will stop the tide!" He slapped his hands down, splashing the water.

"We'll stop the tide," Marina yelled, delighted. She grabbed him around the neck and scissored her legs around his midsection. Then she brought her face to his face, and her lips touched his lips, a solidified fantasy in the liquid, his tongue on her tongue, exploring, tasting, sucking, waves breaking, beating, heating, heart pounding out of his chest, blood rushing, salt tasting, coconut smelling—her aquamarine eyes staring into his eyes.

A Star Is Born

Gabriel sat with Jesus in the Big Time Productions trailer parked on the beach. A woman, who looked like a model gone to seed, plucked and shaped Jesus' eyebrows.

"In Cuba, this lady, Helena Ruth, pay me to let her pluck out my public hair."

"Pubic, not public hair," Gabriel corrected him. "And why?"

"Helena Ruth said she wanted to make me stay a boy, to not turn into a man, because all men hurt women."

"She's damn right," the makeup artist said as she plucked out a final stray hair. Then she curled his eyelashes and combed his eyebrows.

"How's my muse?" Fabrizio asked, walking into the trailer. He stepped back and seemed to tremble as he stared at Jesus. "You are perfection! You are Fabrizio!"

Then they all strolled to a ten-foot-square raft wrapped in baroque-printed Fabrizio silk fabric and laced with a netting of golden cord; it was like the raft Jesus floated in on dressed in drag. Thirty more models came out of the other trailers, all wearing identical white robes. Fabrizio whispered something into an assistant's ear and she took their robes and soon all of the beauties were standing nude on the sand.

Fabrizio took the hand of an angelic-looking blond boy with sleepy green eyes. He led him over to the raft, told him to lie flat on the sand, one arm stretched out and one hand covering his genitals. He bent one of the boy's legs up under his body and bent the other leg and hooked it to the raft. Then he scrutinized the group and picked out a girl. He had her lie on the raft, and grab the leg of the boy. He placed the other models, one at a time, on the raft, molded them into each other. At first, the mass of models just looked kind of clumsy, but then it all came together and turned into a human sculpture, turned into a modern *Raft of the Medusa*. Gabriel was amazed that the man with the gaudy clothes had such an elegant touch with human choreography.

Fabrizio sauntered up to Jesus and peeled off his robe and handed it to an assistant. Then he stood back and gazed at Jesus as if he were a huge diamond or a perfect sunset. He led him to the top of the raft, to the highest point, where he had two boys and a girl grab him around the waist and legs, just covering his genitals. Assistants then misted the models with big white cans of Evian, as if they were gigantic ferns, and someone carried out a silk scarf covered with the Fabrizio lion's head logo.

"There is a storm," Fabrizio shouted to the models, gesticulating wildly. "The raft, she is sinking, you are crawling up, so you no drown. You see a boat, you point, look at Jesus, see him waving the scarf." He paced, full of adrenaline. "It is up to Jesus to save you." Fabrizio took the scarf with his logo from his assistant and placed it in Jesus' outstretched hand.

"Fans," he yelled, and five gigantic fans were turned on. The sail smacked in the faux gust. The scarf flapped in Jesus' hand, like a flag in the wind. "Struggle! Struggle!" Fabrizio screamed as the photographer clicked away. "The scarf," Fabrizio yelled. "Look to the scarf." He seemed possessed. "Emotion, emotion," he shouted. "You die if the ship no see you!"

The photographer just kept taking pictures, moving around the raft as Fabrizio strode back and forth, kicking up sand. "More," he yelled. "I want more."

That's exactly what I want, Jesus thought. *More.* He loved being in front of the camera. He knew the exact look to put on his face — a combination of fear and desire and desperation. He'd learned how to act from being a good whore.

Then Fabrizio yelled, "Rain," and a truck pulled up and sprayed streams of water over the models. Jesus opened his mouth and started to drink.

"*Fabuloso,*" Fabrizio yelled. "Keep drinking! That's it!"

The photographer continued to shoot until Fabrizio whispered something in his ear. Then he put down his camera and everything stopped, went silent. The models stood shivering in position.

"You can now dry," Fabrizio said softly, breathing heavily. Then, he strolled over to Gabriel. "Now, I must ask the million-multidollar question. Will you sell me your Venus With No Arms?"

This was the question Gabriel had been dreading. He looked over at Jesus. He thought of the rest of them: Miss Levy, Pandora, Skip and, most of all, Marina. He could not break them up. Finally, he thought of his grandfather.

"I'm sorry," Gabriel answered.

"Do not be sorry, my boy. When you possess beauty, you should try to do everything you can to keep it, to own it." Fabrizio glanced over at Jesus. "The Venus Without Arms. She is beauty!" Fabrizio walked away.

Jesus, who was now wearing a white robe, walked up to Gabriel and flicked some water at him.

Gabriel laughed and said, "A star is born."

"I hope so," Jesus said. "That's why I came to America, the land of dreams—so that all my dreams would come true."

And it was in this moment that Gabriel knew that in fact Jesus would become a star. And for some reason, he felt scared for him.

SUNSTROKER

by Skip Bowling

It's another South Beach Saturday night and so many things are opening, my head is spinning. Clubs, clubs and more clubs! So many new faces. So many famous faces, jet set faces, royal faces. I used to know everyone in this town. Now, the street, like model Mardi Gras, all beautiful but few chosen. Skip, Skip, please take my picture. Write about me! I'll blow you! South Beach has become a fame factory.

REM, Burning Flames, Ashton Hawkins of the Metropolitan Museum, **Suzanne Bartsch** with entourage of imported twisted drags including the talented **Joey Arias** who channeled **Billie Holiday,** attended the opening of the **Marlin Hotel,** owned by **Chris Blackwell** (Mr. Island Records). The dripping shell-encrusted melting deco meets Caribbean wonderland is the work of designer **Barbara Hulaniki** (of **Biba/Carnaby Street** fame). At a U2 postconcert party later in the week, **Clash** legend **Mick Jones** and **Public Enemy's Chuck D,** photographer **Herb Ritts, Russell Simmons, Quincy Jones, Jimmy Buffett** and a bevy of fourteen-year-old girls waiting outside for glimpses of **Johnny Depp** and **Kate Moss.**

And if we didn't have enough queens in town, now we have their children. **Filipe de Borbón, Prince of Astúrias** and heir to the Spanish throne, being chased by Euro paparazzi up **Española Way**. America's own Fresh Prince, **Will Smith,** seen munching down at **Pacific Time**. **Prince Egon Von Furstenberg** with **Regine** at **Love Muscle**. **Baroness Joanna Wittgenstein** held a regal party for **Miami Light Project**. **Prince Albert of Monaco** seen buying edible male and female underwear at erotic boutique **Sex Sells** on **Washington Avenue**.

The most royal of them all, none other than **Prince, Mr. Purple** himself, opened his club, **Grand Slam,** on his birthday. Door scene, an attitudinal war zone of hysterical desperation of historical proportions. Then inside, two huge screens where we had to watch our motley selves, most disheveled from the entrance war. Then Prince and his symbol-shaped guitar hit the stages for an indescribably difficult rock-operatic performance. Still trying to regain my hearing.

Hottie **Chris Paciello's** once hot, now so-over club **Risk** turned red hot when it caught fire and burned to the ground. Very convenient. Rumor has it that the inferno was started by a lit cigarette stuffed into a couch long after Risk closed. Rumor has it, Mr. Paciello received mucho moola from his insurance company. He is scouting a space for a new club he will call **Liquid** with his new partner, celeb gal pal **Ingrid Casares,** who was observed cavorting around town with handsome **k.d. lang.** This may be the answer to the short shelf life of clubs and everything else in the New South Beach. When they are not hot anymore, they spontaneously combust!

But You Are Nude

"I ask for the most big," Jesus said as the super-stretch white limo, with neon trim, pulled up in front of the Venus de Milo Arms.

"It's f-a-b-u-l-o-u-s," Pandora signed to Miss Levy, and her fingernails were painted glow-in-the-dark green. Miss Levy translated the finger movements to words so they could all understand. She had learned sign language so she could help Pandora communicate.

"I think the limo is just lovely," Miss Levy said as the chauffeur got out and held the door open. She was dressed in Liz Taylor–style vintage chenille and black toile slacks with black pillbox cap and matching purse. "But Jesus, you should save your money for a rainy day."

"Don't preoccupy yourself," Jesus said. "This is America. The streets, they make out of gold!"

"Where are we going?" Marina asked as the limo whizzed north up Meridian Avenue.

"I want to make you a surprise," Jesus answered, grabbing Marina's hand and holding it, and looking so happy, so handsome in his white Fabrizio tuxedo.

Gabriel peered at Marina in her simple little no-name black dress with spaghetti straps, and his eyes rested at the delicate hollows between her neck and shoulder blades and he felt his heart skip a beat. He wanted to grab her hand away from Jesus. He replayed the kiss in the water over and over in his head.

They pulled up to The Forge, a restaurant that looked like a Disney version of the Palace of Versailles. As they were led to their table, they could hear people asking, "Who are they?" They were seated in the center of the room under a fake stained glass dome.

"This is the A table in the A room," Skip said.

"What you mean?" Jesus asked.

"It means it's the best one," Skip answered.

"But all the tables. They are the same," Jesus said.

"No, it's the best because of the positioning," Skip said, as Miss Levy took the packs of sugar from the silver holder and stuck them in her purse. She had craved sugar so much in Auschwitz that she could not resist taking some whenever she saw it.

Jesus shook his head. "This America, it have so much that people need to think one thing is better than another even though it the same."

Light was streaming, bouncing, flaming, all over, through stained glass, from crystal, off mirrors and on candle tips. Everywhere Gabriel gazed, he saw old men with young women, turkey wattles hanging and cleavage protruding.

"What are we celebrating?" Gabriel asked as they were served a microgreens salad.

"My six-month anniversary in America, and this," Jesus said, pulling out a *Vogue* from a paper bag. He opened it and held a page up for them to see. It was a photograph of Jesus on the raft. He stood out from the other models, looked three-dimensional, as if he were coming out of the page. Waves had been superimposed around the raft and an aura of light seemed to envelop Jesus. He looked like a cross between an angel and the devil, a cross between decadence and innocence. He was a beautiful Satyricon. Across the bottom of the page was written, "Risk it all, Fabrizio."

"Fame," Skip said, looking at the striking ad. "Now the shit's gonna hit the fan."

Miss Levy put on her reading glasses, whose oversized frames she had painted black and white to match the color of her outfit, and studied the picture. "But you are nude. I thought you were selling clothes," she said, remembering when she was young and beautiful and used to dance at the Latin Quarter on Palm Island. She drifted back to the translucent stage, the mirrored ceilings, her beautiful outfits. She remembered owner Lou Walters' little daughter Barbara helping to zip up her skimpy costume that would be so tame by today's standards. She remembered all the men falling in love with her and her wanting none of them, her heart having already been shattered by Gabriel's grandfather.

Then six waiters surrounded their table, each holding platters covered in silver lids. They lifted them up at the same time to reveal gigantic lobsters, red and prehistoric-looking. The waiters put plastic bibs on everyone.

Jesus tapped his glass with his fork. "I brought you all to dinner to celebrate that today I sign a year exclusive contract for much money to be representing Fabrizio," and then he looked really serious. He took a deep breath, held up his glass. "In Cuba, I thought that everything in America was made of gold, and I was right. You are all made of gold." Everyone clinked glasses.

"I'm into Pain"

Gabriel and Jesus scraped paint off the walls of one of the remaining vacant apartments in the Venus de Milo Arms. They had all been fixing up the Venus for a month now. Gabriel had the roof repaired, removed all the flock wallpaper and shag carpeting in the lobby, polished the terrazzo underneath till it gleamed. All the walls were given a fresh coat of smooth paint. Marina chose the colors using Leonard Horowitz's palette of pastels: peach, aqua, lavender and salmon. Skip helped Gabriel hire homeless workers for minimum wage from Camillus House across the bay. Miss Levy and Pandora made them all coffee and sandwiches and snacks. So many people were flocking to South Beach that Gabriel had a waiting list of prospective tenants. So far, he had rented to a bartender, an author, three air hostesses, a chef, four waiters, a club promoter, two models, a country music singer/clown/mime, a construction worker, a dental hygienist, a stripper and an Elvis impersonator.

Gabriel painted "MARINA" on the wall in pastel pink paint.

"You are obsessed," Jesus taunted.

"I know," Gabriel agreed, painting over her name. He wished he could erase his feelings for her as easily as her name.

"*Estúpido*," Jesus pronounced, dipping his brush into the paint. "This America has too many hot *chicas* to be crazy over one."

"I kissed her and now she seems to avoid me. Do me a favor? Ask Marina how she feels about me?"

"*No problema,*" Jesus replied.

"Thanks for paying your rent in advance so I would have extra money to fix up the Venus."

"*De nada,*" Jesus said. "You save me."

Then the door to the apartment opened. "Time to go, studs," Skip said.

"We no need to change?" Jesus asked.

"Not necessary," Skip said. "You guys look perfect for where we're going. Tonight, the king of the night is escorting you boys to the edge."

"To the edge of what?" Gabriel asked as they followed Skip out of the apartment.

"Miami—the edge of Miami, which is itself the edge of America, which is itself the edge of the world," Skip pronounced.

They walked to Gabriel's Cadillac convertible. It was a picture-perfect, moon-over-Miami night. As Gabriel drove up Ocean Drive, Jesus pulled some pills from his pocket. "This *chica* I make sex with last night give me these X." He swallowed a pill, handed one to Skip and then stuck one into Gabriel's mouth. They drove over the Julia Tuttle Causeway into downtown Miami and then by the Miami River into a neighborhood full of warehouses and pulled into an alley behind the Sanitary Beef Company Inc. They walked over puddles of dry blood mixed with sawdust to a back door with a painting of a dripping red cross. It smelled of putrefying cow. Skip rang a bell, said into the intercom, "I'm into pain."

"Pain!" Jesus exclaimed. "I'm into pleasure."

"No pain, no gain," Skip giggled, grabbing his arm.

Gabriel could not help but laugh, the X tickling his brain. He followed Skip and Jesus into the darkness. The air was thick and wet, like a locker room. It reeked of decomposing amyl nitrate mixed with sweat, oiled leather and stale smoke. The thud of paddling and whipping combined with the sound of begging and grunts and sobs and groans and sighs and slurps and gobs and yelps and mechanical music. The sound of pleasure mixed with pain mixed with boredom mixed with hunger mixed with faux terror.

"Hi, Skippy," a woman dressed like a New York City cop said as she grabbed Gabriel by the collar. "Spread them, blondie," she demanded. Her pierced, silicone breasts flopped out of her open shirt. Gabriel stood there as she patted him down and gave his genitals a gentle caress.

When their eyes adjusted to the dark, they could make out slings, cages, racks, bondage chairs, suspension bars, a St. Andrews cross and people dressed like babies, bikers, construction workers, soldiers and naked slaves. Packs of hungry-looking men surrounded the few women in the club. Others milled around like zombies.

Skip's face lit up like an addict about to get a fix as he watched some nude, pumped muscleman flexing. "Don't worry, this place is soft-core," Skip said, "just Sears leather and game playing." Then Skip walked ahead, leaving Jesus and Gabriel together.

A man, arms tied tight and stretched above his head, suspended from the ceiling, was being wrapped in bandages, slowly being mummified. The only thing not being wrapped was his genitals, which hung out like some kind of puny afterbirth. A lanky woman dressed as a nurse inserted an IV into the balls of a buff naked man who lay on an old operating table. The IV was connected to a bag full of clear liquid. The nurse stroked the expressionless man's balding head as if he was a kitten as he lay back and let the solution drip into his ball sac.

"That make him feel good?" Jesus asked Gabriel.

"I've seen a lot of messed-up crap but . . ."

"I think it might be some American custom," Jesus said.

Gabriel burst out laughing.

"Are you the Fabrizio model?" a cross-dresser who looked like early Cher on steroids asked Jesus.

"*Sí,*" Jesus answered.

"Please punish me, sir?" she begged, handing Jesus a wooden paddle with holes in it branded with Greek lettering.

"No, *gracias,*" Jesus said.

"I'll pay a hundred dollars," she said, yanking out a bill from her bra.

"A hundred dollars?" Jesus exclaimed, grabbing the money. "You got to love this America," he said, grasping the paddle, winking at

Gabriel as they walked over to a wooden horse. The cross-dresser slid down her skirt, bent over and spread her legs, exposing a hairy crack. Jesus tapped the cross-dressers' flabby ass softly with the paddle. Her shaved balls hung down.

"Harder!" she demanded in a man's voice.

Jesus hit her a little bit harder. He didn't want to hurt her, but some work ethic from being a good whore made him want to give the man dressed like a lady her money's worth. He hit her harder and harder until he was sweating, and the cross-dresser kept screaming for more. Jesus felt like he was in another world, and he stared at the faux jail cell and thought of all the people who hurt him when he was in real jail, and stopped. He was out of breath.

"Let's find Skip and go," Jesus said, grabbing Gabriel's hand, pulling him into the next room, where a man lay on the floor, naked, spread-eagled, facedown. A young guy dressed in a Nazi uniform ran a butcher knife delicately over his skin, the tip leaving little scratches in the shape of a swastika.

"That's Skip," Gabriel whispered to Jesus. And he realized the guy in the Nazi uniform was Butch.

"Let's get the hell out of here," Jesus said, trembling.

"OK," Gabriel said.

They left, passing the man on the operating table, whose scrotum had blown up to the size of two cantaloupes. They drove back to the Venus and went into Jesus' apartment for a drink. Jesus gulped on the bottle of Bacardi 151. "That club freak me because it remind me of jail, El Moro," Jesus said, sitting on the couch. "I was raise up by my grandmother after Castro kill my parents. And then she die when I am fourteen and I have nobody. The government move in another family to our house. I keep my room. They have five children. The father come into my room one night and try to rape me and I fight him. He say, 'I'll get you. I let you live in my house and this is how you do me,' and it is my house."

Jesus spoke as if he had slipped into some sort of trance. His eyes were shut. He trembled slightly. "The father never come back into my room but his wife did, after he beat her and leaves. She cry and I hold her. One night, we have sex. She is the first time."

Jesus was watching a movie of his own life under his eyelids. He took swig after swig of rum, to feel numb. *Relax*, he told himself: *You're in Miami, no one can hurt you now.* "The husband have me arrest. He say I steal a radio. *Communistas* love with trials. They put the wife on the courts and they ask her if I had steal and she cry but finally say yes. I tell myself, I never love again. I learned that love was betray." Jesus opened his eyes. "Being torture in jail was nothing compare to the pain of her say yes." Then he stopped speaking and his body shook and one lonely tear escaped from under his closed eyelid and struggled against five o'clock shadow as it flowed down his cheek.

Gabriel got up and sat next to him on the bed, and Jesus said, "Until you sit next to me, the room was go round and round; until you grab me out the water, my world was go round and round."

Gabriel heard a noise and looked up, and it was Miss Levy, and she was standing there at the door connecting the two apartments, crying quietly. Jesus' story of jail had taken her back to Auschwitz.

Gabriel couldn't look at her, so instead he focused on her nightgown: white, covered in white roses, white on white, and the flowers started to blur together as he stared and he realized tears were coming out of his own eyes. And he was shocked because he'd thought his eyes had dried up forever.

Gabriel's Fantasy Almost Turns to Reality

Gabriel jogged along beachside Lummus Park, bathed in the soft peachy early morning light. He stopped to catch his breath and watched an exercise class of ten senior citizens stretch in unison, slack and bony arms raised triumphantly into the cloudless sky. A group of Goths, all dressed in black, with heavy black eyeliner, and black lace-up Doc Martens, stumbled past. They looked like vampires caught in the light.

Gabriel cut over to Washington Avenue and then was stopped dead in his tracks by Friedman's Kosher Bakery #1. He couldn't believe it. The bakery had been painted in pastels. It had morphed into a delightful birthday cake with mint green, periwinkle blue and flamingo pink icing. Leonard Horowitz's drawing had jumped off the page, had come to life.

A bunch of hotel chambermaids got out of a metro bus and started to clap.

"I must still be really high," a faux-punk cutie with a Mohawk said to a beautiful Asian hip-hopper with pink hair. "The bakery has turned into a giant cupcake."

Then Gabriel heard a series of loud booms. He jogged toward the noise. It was the Senator Hotel. He stared in disbelief, gritted his teeth as the pear-shaped wrecking ball swung and smacked and then crushed. A shower of foam-green chunks crumbled down, as the ball swung back. He inched closer, in a trance, like the wrecking ball was a giant clock swinging before his eyes, hypnotizing him. He watched porthole windows etched with seagulls, banana leaves and palm trees shatter, a keystone fireplace explode, a relief of a voluptuous mermaid sink, chrome nautical railings tangle and the curved corners flatten.

A black limo pulled up and parked by him. A tinted window rolled down. Gabriel saw the leisure-suited German, Heinz Lerman. He was smiling and talking on a cell phone. Then, Gabriel saw Marina leaning against the chain link fence surrounding the Senator, clutching it like a prisoner grasping jail bars.

"What's wrong with people? Why?" she asked, shaking her head. A tear slipped down her cheek.

"People are greedy," Gabriel replied as the Senator's proud upward-thrusting finial fell and lay limply on the ground.

"I want to remember," Marina said. "So it gives me the strength to fight."

He grabbed her hand and guided her up Collins. They walked a couple blocks in silence, then Marina stopped and turned around. "Look," she said to Gabriel, pointing up the street. "See how all the corner buildings from where the Senator stood to the Essex House look similar. They all have curved keystone corners and spires rising into the sky. The architect, Murray Dixon, designed them to all fit together. Destroying the Senator messes up the whole rhythm of the street."

"Like pulling a tooth from someone's mouth," Gabriel said as they continued up Collins until the sound of the wind and the ocean almost completely muffled the cry of the dying Senator. They walked into Your Everything Store, and Gabriel bought two café con leches, two fresh-squeezed orange juices and some *pasteles de guayaba*. A yellowed poster left over from the 1940s with a drawing of a man with his nose in the air on the back wall said:

For Heavenly Relief from Hay Fever, Miami Beach

They kept strolling until they reached the tip of Miami Beach, South Pointe Park. They walked on a path through a grove of trees. Sunlight streamed through the canopy of circular leaves. Clusters of purple and green sea grapes dripped down. Wild palms pierced through the canopy. They walked over a small bridge, then Gabriel led Marina off the path into a break in the brush. Leaves and branches crumpled below their feet. It smelled fertile, of salted decay.

"You know where we're going?" Marina asked.

"Yep," Gabriel answered as they walked up a ridge and the thicket changed into a field of sea oats with a huge, flat, smooth, pale gray rock in the center. They climbed to the top of the rock.

"How did you find this place?" Marina asked, looking below at the waves breaking on the beach, at the gigantic cruise ships heading out of Government Cut, at the buildings of South Beach, jutting up in the distance like scattered pastel marshmallows.

"Skip brought me here. He calls it Paradise Beach," Gabriel said, taking off his shirt and using it as a tablecloth. He arranged the food on it. "It's his favorite place in the world."

"Let me make a toast," Marina said, raising her carton of orange juice. "To you."

"What for?" Gabriel asked.

"For working so hard, for fixing up the Venus. For not being a sellout like everyone else in South Beach."

"It was nothing, and everyone helped."

"You could have sold the building, made lots of money."

"Stop," Gabriel said. "You make me sound noble."

"To you. To Gabriel Tucker. The knight in shining armor who saved the Venus de Milo Arms from the dragons." She held her orange juice in the air.

"To us," Gabriel toasted. Carton rims kissed.

"To us," Marina repeated, and this scared her. Deep down inside, she had fantasized about them being an "us." Even though it scared her to death.

Gabriel leaned toward her. He saw his face in miniature reflected back at him from her mirrored sunglasses.

"I love this place," she said. "Thanks for bringing me here, for the feast." A flock of laughing seagulls floated overhead.

"Anytime," he said.

They continued eating and talking. Everything tasted delicious, their senses heightened by each other.

After they finished, Marina curled up and fell asleep in the sunlight. It was an escape for her. She had to get away from the senseless destruction of the Senator, from her desire for Gabriel—from the feeling that her body needed something from him.

Gabriel watched her sleep. He listened to her breathing, breathed along with her, matched her rhythm. He shut his eyes and imagined going inside, getting beneath the flesh, beyond the physical, getting to the essence, to the answer, to what it was that had so much power over him.

Gabriel noticed the sunlight bouncing off her face and was afraid that she would get burnt. She looked so peaceful. He didn't want to wake her up, didn't want to disturb her, so he linked his hands and held them up, shading her face while she slept.

Then she woke, opened her eyes and saw his linked hands above her face, his thumb and finger forming a heart, shielding her, protecting her. And that was it. This was the sign. Her heart beat fast. She had told herself she would never need anyone again and now realized this was bullshit.

She reached up and touched his fingers. She held them tightly. He met her eyes. They were begging now. She froze, petrified. He leaned forward, his lips moving toward her lips, and then she turned away from him even though she wanted him to kiss the sadness and fear and loneliness out of her.

Jesus and Gabriel
Play the Field

Gabriel, Jesus and Skip sat on the front porch of the Venus de Milo watching the passing parade of people on Ocean Drive. A man, his bone-thin legs in braces, rode by in an electric wheelchair. He was guiding a blind man wearing jet black glasses, who was holding on to the back of his chair. He led the blind man into the curb.

"What's wrong with you? Are you blind?" the man in the wheelchair exclaimed.

"Shut up, you old cripple!" the blind man replied. Then they both laughed and continued up the street.

Then the German man, Mr. Heinz Lerman, sauntered up and stopped right in front of them. He opened his leather briefcase, took out a pad, looked up at the Venus and started writing. Then the thuglike man with him unrolled architectural plans and spread them out on the hood of a car.

Gabriel snuck up behind them and peered over their shoulders at their plans. It was a rendering of an ugly LEGO-looking high-rise condominium-hotel.

"We have to get this Venus building to make up the parcel. Make the owner an offer he can't refuse," Mr. Lerman said, chuckling.

Gabriel heard the thug whisper, "Press," to Mr. Lerman and point at Skip. The German peered over toward Skip and frowned. Then they skulked away.

"The stupid politicians are going ass up for Heinz Lerman because he's throwing money around, buying them all off," Skip said. "All the commissioners are Jews and they're selling out to a German." Skip coughed. "Follow them," Skip said, "see what they're up to. I want to write a feature and expose him."

"Let's go," Gabriel said, grabbing Jesus' arm, and they followed Mr. Lerman up Collins Avenue. They passed the little coral house covered in oolitic limestone, the only freestanding house remaining in this part of South Beach. Then a limo pulled in front of a little boarded-up deco building that looked like a giant Electrolux vacuum cleaner with a sign in front of it that said, "Coming Soon, Armani Exchange." Mr. Lerman and the thug got into the limo and drove away.

"You want to go to the Deuce for a *cerveza?*" Jesus asked.

"I don't feel like it," Gabriel answered.

"*Que pasa?* Let me guess. Is Marina, no?"

"Yep," Gabriel replied, frowning. "Her cat-and-mouse game is driving me crazy!"

"Just forget. Find someone else. When last you have sex?" Jesus asked.

"Can't remember."

"See that white BMW without a top?" Jesus said. "It have follow us since we left the Venus. In Cuba, you learn to notice things like that."

"You're just paranoid," Gabriel said.

"It's one of his people."

"Whose people? The German?"

"Fabrizio's people. I think he have me followed. He obsess with me. He grab my ass at the shoot today."

"What did you do?"

"Got the hell away."

"Good."

"I am fraid Fabrizio will fire me if I don't fuck him."

"He's making money off of you and you have a contract. Don't worry."

"I hope you right."

Then the BMW cruised back around the corner in front of them and slowed down and stopped.

"Continue to walking," Jesus uttered. He was nervous.

"Excuse me," the woman in the BMW said hesitantly, raising her sunglasses and flashing a nervous-looking smile. "Aren't you that Fabrizio model guy?"

"Yes," Jesus responded, clearly thrilled to be recognized.

"You're beautiful," she said. "I love that picture of you on the raft and that other one of you in the chain mail vest with your chin on that girl's thigh."

"*Gracias*," Jesus said, and he beamed and stood up taller, and stuck out his chest a little. He got more bounce in his step. Gabriel trailed behind.

The woman just continued staring at Jesus, and smiled. Her smile was like an invitation.

"Your friend's very hot also," she flirted, finally taking her eyes off Jesus for an instant to look at Gabriel. "Is he a model, too?"

"No, he is a man of business and my best amigo."

"Would you guys like a ride somewhere?"

"Let's do it," Jesus said, turning to Gabriel.

"Why not?" Gabriel replied, thinking of Marina, of her pushing him away.

Jesus jumped into the front seat. "Get in," he told Gabriel. Gabriel climbed into the back.

Gabriel felt alive, as if he were free, about to go on another adventure. Once again he felt like he was in some strange country, and then he thought about Jesus, and realized *he* actually was in a strange country. He felt as if he had to protect him. He felt like his older brother.

"Look in the glove compartment," the woman said to Jesus, and he opened it and pulled out a ziplock bag of various pills.

"Pass me a white one," she said.

"What are they?" Jesus asked.

"Diet pills," she answered, and laughed.

Jesus swallowed two pills and then put one between his teeth and kissed her, pushing the pill into her mouth.

"You want?" he asked, handing Gabriel the bag.

"No," Gabriel answered, getting more and more alarmed.

"What's wrong with your friend?" the woman asked Jesus.

"He is to become a priest," Jesus said.

"Yeah," Gabriel said, "I hope we're on our way to church."

"We're on our way to heaven," she said.

Jesus laughed and said, "Miami *is* heaven!"

She stopped, pressed a clicker and a massive wrought iron gate opened. They pulled into a gigantic Mediterranean revival house, a Hollywood version of a Spanish castle. She led them through room after room, a blur of Persian rugs, gilded gold frames, crystal chandeliers and heavy Italianate antiques that all screamed "rich." They walked into the kitchen, and she opened the fridge and handed them each a bottle of Cristal and kept one for herself. They followed her outside to the pool, which had a waterfall, a Jacuzzi and five concrete statues of Michelangelo's *David*.

"Let's go for a swim," she said, and she reached around and unbuttoned and unzipped and then her dress fell to the floor, and she had on no underwear and she had a fantastic body, one of those perfect gym–plastic surgery bodies—tight, with massive tits and teardrop ass.

Gabriel was more shocked than turned on, until the woman took off her glasses and loosened her hair. It was in that split second that he began to feel desire. The way the last orangey rays of sunset stuck to her hair turned him on.

Jesus popped open the bottle of champagne and sucked and then he handed it to Gabriel and he swallowed some, and the cool bubbling liquid dripped down his throat as he looked up at the darkening sky. The city of Miami sat across the twinkling silver-black bay.

The woman swam to one side of the pool as Jesus opened another bottle with a pop and the cork fired and landed in the water. It floated.

"Aren't you guys coming in?" she asked, and her skin was tan and smooth with not one tan line.

Jesus put down the bottle, pulled off his tank top and then his baggy shorts and then his red Fabrizio briefs. The woman watched him from the side of the pool. She looked like she was going to swoon. The moon acted as Jesus' personal spotlight. His *dulce de leche*–colored skin glowed. Jesus put his hands on his hips and smirked at Gabriel and said, "Come on in."

"OK," Gabriel said, pulling off his clothes. His blond hair looked golden. He had a real masculine man's fit body, the right amount of body hair in all the right places. He didn't have the shaved, tricked-up musculature of all the fem queens with designer pubic hair who were invading South Beach.

Gabriel took a deep breath and swam to the deepest part of the pool. He exhaled, pushed all the air out of his lungs, hugged himself and sat on the bottom, balled up, in the fetal position, feeling so good, so calm, wishing he didn't need air, wishing that he didn't have to surface. He thought of Marina till his lungs screamed. He couldn't take it anymore. He pushed off from the bottom, torpedoed to the surface and gulped huge breaths.

Gabriel wiped his eyes and then saw Jesus and the woman in the shallow end, where the woman was kissing Jesus, holding him by the head, by the hair, her eyes shut, his eyes open. Gabriel felt so lonely watching them, so left out. He wondered why he'd come along.

"Come over here," the woman flirted.

Gabriel swam over, and Jesus took the woman and pushed her through the water to him, sort of pushed her face into his, like he was giving him a gift.

She grabbed Gabriel by the neck, and she seemed really high as she bounced her lips to his. Their teeth clacked. He felt his insides shake and he was turned into lips and tongue and he no longer cared who he was. He was lost in her mouth, exploring, his heart beating hard. She was now the oxygen and his body screamed for her, every molecule reached up for her, hard, demanding. His mouth danced with hers, tasting chlorine and heat and tongue. Her grip got tighter and tighter and he thought of Marina saying, "The water is like God licking you," and he pretended the nameless woman was Marina, as she pushed her body up against his, as if she wanted to push her body into his. Then he thought of Jesus and he pulled away.

Jesus was at the side of the pool chugging from the champagne bottle. He swam over and handed the woman the bottle and she took a couple of sips and passed it to Gabriel and he took a sip and that was all that was left and he thought that was probably for the best because he felt drunk, felt like his head was filled with water, and even when he left the pool and was following Jesus who was following the woman, he felt like he was still in the water.

The next thing Gabriel knew they were in a very white bedroom on a very big, tall canopy bed with sheets that felt like they were made from T-shirts. Jesus shoved some kind of pill into Gabriel's mouth and Gabriel asked him what it was and Jesus told him it was Special K.

Gabriel wanted to spit it out but he told himself it was easier to swallow it and if it was called Special K, it must not be bad, must be healthy, like the cereal, which of course was ridiculous, but in his drunken stupor it made total sense. And it was like he was watching a porno movie as he watched the two of them, and she was on all fours going down on Jesus and he was disappearing into her, into her mouth, and it looked like some kind of magic trick. Gabriel felt like he wasn't there, like he had disappeared. He tried to move, felt paralyzed, lobotomized. The only thing moving on his body was his pulsing dick.

Then Jesus opened his eyes, and it was like he was coming back from somewhere, and he sat up and pulled the woman's head off him and looked over at Gabriel. The woman gazed from Jesus to Gabriel and then from Gabriel to Jesus as if she was watching a tennis match, and then she just moved her head over and swallowed Gabriel in one gulp.

Gabriel shut his eyes and concentrated on the feeling, trying to forget how weird the situation was, and he couldn't, and he opened his eyes and Jesus was between her wide-open legs, licking and licking, as if he were trying to lick his way out, as if he were trying to jam his head up, as if he were performing some kind of job.

Then Jesus stopped and came up for air. His face was covered in juice. She stopped, spat out Gabriel's dick, looked at them and said, "Fuck me."

They took turns fucking her until she screamed, "I'm fucking the Fabrizio model!" as she came even though Gabriel was in her at the time and he came along with her even though he was flooded with jealousy as Jesus shot all over her face.

Pandora Turns into a Drag Queen

Jesus pushed himself through the dancing, frenzied smorgasbord of beefy hairless hard bodies, anorexic models, surfer dudes, twinks, hippie chicks, slumming millionaires, developers, artists, Goths, punkers, whores, neighborhood freaks, street people, hustlers, Euroscraps, gangster girls, gang bangers, ravers and drag queens. The sunset was a watercolor of orange and pink sky, a burning ball of sinking sun with coconut palms in black silhouette. People spilled out from the lobby of the Winter Haven Hotel onto the balcony and down onto the sidewalk. Traffic on Ocean Drive slowed down and stopped. A crowd stood across the street gawking. Music blared. It smelled of suntan oil, alcohol and sweat.

Jesus searched the crowd for Gabriel and Skip. Strangers smiled at him as if they knew him. Someone handed him a drink. He sucked it down. Sweat covered his body, so he pulled off his shirt.

"Take it off, model boy," a pumped-up muscle queen with perforated nipples yelled while an overtanned Lolita dressed in Victoria Secret lace bra and panties handed him a vial with a tiny spoon attached to the cap. He sucked some of the white powder up, thinking, *I'll feel better soon.* He handed the girl back the vial and she grabbed his hand and pulled him against her and she looked up at him as if he were some kind of god, as if he had some kind of answer.

Her face was so sweet and soft-looking. Her tongue was pierced, a gold bead at the tip. She kissed him. He tried to concentrate on the feeling, but he didn't feel anything but full. He tasted metal-tinged stale liquor cigarette breath. He pushed away. Then he began to feel woozy, to feel the power of the powder and liquor hit his brain. He worked his way through the crowd and sat on the curb and watched the sun disappear as if it was falling off the edge of the earth.

Then the music shut off, and it was absolutely quiet for a half minute that lasted forever. A spotlight from the second floor of the Winter Haven Hotel flicked on and searched the sky and the crowd and then settled on a giant skin-colored Martian-looking pod thing perched on top of a van. Drums pounded. A hand pierced the pod, then an arm and then another one, and it was like an alien escaping, a giant Kafkaesque hatching insect thing. Then a head pushed through and hands ripped apart the pod and a woman broke out and stretched. She was over six feet tall and dressed in a skintight leopard gown, tiger cape and acrylic super platforms with goldfish swimming in them. She had a bigger-than-life blonde Afro. The crowd freaked, screamed. Her cape blew in the wind. Jesus clapped along with the crowd, then suddenly realized it was Pandora. She had exaggerated herself: glittered her beautiful lips, accentuated her makeup, put on ridiculously long eyelashes, transformed herself from woman to drag queen. She had gone from female to female impersonator. She had turned herself into a caricature of a woman.

Music blared. Pandora started to sing, mouthing the words, lip-synching the lyrics with perfect timing. It was as if she was possessed by the music, as if she was channeling energy to the crowd. She worked them, dancing, gesticulating. Her face was animated, elastic. She became the song. Just when she had the crowd going full blast, she ripped off her super-Afro wig and threw it high into the sky. As the wig flew through the air, she was more naked than naked, exposed, skinless, a bird, an egg, a half man–half woman creature. She had shaved her head. Jesus caught the wig as the music died. Pandora dropped down flat on top of the van as if she had fainted and covered her naked head with her hands. Then the spotlight flicked off and the van sped away and the crowd went crazy, clapping and yelling, and then the music kicked in and people partied with a new intensity.

Jesus stared at the blonde wig on his lap and tried to get the picture of her bald scalp out of his head. Suddenly, Fabrizio's stretched black limo pulled up beside him. "I need my muse," he said, jumping out, hugging him.

Jesus froze from his touch. *I can't do this*, he thought, wondering how to get away from Fabrizio without making him angry. Then Fabrizio grabbed his hand and yanked him toward the limo. "You must see my new home, the future Palacio of Fabrizio. Here in Miami, I finally find my paradise."

Jesus felt high, like he was floating, like he was a balloon filled with helium and Fabrizio held the string. He sat in the limo. He wondered why Fabrizio was so repulsive to him. He was handsome. He was so talented. He was cultured. He had given him everything. Jesus missed Fabrizio, the Fabrizio he knew before he'd started making passes at him.

"What can I get you?" Fabrizio asked, opening the limo's bar.

"Rum," Jesus answered.

"With what?"

"The bottle."

Fabrizio chuckled, handed Jesus the decanter. He pulled out the stopper, took a sip and then another. He patted Pandora's wig on his lap. The air in the limo felt rarefied. He wanted one of these cars for himself; he did not want to be the toy of the owner of one.

"My beauty," Fabrizio cooed, putting his hand on Jesus' knee. His touch made Jesus feel like a whore, like a bad whore, one who didn't deliver.

The limo stopped farther up Ocean Drive, in front of a ramshackle, crumbling, three-story 1930s faux palazzo. It had a copper-domed observatory and a giant stained glass window of Columbus discovering America, Gothic arches and marble busts of Ferdinand and Isabella, Gandhi, Caesar, Cleopatra and Lenin.

"This building," Jesus said, "it look like Havana."

"It's mine!" Fabrizio said excitedly, grabbing his hand and pulling him across the street through a massive towering arched door, into the cobblestoned courtyard. "I turn it into a showplace of Fabrizio."

In the courtyard, an old lady read the *Jewish Daily Forward* in Yiddish to a group of even older-looking people. An alternateen girl in black clothes and white pancake makeup stared down at them from a balcony above. She played with a pet white rat. A guy who looked like the Marlboro man, dressed in Levi's, chaps and a cowboy hat, sat on the edge of a fountain strumming a guitar.

"What happen to the people who live here?" Jesus asked.

"You can send them out in one minutes. In Italy we need ten, twenty years." Fabrizio smiled. "The House of Fabrizio will make South Beach famous."

Jesus followed Fabrizio back to his limo, remembering how they took the rich people's houses in Cuba and moved lots of poor people into them. In America they do the opposite, he thought; they take away the poor people's houses and move in a rich person. This capitalism can be as hard as communism.

"I will live here like a royal. Salvatore Fabrizio is the new Medici."

Back in the limo, Jesus drank, till the burning liquid extinguished something that was burning deeper inside. He lay back against the plush interior, inhaled the leather smell, shut his eyes. It was spinning inside his head. He was on a carnival ride that would not end. Then he felt Fabrizio's hand stroking him with disarming tenderness. He tried to relax into his touch but then Fabrizio's hands began to feel like slimy snakes, slithering all over, and he told himself to calm down, to let it happen and then he would keep getting things, then he would continue to get famous and rich. He clenched his teeth and tried to separate from his body like he used to do when he was a whore. But he couldn't. Fabrizio's hand started to fiddle desperately with the buttons on the fly of Jesus' Fabrizio white jeans. Then he felt the scratch of Fabrizio's beard, then sloppy lips on his lips.

"No," Jesus said, and he felt like he was back in jail. He used all his strength to open his eyes and get away from Fabrizio, his head jammed up against the limo window.

"I love you," Fabrizio murmured.

Jesus shoved open the door. Hot air rushed in. He rolled out of the car, hit the sidewalk with a thump, as he thought, *I will not be a whore.*

Marina ran up to him. She'd just happened to be there, at exactly the right spot, like some sort of guardian angel. The limo stopped. Fabrizio got out.

"Leave him alone," Marina yelled, flashing Fabrizio an angry look. He froze for a second and then shook his head and got back in the limo, slammed the door and drove away.

"You all right?" Marina asked, kneeling down.

"I'm OK," Jesus slurred. He sat up, started to cry. The spinning continued. Marina hugged him. The spinning stopped.

Jesus and Marina Go to the Promised Land

"What happened?" Marina asked Jesus as Fabrizio's limo fled up Ocean Drive.

"Nothing," Jesus replied, touching his palm, then looking at his finger, at the red blood. Another cut under his heart dribbled, forming a red splotch on his ripped Fabrizio T-shirt. People stopped, stared at them and then kept walking.

"Don't touch it," Marina said, "Let's go home and we can clean you up." She grabbed his good hand and pulled. Jesus stood up.

"What's wrong?"

"I'm really messed up."

"So what's new?" she scolded, hailing a cab.

"Do not be mean," Jesus said as they got into the taxi. When they arrived at the Venus, Marina paid for the cab.

"Come with me," she ordered, and he followed her into her apartment.

"Sit down while I go and get some stuff," she said.

Jesus sat, looked around Marina's apartment. It was divided into two sections. There was a minimal living section, like a monk's cubicle, all in white. It contained just a table with a squat tallow candle, a chair and a bed. Taut white cotton sheets covered the bed—perfect hospital corners. Separated from this section by a white curtain was her studio: a mad scientist's laboratory of appendages, phallic tendrils, knobs, lumps, bulges, protuberances—a woozy labyrinth of psychosexuality. There was a wax figure of a woman sucking her own breast and a man sucking his own penis, like they were pleasuring and devouring themselves simultaneously.

"Take off your shirt," Marina said, carrying cotton balls and antiseptic.

Jesus pulled off his shirt and stared at her, looked into her big blue eyes, looked for the sadness he saw in her art, but there was no trace.

"You're a sculpture. Sculptures shouldn't bleed," she said.

"Now that I'm in magazines, people don't even think I'm human," he said, touching his bloody T-shirt. "It's like they think I have some kind of answer, because I get my photo taken."

"I know," she said, shaking her head. "I couldn't take it."

"What?" he asked, and she saw concern on his perfect face, and this made him look even more beautiful.

"I am . . . was famous, for my art. I had always dreamed of making it. Then it happened. I had a show in this little gallery and the next thing you know, I get this amazing review in the *Times* and then I'm in the Whitney Biennial, and then MOMA buys the piece." The more she talked, the more fragile she looked. "It all happened so fast. Everyone wanted something, like you said, thought I had the answers. I got really depressed. I thought I was a fraud. I thought I was going to have a nervous breakdown."

"I am scared all the time, scared it will go away."

"I was married to another artist. I got very sick, with breast cancer. He left me."

"Well, then he not worth it," Jesus declared, and he wanted to hug her, to help her, to stop her hurt.

"I had to get away from him, from there, from New York, the art world. I just got in my car and started driving. I stopped when I reached South Beach. It cast some kind of spell on me."

"You run away?"

"No," she said. "I did the same thing you did. I escaped."

"You are different. You become famous for something you do. I become famous for something I am. It have not a thing to do with me. You are a genius."

"I even got a genius award," she said, laughing. "It's called a MacArthur. They gave me a quarter-million dollars. That's what I live on." She shook her head. "Now," she said, "let me fix you up."

"Nobody can fix me."

"I'm gonna try," she said, pouring antiseptic on a cotton ball and dabbing it on his hand.

"Ouch!" Jesus cried.

"You're a baby," she teased, blowing on his palm, on the cut, and he watched her lips, the perfect, plump, pink O, as she blew. Her eyes were shut and her eyelids trembled. He felt the tingling rush of blood down below.

She put a Band-Aid on his palm. "Now your chest," she said, dabbing and then blowing. He concentrated on the pain and then the pleasure of the pain disappearing as he willed his hard-on to go away. He wanted her breath, wanted it in his mouth. He wanted her goodness. He wanted her strength. He wanted to find out if she could take away all his pain. He wanted to take away her pain.

"All done," she said. "Now tell me what happened with Fabrizio."

"It was nada."

"Yeah, like nothing made you jump out of a moving limo?"

He shrugged, shaking his head. "You have something to drink?"

"I'll make you lemonade," she said, going into her little kitchen.

"I mean a real drink."

"I know," she said, squeezing the juice from two plump lemons into a glass, adding water and sugar and then stirring. She handed him the drink.

He took a sip. The ice tinkled. Frost smoke floated.

"Fabrizio touch me, kiss me. I allow him. First. I think if I stop him, it will all end. I feel like I owe him, like he own me." Jesus' right knee jiggled up and down. "I just try to give up my body. But I cannot. I feel like trapped."

Marina touched Jesus' knee, the one that was bouncing up and down. It stopped. Jesus craved her touch, wanted her hands all

over his body. He wanted comfort. He inhaled and smelled sugared
lemons.

"He's paying you to model," Marina said. "Whatever you get from
him, you're earning."

"I think he's paying me 'cause he wants to fuck me," Jesus said,
thinking, *That's all I am, a fuck, that's all I ever was, that's all I'll
ever be.*

"He's paying you because you're beautiful." She grabbed his
hand and pulled him over to the full-length mirror on the wall.
"Look," she ordered.

Jesus stared at himself. Sadness washed over him in thick waves.
He felt so alone. He felt like he was not in himself, not connected
to himself, like the person in the mirror was not him. The person
in the mirror was the Fabrizio model and if he didn't fuck him he
would go away.

"You're perfect."

Jesus felt like he was going to faint, and sat down on her couch.
Marina sat next to him. He grabbed her feet, to stop from sinking.
He needed to touch her. He started to massage them. She sighed,
shut her eyes. She had beautiful toes. Her toenails were painted with
clear varnish. He concentrated on her feet. His heart beat hard. He
would not stop until she said so. He was afraid. He took deep breaths.
His hands began to wander. He couldn't stop them. They had a life
of their own. One inch at a time. Her eyes stayed shut. He explored:
calves, the soft skin behind her knee, thighs. Goose bumps. His
hands went under her dress. He pictured her lips blowing on his
cuts as his fingers caressed farther up. She trembled.

Her eyes snapped open. His hands froze.

"What are we doing?" she asked, shaking her head. She breathed
heavily. She had not had sex in so long she had forgotten this feeling. She hadn't had sex since her husband left her when she was in
the middle of her chemo for breast cancer.

He didn't know what to say. His mouth wouldn't move. All he
knew was that at first he'd wanted to give her something and so he'd
started to give her the only thing he thought he had, his body, but
now he wanted her.

Then she smiled at him, a smile that was so pure and friendly that his voice unlocked.

"Please," he said. "I don't know what the English word is." He took a deep breath.

"What?" she asked.

"Yes," he said. "Joy. That is the word. You make me full with joy."

She stared deeply into his eyes as if she were searching for something. He stared back, and it was like looking into the sea: an endless hazy shade of blue, black pupil—a raft. Only she could save him at that moment. She touched the back of his head, stroked his hair.

He brought his head down, down, into her lap, the most luxurious of pillows.

Gabriel Screws a Floor

Gabriel finally finished scraping the paint from the wall of the last vacant apartment in the Venus de Milo Arms. He started to paint the walls pink. He was excited and nervous because tonight he was going out with Marina. He had got his hair cut and even paid five dollars for a manicure from an old lady who told him she was a retired mermaid from Weeki Wachee Springs. She told him she could still hold her breath for over two minutes.

Then Gabriel thought he heard Marina's voice. The sound was emanating from behind the wall, from her apartment next door. He stuck his head, his ear, against the wall. He felt desperate doing this, but he couldn't help himself. He listened. He thought he heard another voice, a familiar voice. Yes, he was sure. He heard Jesus. He heard him moaning, her moaning. Sex!

Gabriel's heart sank. His chest became a deep hole. He threw the paintbrush onto the floor, sat down, leaned against the wall and hugged himself. He shut his eyes, strained to hear. He heard them fucking. The noise was like a bullet that shot from his ear to his heart. Fuck her! Fuck him! Fuck them! Then he pictured her beautiful body. He imagined grabbing Jesus, stopping him in midpump and grabbing his legs, ripping them apart like a chicken's wishbone. He imagined throwing him off the raft, letting him sink, pictured tiny bubbles emanating from his mouth, getting larger as they rose to the surface. Why is he doing this to me? Why Marina? He can have anyone. His beauty. It cut like a knife.

Gabriel couldn't help himself. He turned his head, rested his ear against the wall. Listened. The sound of their pleasure. He heard their rhythm, heard the creak of the bed, the escaping moans.

He imagined it was him and not Jesus, that he was the one, going in and out, slipping, being gripped, down there, feeling the pleasure. Her face. What was it about her face? It was just a face. Fuck her face! He imagined her lips, the way they'd felt against his as if he was finally where he belonged, as if he'd finally surrendered. It stopped hurting. He felt himself hardening. He was back in the water with her.

He felt his hard-on inside his shorts, begging for release. I'm so messed up, he thought, as he pulled down his pants, accidentally kicking over the paint can. Pastel pink paint flowed across the floor, painting it, painting him, a small blob on his midsection. He started fucking along with them. He fucked the floor. The paint felt wet and sticky against his dick. He was going in and out of her in his head, grinding the floor. He moaned.

On the opposite side of the wall, Jesus shut his eyes and tried not to think of Gabriel, tried not to think about how much this would hurt him. And Marina shut her eyes and also pictured Gabriel and imagined she was making love to him, remembering the way his lips had felt against hers—his kiss, like he was sucking out her soul.

Then it happened. Gabriel heard her scream, heard Jesus moan. Gabriel felt unbearable pleasure. Pleasure that was so powerful, it had to be released. He came with them. They all came together. White squirted on pastel pink, stuck to Dade County pine floor.

"Fuck!" Gabriel yelled, coming to his senses. He punched the wall as hard as he could. His fist crunched drywall; his middle finger cracked as his fist went right through the wall. He screamed in pain.

Risk Your Anus, Depends

Gabriel's hand was powdered in white drywall dust. He peered into the hole he'd punched in the wall of the Venus. An eye stared back at him. He ran into the hallway.

A door squeaked open. "Gabriel!" Jesus yelled. He was naked.

Gabriel ignored him, ran outside and hailed a cab. His hand throbbed, as did his heart.

In the emergency room of Mount Sinai Hospital, Gabriel took deep breaths and tried to ignore the pain. He shut his eyes again and didn't open them until he heard his name called.

He followed a tough-looking male nurse into a cubicle. The man pulled some curtains and told him to wait on a paper-covered examining table. Gabriel craved something to kill the pain.

"I think I know you," a very butch doctor with a shaved head said. "You hang around that Fabrizio model."

"Yes," Gabriel said.

"Does this hurt?" the doctor asked, pushing his finger back and forth.

"Yes!" Gabriel moaned, feeling like he was going to pass out.

"It's sprained, not broken," the doctor informed him. He wrapped Gabriel's finger in a skin-colored bandage, gave him some Vicodin. "Is that Fabrizio model your boyfriend?" he asked.

"He's my friend," Gabriel answered, thinking. *He was my friend.*

"He's so hot," the doctor said. "Can you fix us up?"

"He's not gay," Gabriel said, frowning and walking away. He took a sip of water from the fountain and swallowed three of the pills. As he walked out, he spotted Skip.

"What are you doing here?" Skip asked.

"I sprained my finger," Gabriel answered. "Fell down, painting."

"Well, I found out my diarrhea is caused by a parasite in my gut, cryptosporidium."

"That doesn't sound so bad."

"It's incurable. Now I'm a parasite with a parasite."

"What?"

"All writers are parasites, especially gossip columnists."

Gabriel tried to smile.

"They gave me some experimental crap," he said. "They got it from Mexico."

"A drug from Mexico to cure diarrhea? From the land of Montezuma's Revenge?"

"Yeah." Skip took a deep breath and then stood up slowly. Gabriel followed him to the door. They made their way up Washington Avenue, passing a drugstore with a dusty window display of Imodium and prunes.

A man, plastic forks stuck in his Afro, handed them two flyers—one for Walgreens advertising a sale on Depends and another promoting a special night at Club Risk called Uranus.

"It's risking my anus that's going to have me wearing Depends soon," Skip said.

Gabriel laughed. They kept walking past a lot of empty stores. The kosher butchers, the mom-and-pop shops, the dollar stores, the old beauty parlors, the junk stores, the Cuban coffee shops were all already shut down or going out of business. They passed a souvenir store crammed full of painted coconut heads and flip-flops and tourist trinkets marked "Miami Beach." There was a banner in the window that said, "Lost our Lease—All Contents Must Go!!!"

"Washington Avenue is going to be to SOBE what West Broadway is to SOHO," a real estate agent said, pointing out an empty old theater to two men wearing black Armani suits.

"*New York* magazine just christened South Beach SOBE — SOHO on the beach," Skip said, as they kept walking on broken red sidewalk.

They looked at the window of the Mr. Excellence Beauty Parlor. Rows and rows of vintage dummy heads stared back at them. Some were bald, others had beehives and one had hair woven into a Christmas tree, complete with bulbs and an angel on top. Then they saw Miss Levy. Dressed in English mod go-go tights, topped off with a little girl romper in matching periwinkle blue with patch pockets and matching blue Carnaby Street hat, she was talking to an old Cuban man dripping in gold chains and rings wearing a helmetlike black toupee. He had on a gaudy galleon-patterned silk Fabrizio shirt that was terribly tight around his paunch.

"That's Angelito, Mr. Excellence," Skip said as they entered Mr. Excellence Beauty Parlor. It looked like it had been frozen in time.

"I have it written down," Miss Levy argued, pulling out a pad. "Hollywood Dog Track, superfecta, four, eight, six, three, Bow-wow, Chubbychaser, Bar Snooty and Bozo, fifty clams, three o'clock post."

"No, that's not right," Angelito replied, shaking his head.

"We will discuss this tomorrow," Miss Levy said as she noticed Skip and Gabriel.

"What's wrong, Skippy?" she asked, concerned, turning away from Angelito toward them.

"I feel like an old man."

"So do I, but I'd rather have a young one," Miss Levy joked. "What happened to your hand?" she asked Gabriel, noticing the bandage.

"I fell when I was painting."

"Come with me. I'll cook, fix you both up," she said.

They dutifully followed her around the corner, passed a group of old people sitting on the porch of the Astor Hotel. Miss Levy smiled and said hello to the group as if they were all one person, as they kept walking.

"Those old people's only pleasure is waiting for me to walk down the street every day on my rounds to see what I'm wearing," Miss Levy said. "Isn't that sad?"

"You give them so much pleasure," Skip said. "You are their tourist attraction."

They arrived at the Venus and went up the stairs to Miss Levy's apartment. She touched the mezuzah to the right of her doorjamb and said a silent prayer for Skip as they entered. She'd seen the look of death in his eyes. She would cook for him, make him better, she lied to herself. Ever since Auschwitz, she loved to cook. She always had to have food around. She even kept cans of tuna and jars of peanut butter and the sugar packets she stole from restaurants under her bed, just in case.

They sat down on her royal blue plastic-covered couch. It crackled.

"What do you boys want to eat?" she asked.

"I'm not hungry," Skip said.

"Oy vey," she said, exasperated. "I have chicken soup, Jewish penicillin." She took a pot from the fridge, put it on the stove. "Worries go down better with soup."

Gabriel picked up a little sepia-colored photo in a pitted gold oval frame. It was a picture of a family: a mother and a father and two identical young girls in sailor suits posed in front of a grand house on a lake.

"Who are these people?" Gabriel asked.

Miss Levy wiped her hands on her apron. "That's my family," she said. "They're dead. Nobody survived but me."

Then they all just sat in silence. Gabriel listened to the sound of the waves, the wind blowing. He glanced at the tattoo on her forearm. The figures had almost faded away, like the family in the photograph.

She poured the chicken soup into three bowls. They sat at the table.

Gabriel looked at Skip, thought how he was starving, the parasite stealing what little food he was eating. And then he thought of Miss Levy starving in Auschwitz and Jesus telling him how he starved in El Moro jail in Havana. He thought of Marina and he felt like his heart was starving.

SUNSTROKER

by Skip Bowling

Once again I schlep down **Ocean Drive,** the runway of SOBE,
the Yellow Brick Road to the absolute opposite of Kansas.
South Beach is no longer America. We have become America's
border town, providing whatever: drugs, sex, drugged-out
sex. A deco **Tijuana.** Hey, you want to fuck my sister for
some fame? Hordes of underage children with fake ID cards
selling their souls to share a bottle of overpriced cheap
champagne in some scummy VIP room with some scummy
nobody who can help them make it, and they do not even
know what it is they want to make. A teenage girl last night
offered to blow my sorry self for a mention in **Sunstroker.**

The city fathers should just sling some red velvet ropes
across the causeway and hang a gigantic disco ball over
South Beach. They should give away the drug and flesh of
choice. Forget giving out the condoms because everyone
knows that sickness is a myth on Planet SOBE. Those
ambulances are only taking away the last of the old people.
Safe sex is for sissies. Come on, baby, bareback me to death.
Destroy me with your dick! Sometimes this petri dish of PnP
valueless values gets to me but I trudge courageously into the
SOBE sleazy sick seductive scene for you, my readers.

Back to bigger and brighter and whiter and more pristine
things: the opening of the **Delano Hotel,** placing South Beach

firmly at the pinnacle of the style hierarchy. Behind the high hedge and billowing white curtains, **Ian Schrager** has upped the ante with this incredible forty-two-million-dollar rehab of the Delano by **Philippe Starck,** with its furniture museum meets **White Mischief** hospital meets **Alice in Wonderland** decor—New Glamour personified.

Then on to the third-anniversary party for South Beach's own super-glossy *Ocean Drive* magazine at **Fisher Island** (**William Vanderbilt's** old domain tarted up and loaded with overpriced superrich condos). I felt like I was playing a fame pinball game as I kept ricocheting from boldface to boldface: **Steven Tyler,** superlawyer **Roy Black,** models **Niki Taylor, Bridget Hall** and the **Riker Twins,** the over-20,000-notches-on-his belt b-ball player **Wilt Chamberlain,** actor **Stephen Dorff,** superdirector **Oliver Stone,** celebutant **Gabriel Tucker,** Italian designers **Salvatore Fabrizio** and **Gianni Versace** with sister **Donatella.** And arriving at the same time as the fireworks, the ultimate fame pyrotechnic, **Jack Nicholson.**

Never knowing when to go home, never knowing when I've had enough, I continued on to **Liquid,** now world-famous. I fought my way into a crowd being driven wild by spin master **Victor Calderone. Liza** with a Z, the iconic **Ms. Minnelli,** was hanging in the DJ booth. She claimed that Liquid was just like **Studio 54.** The king of South Beach nightlife, **Chris Paciello,** was seen holding the hand of fame itself, **Madonna.** Rumor has it he is getting sloppy seconds from the other half of the hippest nightlife duo of the nineties, his partner, celeb gal pal **Ingrid Casares.**

Another Shattered Heart

Gabriel lay in his bed with his pillow smothering his head. It was noon. He didn't want to get up. He had been depressed for weeks, ever since Jesus screwed Marina.

He fantasized about running away. But for the first time in his life, he had responsibility. He had the Venus de Milo Arms.

In the apartment down the hall, Jesus sat in the overflowing profusion of Marina's studio. Marina sat on the floor in front of him, pulling pieces of rising dough from a big aluminum bowl. She rolled them into balls and then bit them in half. Each contained a ghost-like trace of the inside and outside of her bite.

Ever since they'd had sex, every time Jesus was with Marina he felt a subtle strangeness, a slight gnawing deep inside. He wanted it to go away. He cleared his throat.

"I feel now different with you. I do not like it."

"I know," she said. She bit a dough ball in two. "I feel the same way."

"Gabriel?" Jesus said.

"Yes," she answered, and she looked so sad.

"He hates me."

"Us," she corrected.

"He loves you," Jesus said.

"Love is scary," she replied. She was so afraid of it that she'd subconsciously done something to try to make it go away: She'd screwed Jesus. "We should talk to him."

"I know," he said, standing up. "I go now."

"Good luck," she said, and wished she had the courage to go and tell Gabriel she loved him.

Jesus kissed Marina good-bye. Gabriel was his best friend, but he had betrayed him; he had broken the male code. He left Marina's apartment and walked down the hall and knocked on Gabriel's door.

Gabriel recognized Jesus' voice. He froze.

"*Por favor*," Jesus begged, as he kept knocking. Gabriel had been avoiding him for weeks now.

Please, Gabriel thought. *Just go to hell.*

Jesus kept pounding the door.

Gabriel got out of bed, wiped his eyes, pulled on a pair of shorts. Opened the door.

"What?" Gabriel asked, in a tone meant to hurt Jesus.

"Can I come in?" Jesus pleaded.

Gabriel moved aside. Jesus skulked in and slumped on the couch.

"You OK?" Jesus asked, because he didn't know what else to say.

"Yeah," Gabriel answered, folding his arms across his chest. Then he walked to the open kitchen and started washing the mountain of dishes in his sink. He gritted his teeth, scratched off the dried food with his fingernails.

Jesus couldn't take this. Gabriel was his best friend. Gabriel had saved his life. He walked into the kitchen.

Gabriel still didn't look at him. He took a deep breath, kept washing the dishes, squeezed some more Joy into the sink.

Then he felt arms grab him, from behind, around his shoulders, pinning his arms against his sides.

"Let go," Gabriel demanded.

Jesus just hung on, said nothing, just hung on.

Gabriel used all his strength to break Jesus' grip. He swung around. A plate flew across the counter, smashed against the floor and shattered into sharp shards.

"Fuck," Gabriel screamed, bending down, picking at the pieces as he thought *This is my heart*. His hands were shaking. "Why did you have to fuck Marina?"

Jesus flinched as if he had been slapped.

"You can fuck anyone you want. Why Marina?"

"I'm sorry," Jesus said, moving toward him. Gabriel stepped back, ran his hand through his sharp blond hair, rubbed his temples. His eyes were steel blue.

"It no mean anything. It just happen. I no mean to hurt you."

"You knew," Gabriel said. "How I felt. It's worse that it meant nothing," Gabriel said, but inside he was thrilled. He had been afraid they were in love.

"It just happen," Jesus said. "I am sorry."

Gabriel had to get away or he would hit him. He rushed into his bedroom and slammed the door.

Jesus walked to the bedroom door, stood in front of it. He didn't know what to do.

Déjà Vu

Gabriel rolled over, woke up in his apartment. His head pounded and his body ached. Inside, his teeth throbbed. He tasted that chemical after-crystal, after-E, after–Blue Nitro, after-whatever-would-get-him-higher taste in his mouth. Then he saw the arm, heard the high-pitched snoring.

He tried to remember last night, tried to remember last month. His life had become a continuous fog of trying to forget Marina, trying to numb himself of desire. He saw a nameless stream of the fuzzy faces of the women he'd screwed last month. They took the pain away and then he came and the pain came back.

Finally, Gabriel forced himself to peer at the stranger sprawled next to him. His eyes zigzagged over her body. She was ebony and bald and had the most beautiful ass he had ever seen. She had on a white bra and panties, and wore a thin gold chain around her thin ankle.

His heart beat fast as the woman rolled over, and then he sunk. Déjà vu! He fought the urge to run. He couldn't believe he'd done this, couldn't remember what he did. Then he heard banging on his door.

Pandora woke up, jerked the sheet to cover herself up and then enclosed her scalp in her hands.

Gabriel had to get away. She looked so fragile, so baby bird–like. He forced himself up. Inside, his head stabbed. He felt dizzy. He felt awkward. He felt embarrassed. He felt stupid. He felt pain. He yanked on a terry-cloth robe, walked out of the bedroom, opened his front door.

It was Mr. Heinz Lerman.

"Yes," Gabriel uttered, thinking, *How could I have screwed Pandora?* He didn't even remember doing it, didn't know how she got in his bed.

"I'm looking for the owner of the building," Mr. Lerman said, pulling him back.

"Yes," Gabriel said, massaging his temples. "I own the building."

"Gabriel Tucker?" he asked.

"Yes," Gabriel answered, wanting to slam the door in his face, but he was curious to hear his pitch and it also gave him time to figure out what to do about Pandora.

"My name is Heinz Lerman," the man said, holding his hand out. Heinz squeezed Gabriel's hand so hard it hurt. "I would like to speak with you please," he said, pushing past him into the apartment. Heinz's eye's searched the room as if he was taking inventory. "This is a very beautiful building. But, it is badly run-down, badly in need of repair." He took a deep breath. "Is it for sale?"

"Maybe," Gabriel answered, thinking déjà vu again, first Fabrizio and now Heinz.

"I want to fix it up," Heinz said, with a phony smile. "It is an art deco gem. If I don't save it, someone else may buy it and destroy it. You can keep living here."

Gabriel remembered having overheard him saying that this was the last building he needed to assemble a parcel to build a huge convention center hotel and condominium.

"I offer you nine hundred thousand dollars," the German announced.

"I already turned down two million."

"I offer you two million and two hundred thousand."

"Five million, cash," Gabriel said, as the door to the bedroom opened and out walked Pandora, wearing a golden Afro and a gold-sequined miniskirt. She looked like a sparkler.

Heinz stood. Pandora walked past Gabriel, dropping a note in his lap. Then she kissed Heinz on the mouth and he touched her ass for an instant. She pulled away from him, smiling.

"I'll let you know," Heinz replied, grabbing Pandora's hand. She stumbled on her golden stilettos. They left together.

Gabriel shut the door, wondering whether he should sell. Then he could get out. Now that he had restored and rerented the empty apartments, the Venus was turning a profit. He was earning more than enough to live on and was putting away money in the bank. And he dreamed of making the Venus nicer, fixing and filling the pool.

Then, he thought that this place, South Beach, was changing, that the original tenants of the Venus de Milo Arms were becoming obsolete, that the building was becoming a museum of the old South Beach. Maybe it was just Darwinian.

He unfolded the note that Pandora had dropped on his lap:

Gabriel,
Please don't sell the Venus and don't worry.
We didn't do anything last night. You were
real messed up. I just put you in bed and
stayed with you to make sure you were ok.
                                        PANDORA

Out, Out, Damn Spot!

Skip stepped out of the shower, stood naked in front of the mirror, wiped the fog and stared as if he was looking at someone else, stared at himself with complete objectivity. AIDS had taught him how to do this.

His bony face with its sunken cheeks and eyes stared back at him. He looked down. His ribs, his pelvis, his hips stuck out. His butt had disappeared. He was flat at the back. He was a stickman. Everything was shrinking except his dick and his head. They looked bigger, now that his body was smaller. Both his heads looked bigger.

Then out of the corner of his eye, he saw it. It came from out of nowhere; it had not been there yesterday. He looked away. He had waited for it. He knew it was coming; every day he'd searched his body for it. And now that it was there, he couldn't believe it. He stared at it until his reflection fogged up, until he became a blur.

"Out, out, damn spot!" he screamed and laughed, and then he just shook his head. He didn't know what else to do. He looked down at the spot, his chin touching his chest. He studied it. It was an alien spore, a UFO. It was a purple-red-brownish wine mixed with shit. It was slightly raised and centered between his nipples — a bull's-eye.

He grabbed a bottle of Johnnie Walker Black from next to his computer and took a few gulps and then looked away and touched it, pressed his thumb into the lesion. He wanted it to hurt, to be sensitive. He wanted it to feel like a zit, ready to pop. Instead it felt like nothing.

Kaposi's sarcoma, he thought. He scratched it harder and harder, as if he could scratch it off. He scratched until tears started.

God, you can have my body, but please don't take my mind. Splatter me with spots but leave my brain alone. Please, you sadistic fucker. Let me finish my book. And then he sunk down into the fetal position on the floor. The pain convulsed out in great sobs.

Skip heard knocking. The door to his apartment cracked open.

"Skip," Jesus said hesitantly. He had heard him crying, wanted to soothe him. Jesus peered into the apartment.

Stop, Skip told himself, seeing Jesus through a haze of tears. Then he shut his eyes as tight as he could. He wished Jesus would go away.

"*Que pasa?* What's wrong, Skip?" Jesus asked, getting down on the floor, stroking him, feeling his ribs pierce through his back, feeling each vertebra distinctly. Jesus thought he had learned to block out other people's suffering; he thought Cuba had taught him this. But he was wrong. He spooned his body up against Skip's and put his arms around him.

"I here," Jesus whispered.

Skip felt Jesus' touch, felt his heat. He felt the tears stop, dry up. He felt the empty spot fill. He opened his eyes, saw spots, dissolving spots. "I'm sorry," Skip uttered, pulling away from him.

Jesus touched his cheek, wiped the tears with both hands and then held his face, softly. "*Por favor*," he said, "tell me what wrong?"

"Nothing," Skip replied, feeling embarrassed and naked. He stood up and pulled on a T-shirt and a pair of Joe Boxers with bananas all over them.

Jesus grabbed Skip's hand and led him to the couch. They sat down. Skip saw the concern on Jesus' face, saw it radiating from his sweet chocolate eyes.

"Tell me what wrong," Jesus persisted.

Skip tried to tell Jesus but he couldn't; his mouth wouldn't move. Instead he pulled away from him, pulled up his shirt and pointed.

Jesus looked and couldn't figure out what was wrong, what Skip was trying to tell him, what he was pointing at. It was just a spot. Skip's finger was trembling.

"I just found this," he forced out.

"What?" Jesus asked, his eyes wide open.

"AIDS," Skip answered, his voice cracking.

"I know you have the AIDS."

"This spot," he said, touching it. It's a kind of cancer. "It's called KS. It will cover me. I'm going to be grotesque, the Elephant Man."

"You are most beautiful," Jesus said. "No is you. It only cancer," Jesus whispered, bending forward. His perfect face, his liquid brown sparkling eyes came toward Skip.

Skip froze, petrified, startled by Jesus' pink, puckering, perfect lips. He forgot to breathe. Everything was in slow motion, felt hyperreal.

Jesus' face moved toward the center of Skip's chest. He wanted to make him feel better. He pulled up his shirt and kissed the spot, over and over, and stuck out his tongue to lick Skip's KS, like a kitten licking cream.

Skip felt something he could not describe, something beyond sex, beyond lust and the satisfaction of lust. He didn't know what it was but it felt so good that his fear dissolved.

Friends and/or Lovers

It was midnight. Gabriel sat on his couch in the Venus and stared through the glass doors at the moon, at the quivering silver sea, and imagined how much more beautiful it would be if he were seeing it with Marina.

Then, he heard a noise in the hall—footsteps. They stopped at his front door. A pink piece of paper slipped halfway through the crack under the door. The paper kept sliding in and out.

Gabriel grabbed the paper. He yanked. It was stuck.

"If you want it," Gabriel heard Marina's muffled voice through the door, "you have to open up."

Gabriel let the flyer go. Froze for a second.

Then he opened the door. Marina stood there. Gabriel's heart pounded. She looked surprised, then embarrassed, then sad.

"Can I come in?" she asked, handing him the flyer, looking down, unable to meet his eyes. She had missed him so much, had tried to drive him out, but seeing him now put her right back where she had started.

Gabriel moved aside, read the flyer:

TUESDAY, FEB 14

THE ARTS ASYLUM
MONTHLY EVENT

Marina
extracts her heart from her vagina

THE AQUARIUM
VENUS DE MILO ARMS
10:00 p.m.

"What are you going to do?" Gabriel asked.

"You have to see for yourself," Marina said, sitting down on the couch, crossing and uncrossing her legs.

Gabriel sat away from her on a chair that looked like half a hollow upholstered egg resting on a white plastic eggcup.

"You look like Humpty Dumpty," she said.

"Before or after the fall?"

"Before . . . ," she pronounced. "And you're not going to fall." Marina got up, started to pace in front of him. She scratched her head, stared at Gabriel. "I need a drink," she sighed.

He poured two shots of Absolut into a glass, added ice and a splash of tonic. Gabriel handed her the drink, sat down next to her. She took two big sips, stared at him.

"What?" he asked.

"I'm sorry." She grabbed his hand.

Gabriel stared at her fingers. Her nails were bitten short.

"Let's go out on the balcony," she said, letting go.

"OK," he replied, sticking his hands in his pockets.

Gabriel sat across from Marina on a wicker chair. She looked at his face and then looked down. He stretched his leg and touched her knee with his foot.

She took a deep breath. "Sex," she said in a voice that sounded like someone else. "Now you're mad at Jesus. And me. I'm sorry. I messed up our friendship."

"But . . . why?"

"I know," she said, interrupting him, rubbing her temples. "I mean, he is so beautiful. I'm not immune to that. But that's not it. And he's so needy, and you know I'm not immune to that. I wanted

to take care of him, fix him." She swallowed. "It didn't mean anything, with Jesus."

Gabriel shook his head. "You could screw Jesus because he
meant nothing to you. . . . Please, don't, that doesn't make any
sense."

"I know," she said, rubbing her temples. She swallowed. "Please,"
she begged. "I want us all to be friends, like before. All three of us."

"Fuck friends!" he blurted.

Her face fell.

"I want to wake up holding you—I want . . ." It was so hard to
tell her how he felt. He was exhausted.

Her head fell against the chair. "Time," she said. "I need time."

He reached his hand out to her. His eyes met her eyes. Release,
he thought. *She didn't say no, she said she needed time,* he thought.
She'd thrown him a lifeline.

"Do me a favor?" she asked, grabbing his hand.

"What?"

"I . . . ," she said. "I don't want this to hurt our friendship or your
friendship with Jesus. Whatever we do, I don't want to mess up our
family."

"I love you," Gabriel said, without thinking, and then he saw the
fear on her face. He brought his lips to her ear, trapping her. He
whispered softly, "Friends," and he caressed her with his breath,
and he felt her shiver and then her lips were on his lips but she didn't
open her mouth.

"I've got to go to bed," she said, pulling away. "I don't. Can't,"
she said, as panic flooded her. Then she remembered Gabriel's
shading her face from the sun, pictured his trembling hands. She
leaned over and kissed him on each eye. Each kiss knocked the wind
out of him. Then she got up and walked away.

Pandora Works Her *It* Off

Pandora sat down at her dressing table. It had a pink pleated skirt of taffeta trimmed with red velvet ribbon. Between her drag performances and her dating, she had half of the twenty thousand dollars she needed for the operation. She refused to think of herself as a whore. She refused to think of herself as a man. She thought of herself as a girl going out on dates.

Pandora finished her makeup, checked her wig. She was flawless. She hated Heinz Lerman. But she forced herself to date him to get the money to get rid of her *it*.

Pandora left the Venus de Milo Arms and took a cab to grandiose Fontainebleau hotel. She glanced at her reflection in the mirror at the entrance. You are a beautiful woman, she told herself. Men checked her out as she sashayed through the lobby. Her heels clicked on the white marble floor puncturated with giant black marble bow-tie shaped tiles. She passed the stairway to nowhere and got on the elevator.

Pandora took a deep breath and knocked on the door. Mr. Lerman opened it. He kissed her on both cheeks. He was dressed in a Chinese blue silk robe covered with dragons, and smelled like fabric softener and musk. He led her by the hand into the huge suite.

Pandora glanced around the room, her eyes getting bigger as she absorbed the richness: Persian carpets, gold gilded furniture, perfect peach-colored roses in a gleaming crystal vase and a spectacular view of the moonlit ocean. *This would have been my world if I hadn't been born with it between my legs*, Pandora thought.

Heinz popped a bottle of Cristal, filled two Baccarat glasses and then they sat on the ostentatious, oyster silk taffeta couch. He toasted, "To the perfect woman."

Pandora smiled. She was happy he'd called her a woman and perfect.

"Perfect woman because you can't talk and you don't have a pussy." He smiled obscenely.

The two things he liked her for not having were the two things she wanted most. She wanted a vagina and a voice.

"You have to help me," Heinz said, grabbing her hand, caressing her fingers softly. Something in his tone scared her.

Pandora sipped some champagne, tried to smile, but it turned into a grimace.

"You have to make your friend, Gabriel Tucker, sell me the Venus de Milo Arms." He pointed his finger at her when he talked, as if he were lecturing a child. "It is falling down. My hotel will allow more people to enjoy the ocean view. More people to pay taxes. The people who buy my condos will be rich. They will spend money in South Beach. Everyone will get richer. It is progress."

Pandora nodded her head and realized Heinz believed what he was saying, believed knocking down the Venus and the rest of the block would improve South Beach.

"You'll help me?" he implored. "Don't tell Gabriel. Don't tell him I want to knock his building down."

Pandora nodded her head.

"Don't lie to me," Heinz muttered.

Pandora took a pad and pen from her purse and wrote: *I will help you*. She passed it to him.

He read the piece of paper and ripped it up and then sat back and stared at her. Pandora couldn't stop herself from looking away.

"Don't lie to me," Heinz repeated, glaring at her—his face turning scarlet, his eyes bulging. Then, he took a few deep breaths and smiled sweetly. "You help me, I will give you a penthouse. You hurt me, I mess you." He leaned over and kissed her firmly on the lips as if to seal the deal.

Pandora froze, felt a pain in her tongue, the tongue that wasn't there, like a phantom limb. This pain was a sign of danger. She got up and made her way to the door.

"Where are you going?" Heinz asked, grabbing her roughly. His fingers dug into her arm, clawing her. She opened her mouth and screamed, reflexively. Nothing came out—just silence from an ovaled mouth.

Heinz released her. She fell forward, tripped to her knee, one of her heels snapping off.

"Make me hard," Heinz demanded.

I will do him. I will get my money. Then, it will be like it never happened. Pandora tried her best to get him hard, doing everything she could with her mouth and her hands. It seemed to go on forever, his dick flopping around in her tongueless mouth.

"Suck it," Heinz commanded, with complete contempt, angry at himself.

Pandora spat him out.

"Please!" he begged over and over as he grabbed the back of her head, knocking her off balance. Pandora tried to grab his hand. She felt more shock than pain. A black button from her dress flew, bounced on the floor. This was how it had started that time. She remembered the button flying, the man, the rape, the beating and then passing out and waking up in the hospital. She remembered him saying, "Don't tell anyone," and he'd fixed it so she couldn't tell anyone anything ever again. She'd woken up without a tongue. He had bitten it off.

"I'm sorry," Heinz said desperately. "I'm sorry, beautiful." He eased off her panties. She kicked him away, covered her *it* with her hands, ashamed.

"Take your hands away," he begged. "Please!"

Pandora rolled over on her stomach, lifted her ass into the air as an offering.

He pushed her over. "I will pay you extra. I love you."

She lay perfectly still with her eyes clenched tightly. She felt him touch her *it*. She cringed. Then he stroked her with disarming compassion. Pandora realized that the only time he could bring himself to take what he craved was when it was connected to a woman. She opened her eyes a slit and watched him, and he was staring at the thing she hated most about herself with such love, touching it as if it were too good to be true. He dribbled and then she felt his breath against it as he gently pressed his lips to it. Kissed it, like a lover, over and over.

This went on and on as she imagined the transformation, imagined her dick a cocoon that would soon give birth to a vagina. Like a beautiful butterfly, she would grow wings. She would fly!

Marina Extracts Death from Her Vagina

The moon was so huge it looked bloated. Moonlight turned the ocean liquid silver. The night was hot—even the wind. The air seemed pregnant with warm liquid, heavy and fungal.

The bottom of the empty pool at the Venus de Milo Arms was sweating, as if the pool itself was tired of being dry. An audience of about fifty people sat on the tiled floor of the pool, staring at a lonely, unmade cot placed in the deep end.

Gabriel felt like he was in someone's stomach, felt his own stomach burn with anticipation, with the anticipation of seeing Marina. He heard Skip coughing next to him. He sounded terrible.

Jesus arrived, smiled. Gabriel ignored him.

A wedding march played as Pandora walked down the steps into the dry pool wearing a pink, polyester bridesmaid dress. Marina paced a few steps behind her. She was dressed in a puffy, traditional, white bridal gown and her face was covered in a spiderweb-like veil. She dragged a five-foot train behind her and carried a bouquet of weeds. The two of them walked in extreme slow motion.

Everyone clapped, moved aside and formed an aisle to let them pass. Marina looked like an animated white tent, like she was floating through the crowd.

When she reached the empty cot, the music stopped. Dead silence. She stood in front of the bed, staring at the audience. Her hands were folded as if she were praying. Marina just stood there, felt her breath going in and out, felt the texture of the wedding dress against her skin, felt her heart beating, felt the taste of her saliva, felt the smell surrounding her.

Then she started to glow. It was as if she were lit from inside, like a lampshade. People clapped. The pool light had been switched on and she was standing over it, covering it with her wedding dress. She looked like the Virgin Mary about to ascend.

Then, Pandora walked up to her and lifted Marina's veil, slowly revealing her face, as a Gregorian chant started ricocheting throughout the pool. Marina sat on the end of the cot. She pulled off her garter belt, stood up, turned around and threw it over her back to the audience. It hit Gabriel in the face. He grabbed it, smelled Marina on it. She turned around, stared at Gabriel. Their eyes locked.

Marina unzipped her bridal gown, and it dropped to the floor. She stepped out of it and onto it in one step. The music stopped. Marina stood before the people in the audience naked, and somehow made them embarrassed not for her, but for themselves. Somehow she made them feel as if each one of them was up there nude.

Gabriel took deep breaths, his eyes grazing on her body, imagining they were his fingers, his tongue. He tried to look at her as if she were a stranger. Her legs: too thin, not shapely enough. Her ass: too big. Her breasts: too small. Even as he was telling himself this, another voice, a voice deep within that went down to his core, was saying she had the most beautiful body ever created.

Then Marina lay on the bed, faceup, staring at the stars. She spread her legs, slowly, slowly, revealing, revealing, and opening herself up. She stayed like that for a few long moments, spread-eagled, stretched and wide. She reached inside and pulled something out. It looked like a roll of film, like a miniature rolling pin. Marina contorted her body, stretched, started to unwind the object, and it looked like she was unwinding a red ribbon. There was writing on the red. It was not ribbon, but paper, a scroll. She held one end inside her as she unraveled the other end. She started to read from the scroll: "John Jacobus, Jose Ramon Diaz, Craig Coleman-Varla, Victor Farinas." She read name after name after name. "Carlos Alfonso, Mark Romero, Silvio Fittipaldi."

The more names she read, the sadder she became, the sadder the audience became. She read "George Tamsitt" and a girl burst into tears. Gabriel didn't understand. He looked at Skip.

"What?" Gabriel whispered into Skip's ear.

"They all died of AIDS. All beach people. All dead." Skip said, and his voice broke.

"Randy Underwood, Leonard Horowitz," Marina chanted.

Then someone from the audience said "Sexcilla," and then someone "Tomata du Plenty" and then someone else "Alan Sasson," and "Michael from La Bomba," and "Martin" and "Fran Wager," and "Steve O'Bannion" and "Joe Mesa" and "Kevin Kirby," and the names kept coming and coming. Marina had transformed the dry pool into a cathedral. Memories of the AIDS dead were swimming around.

Marina relaxed, pulled the scroll from out of herself, stood up and spun until the ribbon twirled around her, and then she kept spinning and spinning and spinning, going around and around and around, faster and faster and faster until she felt no pain, until she was so dizzy that she crashed to the ground. She hit the deep end of the dry pool with a thump.

The audience was in a daze. Dead silence. Sensory deprivation. Then someone started to clap. Others followed. Applause bounced off the pool floor like slaps.

Marina stood and picked up the wedding dress, wrapped it around herself, walked back through the crowd and up the steps. Pandora followed her.

"I've got to go," Skip muttered, staggering away fast, fighting back tears.

Jesus wanted to tell Gabriel about the KS, about how he was worried about Skip, but all he could say to him was "You go."

Gabriel felt Jesus' concern for Skip. It reached into him and tugged on something inside.

"Yeah," Gabriel uttered, and he realized how much he had missed Jesus' friendship, how much he really cared about him, like a little brother.

Snuffme

Skip sat at his desk, pulled off his T-shirt, stared at his KS. There were now more spots—an archipelago of lesions. He touched them, felt terror. *Just give me time to finish my novel,* he begged. He didn't know who he was begging. He didn't believe in God. No merciful god would give him AIDS.

He booted up his computer, typed in his password, *FEAR*, and his screen name, Snuffme, logged onto the AOL chat line miami *BDSM-FETISH-KINK M4M.*

Snuffme: This is Snuffme.

He heard a ding and then got an instant message from HOTKILLER.

HOTKILLER: What kind of action?
Snuffme: I'm ready to die.

Skip read HOTKILLER's profile:

Member Name: Damian: looking for someone to absorb my anger; the means to this is bndg, s/m, cbt, this is an acquired taste, but there are some of you pain pigs who would appreciate this kind of attention. Enjoy making a sacrifice of yourself? It's an interesting way to let yourself be loved, sometimes it feels like the ultimate giving, give till you're gone—I don't do phone unless you want it shoved up your ass

Location: your pleasure zone/Miami

Sex: all the time

Marital Status: smooth, younger and smaller than me. the more attracted to you, the harder I will be on you.

Computer: If you are hot enough, I will kill you. my stats: 45, 6'2", 200, salt and pepper/bl, very hairy, muscular (no fat). . . . South Beach, FL

Occupation: edging it, really thin goes to the head of the line

HOTKILLER: I'll fuck you to death. With pleasure :-)

Snuffme: First I want you to hurt me

HOTKILLER: PIC?

Snuffme: Sir Sure Sending Sir

Skip e-mailed HOTKILLER a picture of himself naked, except for his Mickey Mouse cap covering his face.

"You've got mail," the electronic voice on his computer announced.

Skip checked out HOTKILLER's pic. He was older and hot and dressed in leather, a hairy masculine muscle-bound Daddy type. He would do.

HOTKILLER: HOT PIC! Talk to me boy, you're getting me hard. I'll hurt you—bad—good.

Snuffme: Yes sir. Drive me into the darkness sir, into the black/drive me to a beach. Thank you sir.

Skip yanked his shirt off, pulled his chinos and Jockeys down to the floor.

HOTKILLER: I'm driving, and every few minutes I slap your fucking face. Boy.

Snuffme: Thank you, Sir.

HOTKILLER: I'm slapping the shit out of you, you little faggot. You piece of pig shit.

Skip started to calm down as he imagined the slaps hitting his face, harder and harder, as he traveled in his mind through the darkness to the fantasy. He felt his face slam back and forth with each slap. He imagined that HOTKILLER was slapping the AIDS out of him.

HOTKILLER: I'm sticking my fingers in your mouth. You're kissing them.
Snuffme: I'm sucking them as you ram them down my throat.

Skip slipped his middle finger in his mouth, kept typing with his right hand. He gagged.

HOTKILLER: We're there, boy. The beach.
Snuffme: You got handcuffs, duct tape, a steak knife—a white sheet.
HOTKILLER: I'm handcuffing you now. Pussy boy. If you don't shut the fuck up, I'll gag you. I cut off your clothes with my knife.

Skip felt the cold metal against his wrists, saw Paradise Beach. In his mind, HOTKILLER was his dead boyfriend. The only way to beat death was to control it.

HOTKILLER: This is what you get for taking it up the ass.
Snuffme: Yes Dad.
HOTKILLER: I'm unrolling the duct tape. I'm sticking this shit all over your faggot body, except your pathetic dick + dirty asshole.

Skip's hand went to his dick.

HOTKILLER: I'm kicking you in the chest— kicking you till you fall on your face. Your nose breaks. Your ribs crack. You cough, spit up blood. I stick my dick in your ass, fuck you till your asshole is a bleeding sore. Then I kiss you, all over, slowly.
Skip: Don't. Stop. Don't STOP.

Skip spat on his hand, started to beat off.

HOTKILLER: I'm rubbing the blade of the knife along your body, lightly scratching into you. I carve the word pig on your stomach. I cut your face, not deep, just break the surface. You leak.

Skip pictured the silver blade, felt the pain, the fear, but felt good knowing it would soon be over, knowing he would soon be dead. He pictured his face covered in a liquid red veil. He pictured Jesus being nailed to the cross, the arrows piercing St. Sebastian, a dead Kennedy. The pain would go to sleep and he would have nothing to be afraid of.

HOTKILLER: I'm stabbing.

Skip jacked harder. The more pain, the more pleasure. Sweat dripped from his body. He imagined it was AIDS blood escaping.

HOTKILLER: Spill your blood for me boy!!!!!!!!!
Snuffme: IIIIIIIIIIIIIIIIIIIIIII

"Ahhhhhhh!" he screamed, come flying through the air, sticking to his chest. Skip shut his eyes, let his head fall forward onto the keyboard, making a clicking sound.

Gabriel heard the muffled moan through Skip's apartment door—opened it. "Skip," he cried, seeing him with his head on his computer keypad. He read the computer screen.

Skip's eyes snapped open. "Gabriel," he said, yanking up his pants. He wiped the come drops on a piece of white paper by the computer. Ink smudged. It was a page from *The Venus de Milo Arms*, his novel in progress. He hit "Sign Off."

"Good-bye," the computer said, and the screen went blank.

Gabriel saw the red wine splotches stretching over Skip's chest. "You all right?" Gabriel asked.

"I knew them all," Skip said, sitting on his bed. "The people Marina mentioned. They all died of AIDS. I'm next. I'll be just another dead person stuck up Marina's crack."

Gabriel forced a laugh.

"I'm afraid I won't be strong enough. . . ." He pushed his mop of greasy hair back off his face and massaged his temples. "Strong enough to off myself."

Gabriel tried to disconnect from Skip's pain, but couldn't.

"When I lose my mind . . . ," Skip stammered. "When I'm really in pain. When I start shitting, pissing all over myself, when I am a vegetable and not a fruit, . . ." He stopped and smiled at his joke. "Do you know what Jesus did when he saw the KS?"

"What?"

"He kissed the spot and licked it and told me I was beautiful."

"He's right," Gabriel said, and he pictured Jesus doing this and he thought it was a beautifully weird innocent thing to do and he tried to release all the bad feelings he had for him.

"Help me?" Skip asked. "Help me die," he said. "When it's time."

"You have me mixed up with Dr. Kevorkian," Gabriel said, forcing a smile, trying to turn it into a joke.

Gabriel stared at Skip. Their eyes met. "You are stronger than the others. That is why I'm asking you," Skip said.

"That's what the 'Snuffme' crap is about?"

"All I know is I want to die a human. I don't want pain."

"But you like pain. Isn't that what your masochistic shit is all about?"

"I like pain when I'm in control." He massaged his head. "With masochism there is a word or a sign that you agree on before you start, you say the word or give the sign and the other person stops. You're in control. With this fucking game of AIDS, God is your partner and there's no sign." He smiled weakly to himself. "God is a bad master."

"I want someone who cares about me to kill me, not some AOL freak," Skip continued. "And not some fucking anonymous virus." He beckoned him with his eyes. "I want to be in control. . . . Will you?"

Gabriel glanced away from Skip, because he couldn't look at him.

"I asked you a question," Skip demanded, grabbing Gabriel's hand.

"Yeah, Skip, I know. I heard you. . . . What do you want me to say, like, 'Sure, no problem, I'll kill you'?"

"Yeah, that's exactly what I want you to say. If you care . . ."

Gabriel hugged him, and he could feel Skip's frailness and wished he could protect him. He imagined squeezing the AIDS out of him.

Where Neon Went to Die

The night was still and dark. The sea slurred. The air smelled still. Gabriel looked at the recently revived neon on Ocean Drive. Neon signs and ribbons of neon tubing had been repaired and were illuminated, causing the whole strip to glow. The buildings had all come back to life, had come out of a coma. Miami Beach had been the place where neon went to die and now it had become the place where neon went to be born again. Miami Beach had been a place where old people came to die, and now the young also came to die, from AIDS. It had also become a place where all ages came to be reborn, to remake themselves. In Miami Beach there was a feeling that you could be whatever you wanted to be.

The blue neon light of the Colony Hotel cast the glow of a gigantic black-and-white television set. Gabriel kept walking past the Clevelander Hotel bar, a celebration of the atomic age, as if stolen from a *Jetsons* cartoon. The bar was surrounded by the aliens to South Beach, the new people who were supposedly normal: frat boys, preppies, college kids, tourists from the Midwest. Gabriel smiled as he thought, *There goes the neighborhood.* Every day there seemed to be fewer freaks and more so-called solid citizens.

Then, Gabriel heard someone call his name. He looked. It was Jesus. A truce had formed between them. They were friends again, but it was different. On the table were two shots of tequila and a beer. He walked over.

"Sit down," Jesus said. "Help me drink these shoots. They just start arriving. The more I drunk, the more they come. Here, take one shoot."

"'Shot,' not 'shoot,'" Gabriel corrected. He sprinkled some salt on his fist, licked it, hit back the Cuervo, sucked a lime.

"Where were you going?" Jesus asked.

"To the Fuck Fabrizio party. To report on it for 'Sunstroker.' Skip is too sick to go."

"What is a Fuck Fabrizio party?"

"Fabrizio bought the Spanish-looking building up the street and has evicted everyone. Some people have lived there all their life. He gave them only one week to leave. Tonight is their last night. They are having a good-bye party."

"Let's go," Jesus said.

"You can't go. You represent him. The people won't like it. Fabrizio won't like it if he hears about it."

"I can go anywhere I want. Fabrizio doesn't own me. No one owns me. America is a free country and I am free."

"OK, but I told you so," Gabriel said, standing. Jesus followed him up Ocean Drive.

As they approached the party, they heard voices and laughter and music emanating from the apartment building. It was ablaze in lights. A big banner hung from the building.

Fuck you, Fabrizio!

They walked through the front gate into the courtyard, passed a life-sized copper statue of a woman covering her privates with a tiny towel. The statue seemed to be staring at Marina, who was sitting right below her. She looked dejected.

"Why so sad, Cinderella?" Gabriel asked. "Your wicked stepsisters won't let you go to the ball?"

"Another one bites the dust," she replied.

"Fabrizio's going to restore it," Gabriel said.

"More like suck the soul out of it," she said. "Come with me. I'll show you."

"I just want to party," Jesus screamed. "Party!" He walked ahead, leaving them alone.

Gabriel followed Marina past people moving about from apartment to apartment, drinking, smoking pot. There was a keg of beer in the hall. It was like being in a frat house, only the people didn't fit together. They were straight, gay, old, young. They all seemed to be friends.

Marina knocked. "It's Marina," she said loudly. "Abe's a little deaf," she whispered as she pushed open the door.

"Meet Abe, the richest man in South Beach," Marina said, kissing him on the cheek. He was sitting in a wheelchair drinking wine from a pink paper cup. On the table was a buttery-smelling cupcake with blue icing.

Abe shook Gabriel's hand and gave him a piece of green paper, a homemade million-dollar bill. "Now you're a millionaire," he said. "If I were a millionaire, I could. . . . I don't want to leave," he said. "I have been here for the last fifty years. My wife lived with me here for forty-nine years before she died."

"They're moving him to a retirement home in South Miami," Marina whispered to Gabriel.

"I curse this man Fabrizio. A pox on his house!" Abe said, shaking with old age and anger. "His blood will flow in this building!"

"Gabriel owns the Venus de Milo Arms," Marina said.

Abe looked up at Gabriel from the wheelchair, and Gabriel could not help but smile.

"OK," Gabriel said.

"OK, what?" Marina asked.

"OK, we can move him into the last apartment in the Venus. You're pretty transparent."

"You're pretty wonderful," she said, grabbing Abe's hand. "You can move to the Venus de Milo Arms."

"I pay three hundred dollars a month here. That's all I have."

"That's all right," Gabriel said to Abe, thinking, *The apartment could rent for eight hundred dollars.*

Marina kissed Abe good-bye and then grabbed Gabriel's hand. They walked past an apartment with the light on and the curtain open. Jesus was standing naked in the window. On the bed was a woman who looked like the Pillsbury Dough Boy, also naked. Marina and Gabriel just stood there gasping, unable to turn away.

Then a man, heavy and red-faced, shoved between Marina and Gabriel and started banging on the window. "I'll kill you!" he yelled. And then as if in fast motion, the glass pane fell, like a transparent sheet. The man, trailing blood from his fist, jumped through the window and slugged Jesus in the face. As Jesus dropped, the man caught him by the throat.

Gabriel tried to peel the man's hands from around Jesus' throat as Marina smashed a plaster mermaid lamp over the man's head. It shattered, tail falling off, as the man and Jesus tumbled down to the floor. The lady came over and cradled her husband's head. "I'm sorry, honey," she repeated over and over.

Marina grabbed Jesus' jeans and shirt. Gabriel yanked him up. "Walk," Gabriel commanded, as they helped Jesus stumble out of the room. Then he dressed, clumsily.

Crazed partiers beat drums, clanked bottles, chanted, "Fuck Fabrizio!" They splashed naked in the fountain, knee deep in bubbles, some of which overflowed onto the courtyard.

A black man, his head shaved, boogied out of the fountain, trailing a Milky Way of bubbles. A gold hoop dangled from his dancing dick—a Mapplethorpe come to life, a nude, black Mr. Clean. He pointed at Jesus. "Fabrizio! It's that Fabrizio model!" His hands balled into fists as Marina grabbed the golden ring hanging from the tip of his perforated dick, stretching it.

"He's not Fabrizio, he works for him. He hates him," Marina yelled as Fabrizio's limo pulled up and the door opened. Fabrizio's bodyguard grabbed Jesus and threw him into the car. Marina and Gabriel followed.

The crowd surrounded the limo, pressing their faces up against tinted glass. Then someone yelled, "Fabrizio! Inside!"

The crowd attacked. Fists punched metal, hands smacked against glass. The black guy mounted the rear window and started humping it, the gold penis ring clinking against the glass, lighting up like a firefly.

"Fuck you, Fabrizio!" the crowd screamed in time to the man's humps.

Fabrizio took four ice cubes from the bar's sterling silver ice bucket, wrapped them in a Fabrizio scarf and applied them lovingly to Jesus' swollen nose. "Those people," Fabrizio said. "I will turn the building into a palazzo. I will make South Beach famous. All the beautiful, the royal, the hot, the glamorous. They will come. Madonna. Sly. Cher. Elton. I will turn South Beach into the American Riviera. Those people, they are . . . ," he said, flicking his wrist, dismissing them.

They drove back to the Venus. Gabriel shut his eyes, lay back on the seat. Marina rested her head on Gabriel's shoulder. Her hair flowed down, showering his shoulder, creating sparks on his skin.

"Jesus. The stubble on your cheek. The blood. So sexy. So brute," Fabrizio gasped. "I got it. My new campaign, it will be 'Brutal Chic'!"

Then they pulled into the Venus. Gabriel, Marina and Jesus got out of the limo, leaving Fabrizio to drive off alone, already planning his next ad campaign.

"You OK?" Gabriel asked as they reached Jesus' apartment.

"No," Jesus answered. "Don't go," he begged as Gabriel and Marina turned to leave.

They followed him inside. Jesus sat on his bed, grabbed the remote and switched on the TV. He surfed the channels, stopping on I Love Lucy. "I want to be like Desi," Jesus said, pointing at the screen. "The Cubano most famous that ever lived."

"What about Castro?" Gabriel asked, sitting next to Jesus on the bed.

Jesus shut his eyes, shook his head, felt his shoulders touching Gabriel's. "Castro isn't Cuban. He isn't even human."

"Can I ask you a question?" Gabriel asked Jesus.

"Sí."

"Why with that woman?"

Marina brought the freshly filled ice bag, rested it on his nose. He gasped.

"Yeah, what were you thinking?" Marina asked, shaking her head.

"I did it for her," he said. "She told me she would fantasize about me. Told me I was her sun, how looking at me warm her up when she feel cool inside."

"So you're like a male model Mother Teresa with a cock?" Gabriel asked.

"Maybe we should put him up for canonization," Marina said, sitting down on the bed next to Gabriel.

"You two are not funny," Jesus said, shutting his eyes, resting his head on the pillow. "*Sol*," Jesus said. "The sun. In prison, sunlight was a treasure. We got only a couple of hours each month. They would take us to the roof of the jail. The feeling of the sun on my skin was heaven. You could not only see the sun from the top of the prison but also Havana across the bay. Everyone would stare at the city, which looked like a paradise, even though we all knew better. I would turn away from Havana and stare out to sea and people would ask me what I was staring at. I would tell them, 'Miami.'"

"They can't hurt you anymore. No one can hurt you, Jesus," Marina said. She reached over Gabriel and grabbed Jesus' hand.

"My friend, the only friend I made in jail. He was just a boy. He was so pretty. Too pretty to be a boy in the real world, far less in jail. The guards, the prisoners fucked him until he was practically ripped in half. He saved me."

"How?" Gabriel asked.

"He jumped and didn't die. He ended up paralyzed. I was afraid to end up like him. So I didn't jump." Jesus opened his eyes, let go of Marina's hand and looked at Gabriel. "He was the first one to save me, and you were the second, Gabriel."

"I didn't do anything."

"You think Fabrizio is really going to shoot me again? For Brutal Chic?" he asked. "He have not use me for months. He don't want me no more. Ever since I jump out the limo."

Jesus pictured himself back in front of the camera and fell instantly asleep. Gabriel glanced at Marina and she smiled at him, and he saw something in her eyes that he thought could be love. Or was he just fooling himself?

Madonna, the Famous One

(Not the Mother of God)

Gabriel went to Skip's apartment to check on him, used his golden key to open his door. It was dark inside. Gabriel pulled up the Venetian blinds. Light rushed into the room, illuminating floating dust, like powder being swirled in clear liquid. The room reeked of medicine, smelled like a hospital. Skip was fully dressed, asleep on his bed. He rolled over, opened his eyes. "Oh shit! What time is it?"

"Two o'clock. In the afternoon."

"By the time I got dressed, I was so exhausted I needed to lie down for a second. I slept till you came in: all last night and today," Skip said, rubbing his eyes.

"I took notes for you." Gabriel pulled out a small spiral notepad from his pocket.

"So?" Skip asked, gingerly sitting down at his desk, resting his hands on his keyboard. Gabriel sat on the floor, leaned against a pile of books.

"I was at the Esther Williams Film Festival by the pool at the Raleigh Hotel."

"They filmed a lot of her movies there."

"I love that pool."

"*Life* magazine called it one of the most beautiful in America."

"I was standing around with Jesus and his usual groupies and this PR lady, Nadine Johnson, came up and tapped Jesus on the shoulder and we were escorted to this suite on the top floor where another party was going on."

"Who was there?"

"The hottest-looking locals, the mayor, developers—and you're not gonna believe who else."

"Who? Who?" Skip asked, and Gabriel could tell he was energized, that this gossip stuff excited him. He even looked healthy again for an instant.

"Madonna."

"*The* Madonna," he gasped.

"Yeah, and I don't mean the mother of God. The really famous one."

"Who was she with?"

"She was with that hot Cuban lesbian chick."

"You mean Ingrid?"

"Yeah, that's the one."

"Did you talk to Madonna?"

"Didn't have to. She came up to Jesus, told him she wanted to use him in a book she's doing about sex. Some sort of illustrated sex guide. A kind of modern *Kamasutra*."

"Wow," Skip said.

"You know what else? She bought a house here."

"I can't believe I slept through the best party South Beach ever had." He looked dejected. "Madonna is my ultimate fantasy."

"But you don't like women."

"Yeah, but she transcends gender. It would be like fucking fame itself."

"You're sick."

"I know," he agreed, smiling. "What else happened?"

"Nothing else. Really. Everyone just sort of hung out and then left. Some guy walked up to me and said, 'Hi, I'm Daniel, I masturbate a lot.' I took that as a sign to leave."

"I've got to call Page Six, sell the juicy tidbits you fed me."

"Bye," Gabriel said. "I don't want to watch you sell your soul to the devil."

"Thank you," he said.

"For what?" Gabriel asked.

"For supplying the 411. If it wasn't for you I would have been fired already."

"Good-bye," Gabriel said as he looked at Skip and tried not to think of him as a condemned man.

Finally

Gabriel sat in Marina's apartment. He crossed and uncrossed his legs, watched Marina as she bent down and grabbed the jar of Vaseline. Her gym shorts grabbed her ass cheeks, climbed up her long tanned legs.

"Take off your shirt," she said, opening the jar.

"Why am I letting you do this to me?" Gabriel asked, pulling his shirt over his head.

"You're doing it for art."

"What's art?"

"A man's name, according to Warhol."

"That's reassuring," Gabriel said, sitting down. Marina appeared so intense, so determined. She finished mixing the plaster. Then she grabbed a gob of Vaseline and spread it on his forehead.

"Yuck," Gabriel cringed.

"Don't be a baby," she teased, as she kept spreading Vaseline over his hair, down to his neck. Gabriel concentrated on her touch. Her fingers were warm.

"Shut your eyes," she said, and then she rubbed some Vaseline on his eyelids. Then she completely covered his head. After this, she grabbed a handful of plaster and smoothed it on his head. It was the texture of too thick pancake batter.

"How long till this dries?" Gabriel asked nervously. His head had started to feel heavy.

"Just about ten minutes," she answered, smearing plaster over his lips. It felt like his face was being covered in warm pudding.

Marina stuck cotton in his ears and then covered them in plaster. Everything turned muffled. Then she smoothed the plaster over his closed eyes and it was darker. She stuck two straws in his nose. He struggled, felt like he was going to suffocate until he told himself to relax and realized he could breathe. The plaster started to dry, started to pull at him. He thought of the Elephant Man.

"You all right?" Marina screamed.

He could hardly hear her. He shook his head. It felt bloated. He told himself that it would soon be over. The things you do for love, he thought. Will she ever love me back? Does she love me already? The tip of his nose itched.

Marina picked up a small hammer and a chisel. "I'm gonna take it off now," she screamed.

Then he heard tapping on the back of the plaster shell. The tapping got harder and harder. He braced his head against each jolt. It hurt. He felt his face covered in sweat. He stood up, tried to grab her. He gasped for air.

"I know," she yelled. "It's stuck."

Then she grabbed his hand. His heart beat fast. He wanted to bang his head against the wall, to crack the thing off. She pulled him up. He smashed his knee into something. He felt all discombobulated. He heard running water and then felt a warm spray stream down his body. He felt her hands on his back, touching his shoulders, reaching up the back of his neck. Then he felt her hand between his neck and the plaster. The plaster started to melt.

She grabbed the softened plaster and pushed and pulled till a chunk crumbled away and then she forced off another fragment and continued, piece by piece. Strands of hair pulled away with the cast. She exposed his head bit by bit, like pieces of a puzzle. Eventually she was able to crack the whole thing in half. Like a chick emerging from an egg, his head plopped out.

He opened his eyes, saw dots and then her eyes staring back at him. She looked so scared, he felt sorry for her. She stood in the shower with him. Her "MOMA" T-shirt had turned transparent. Gabriel struggled not to look at her large hard pink nipples staring back at him through the "O" and the "A."

"I'm so sorry," she said, scraping the remains of the Vaseline off of him. "I don't know what went wrong. Did I hurt you?"

"Yes," he replied. "All over."

"Kiss and make it better," she teased, and she started kissing him all over his face. She kissed his neck, his eyelids.

Then, her lips touched his lips and sort of stopped, and he grabbed the back of her head and held her there. His lips were on her lips and they sort of just rested, lips against lips, like two pillows against each other, soft against soft, and he willed all the feelings, all the heat he had in his body into hers and he could feel her start to relax in his arms. Her breath quickened. She shivered and then her mouth opened as she wrapped her arms around him, resting them on the small of his back. He felt the blood pulsing through his veins, his heart beating fast. He dove in, like diving into a rapid. Warm water showered down on them.

They kissed, tongues exploring, and then hands exploring, and Gabriel was afraid to stop the kiss, afraid she would change her mind. Tongues everywhere. Hands everywhere. In one movement he dropped to his knees and yanked down her gym shorts and panties and kissed her other lips. Sealed it with another kiss. She moaned. He imagined she had just given birth to him, to the new Gabriel, to the one who was able to feel, to the one who was able to love. He licked and sucked and tasted and he wanted to stay there forever. He could feel her trembling with pleasure, and he just wanted to give her more. She stroked his hair, softly at first, and then her nails were digging into his scalp and then she was grabbing his hair, trying to pull him up. He refused. He was in his tongue and her pussy was his world. He grabbed the cheeks of her ass, and pushed himself in even farther.

She moaned, yanked so hard that he felt lifted up by the hair.

He stood and in one motion slid his shorts down and his dick into her and he watched the look on her face as it slipped in, her lips clenched, her face flushed, her eyes wide open, and she looked so beyond beautiful to him that he knew in that moment that he would never be the same.

SUNSTROKER

by Skip Bowling

From the worship of God to the worship of Pussy and Cock.
From piety to depravity, South Beach's pact with the devil
continues. Another obsolete synagogue morphs into a club. God
and the old Jews pack together and flee across the causeway.
They didn't look back or they would have turned to pillars of
salt. **RuPaul** performed where once stood a rabbi at **Van Dome**.
From the altar, she preached the ecumenical doctrine of
"Sashay Shante, You Better Work, Girl" to the unconverted. No
one in SOBE has a job so how can they work? Though one guy
had on a T-shirt that said, "Will Work for Pussy!"

Here I sit licking my wounds, actual wounds, inflicted at
the Last Helicopter out of Saigon meets Generation X door
frenzy of **Liquid,** where a drag queen with a seborrheic
scaling shaved scalp grabbed me as I was crossing the finish
line, the velvet ropes, latching on to me until her fake nails
gave way and stayed embedded in my arm. Blood dripping as I
yanked the faux nails out. Liquid dripping at the opening of
Liquid. I bleed for you, my readers.

Liquid, even though it is next to **Payless,** is destined to be
the new **Studio 54.** Like it or not, folks, our two-bit beach,
now the hottest fifteen blocks on the planet, will become
brand name. How long before there is SOBE soda, SOBE
Absolut ads, SOBE diets, a line of **Martha Stewart** SOBE butt
plugs in **Kmart?**

Outside Liquid, a smoothie of swirling spotlights, limos, models, boldface and begging VIP holding invitation mob! But inside, after passing through the glass, steel and multiple video screens beaming nude Japanese animation and then moving on to the very inside, into the inner sanctum of VVIP rooms, none other than fame herself, none other than the Material Girl materializing in the flesh, **Madonna,** and I don't mean the mother of God.

Confirmed rumor has it that **Chris Paciello** is presently juggling the luscious MTV veejay **Daisy Fuentes** and super-model **Niki Taylor.** Chris and Niki were seen frenching in the DJ booth of Liquid. Mr. Paciello is not only a lover, he is also a fighter. At **Bar None,** he decked former Arena football star **Matt Martinez,** Niki Taylor's estranged husband, with one punch. Who cares? He's so butch and he's King of the Night.

Confirmed rumor has it, Madonna has bought a home on the bay in Miami. And guess who has already bought the house up the street from her? **Rambo** himself, **Mr. Sly Stallone.** Who is going to borrow the sugar from whom? Then right outside South Beach the original Ms. One Name Fame herself, **Cher,** has bought a mansion. We've entered the big bang. South Beach has gone from a Cracker Jack box of people with no place else to go to a floating menagerie of people who could go anywhere. God help us all!!!!!!!!!

And just when I thought life on SOBE, the end of America, the last resort, was an endless party, our own **Venus de Milo Arms** artist in residence, **Marina Russell,** made it real in **The Pool.** She birthed the PC cult of the red ribbon from where the sin doesn't shine, pulling the dead from her birth canal. Yes the dead do live on in us. She released memories of fucking recklessly and chaste kisses. She released the dead fairies of our little town to swim in our plague-filled tears in the dry pool of the Venus de Milo Arms. Marina made me realize that we are us and you are them. Her performance made me remember what love feels like and I fear that feeling is here to stay.

The Snake Brings
the Apple to Eden

Gabriel woke up. He smiled, spooned against Marina, felt his naked skin stick to her naked skin and thought, *This is my favorite part*—waking up next to her. He replayed the last month. They had slept together every night. It was like they couldn't stay apart, like they weren't complete unless they were entangled. Gabriel peered out of the window at a plane floating by, pulling a sign:

Penrod's, Wet T-Shirt Contest,
Five hundred dollar prize.
Saturday, 5:00 p.m. Jugs galore!!!!

Gabriel got out of bed and walked to the bathroom and started to pee. Then he felt arms wrap around him as he heard her sleepy voice caress his ear.

"Let me hold it," Marina teased, grabbing his dick. The pee stream stopped in midair, a broken golden arch. She held his dick gingerly, as if it was very fragile. He felt her body against his, so delicate and soft, so sweet-smelling.

"See what you did. It quit."

"Just keep pissing. I want to pee standing up. I'm pretending I have one."

"You do have one. You have mine," Gabriel said, laughing. He felt her heat as he forced the stream, but nothing came out.

"Well then do what I say. Pee!"

He tried. He couldn't. "I'm pee shy," he said.

"Just relax," she said.

"Is this turning you on?"

"In a very weird way, 'cause it's bringing me closer to you."

He shut his eyes and imagined she was making art because he loved to watch her work and the pee shot out.

He finished and she shook off his dick as she stuck her tongue into his ear and his dick expanded and filled up her hand and he turned around and saw the playful gleam in her eyes and he kissed her and kissed her and kissed her. He wished he could just kiss her for hours.

Then he heard pounding on his door.

"Answer it," Marina said, letting him go. "Please."

"OK," Gabriel said, forcing himself down. He pulled on a pair of cutoffs and walked to the door. "Who is it?"

"Heinz Lerman."

Gabriel opened the door.

"I'm sorry I just come over, but I want to talk to you in person," Heinz said, holding out his arm. Gabriel shook his hand.

"I still want the Venus de Milo Arms."

"I left you the message that I'm not selling."

"I know, but I want to make you an offer you can't refuse," he said, chuckling.

Gabriel shook his head. "It's not for sale."

"Three million dollars."

"No," Gabriel answered.

"Four million cash U.S. dollars, immediate closing and that's my final offer."

"No," Gabriel answered. He pushed the thought of the money out of his head, picturing last night: Marina's body, pale perfection, naked in the moonlight. Now that he was with Marina, there was no way he was selling the Venus.

"I'm offering you two million more than this building is worth," Heinz said, exasperated.

Gabriel shrugged.

"I want to save the Venus."

"No you don't," Gabriel said. "You want to knock it down and build a high-rise hotel and condos."

The German looked shocked.

Then, Marina walked into the living room and rested her hand on Gabriel's shoulder. Heinz's expression changed from frozen fake smile to uncontrollable grimace. Marina was the enemy. He knew she was the one organizing to save the deco buildings.

"Listen, I will build a beautiful building," Heinz said, changing his tactic. "It will be modern, yes, but also exquisite. It will allow more people to enjoy the ocean. It will bring lots of tax dollars into Miami Beach. The money can be used to help the old and the poor people. It's good for everyone."

"But you don't understand," Marina said. "The Venus de Milo Arms is a piece of South Beach history. Knocking it down destroys the past."

"Exactly," Heinz Lerman said. "America is about the future, not about freezing the past. You want to stop progress. These old buildings are just old. They are not special. The people who live in them are all dying. Why should these poor old people have to live in decaying buildings?" Heinz said calmly. "With the money the city will make from new construction, they could build true care facilities and let these people live in dignity. Some of them live on dog food. This land is too valuable for small buildings. This place is dying. I want to pump some real life back into it."

"You are shortsighted. The architecture of South Beach is what will cause the renaissance of South Beach," Marina said.

Heinz turned to Gabriel. "If you don't sell me this Venus, I will dwarf it with my new building," he said, giving up on Marina. "I will cut off all your sunlight. I will surround you and box you in. The Venus will be worthless."

"I think you should leave now," Gabriel said.

"I have friends in this city. This building will never pass inspection. They will condemn it."

"Don't threaten me!" Gabriel said.

"Please," Heinz replied. "Be reasonable," he pleaded. "Four million is much money."

"Good-bye," Gabriel said as he held the front door open. The German left reluctantly.

Marina hugged Gabriel. "You are my hero," she said.

He kissed her and wondered if he had just made the biggest mistake of his life.

Then she smiled and pulled off her shirt and removed her shorts and panties. Her panties had little silver stars on them. She put her hands on her hips, looked at him. She just stood there naked, staring at him.

He swallowed, felt a jolt, felt blood rush to his dick. Felt dick against fabric. No matter how many times he had her, he was insatiable. He just marveled at her naked body. He could not resist. It was Kryptonite.

She held out her hand. He stood up, and she led him to the bathroom and turned on the shower. He pulled off his clothes. He stepped into the shower after her. He hugged her, his naked body against her naked body, skin sparking against skin, the shower spraying, warm water dripping down. His lips against her lips, his tongue touching silky, soft, his dick as hard as a diamond, pushing, pulsing against her as he pulled her to him. Then she pulled away, grabbed the soap. The smell of musk.

She soaped him, starting at his toes and working her way up: his calves, knees, thighs and then his stomach and chest, his neck and hair, then his nipples and ass and between the cheeks of his ass and his balls and then his dick. Her fingers, the soap—on his dick. He felt about to shoot, felt about to pass out. His legs shook. He couldn't take it anymore. He grabbed the soap from her, pulled her up off her knees.

He got down on his knees and buried his head into her pussy, soaped her ass as his tongue found home, and he had never before felt this close to anyone or anything. As he licked inside of her, he thought, I want to spend forever and ever with you. He loved her taste, lapped up the silky softness, loved the feel of her fingers stroking his hair.

He licked and he licked and he licked as he thought, *This is where I belong. After all the places I've traveled to, after all the searching, I've finally found the place where I'm happiest—in between her legs.*

Marina moaned. With each lick she moaned. All he wanted was for her to trust him, to love him. All he wanted was to take care of her. All he wanted to do was give her pleasure. He thought of Miss Levy telling him she felt the pain of her twin sister in the concentration camp and he understood this as he felt Marina's pleasure. He understood for the first time how if you cared enough for someone, you could feel what they feel. Her pleasure was his pleasure.

It was as if her pussy was a pool and he was swimming in waves of pleasure. His tongue and face had become an extension of her. She stopped stroking his hair, dug her nails into his scalp. He grit his teeth. She moaned, tried to pull him up by the hair. He looked up, through the water, at her face—red, flushed.

He surrendered, stood up, lifted her and carried her wet to the bed. He looked at her as he made love to her, watched his thrusts reflected on her face, in her clouded-over eyes, echoed in her moans. He relaxed into her, became a part of her. They trembled. Her orgasm exploded into him as he exploded into her. It was as if they had exchanged souls.

Save South Beach

"It's war," Marina announced from a makeshift podium to the ragtag group of about fifty people comprised of interior designers, artists, housewives, gay guys, elderly activists and architects. They sat on beach chairs in the lobby of the Venus de Milo Arms. "It's time for organization, time for action." Marina's voice trembled with passion. "We have to stop the wrecking ball in the name of future generations. I call to order the first meeting of the Miami Design Preservation League."

Everyone clapped. Gabriel whistled, thinking, *This group couldn't stop a spitball.*

"We will not let our neighborhood be destroyed by this single-minded, petty greed and bad taste," Marina exclaimed.

Gabriel stared at Marina, and she looked like she was glowing. Her hair was pulled into a tight bun and she was dressed in a business suit, which made her look very serious, very grown-up. *She's the opposite of me*, Gabriel thought. Where he had gone through most of his life not caring about anything, Marina was a bundle of care. He was like a magnet attracted to her opposite life force. *That's why I'm stuck in this strange place with this strange woman*, he thought.

"We need to organize the grass roots of this community," Marina said.

Skip coughed and wiped his mouth as he took notes. "Poor old Jews, unemployed Cubans and gays who are either too sick or too busy partying and pumping iron to notice the buildings going up and down around them," Skip whispered to Gabriel. "You mean those grass roots. Miami Beach is not a community, it's a crowd." He sat on a rocking chair which seemed to dwarf him, to accentuate his frailness. This was the first time in about a month he'd left his apartment, except to go to the doctor. Gabriel had been going out and reporting back to him so he could write "Sunstroker."

"Now they want the Sands Hotel," Marina announced. "They want to turn it into another parking lot. We have to make them realize that tearing down a building in South Beach is just like tearing down a building in Charleston, Savannah or New Orleans. We need to save our city, to save South Beach!"

The group clapped again. Marina had a determined expression on her face, as if she was going into battle. Gabriel felt sorry for her and her ragtag army of preservationists going to war against hundreds of developers, property owners and corrupt city officials. It was David and Goliath.

"We need to preserve the neighborhood, establish a historic district called Old Miami Beach. Instead of tearing buildings down, we have to show the owners that it's just as profitable to fix them up," Marina said. "The smaller hotels could be turned into restaurants or housing for the elderly. Our first task is to survey the buildings—"

Suddenly the doors swung open and a building inspector, escorted by a police officer, marched into the lobby, interrupting the meeting. Everyone stared. Silence.

The inspector, a short, overweight man in neat khakis, polished brown shoes and a short-sleeved white shirt bearing the words "Miami Beach Code Inspection," looked casually self-important. The policeman, tall, overmuscled and tanned, seemed mildly embarrassed and tried to avoid eye contact with the occupants of the lobby.

"Can I help you?" Marina asked from the podium.

"I'm from the Building and Zoning Department of Miami Beach, code compliance division," the inspector announced, walking up to Marina. He wiped the sweat from his triple chins. "We've had complaints that this building is unsafe, that there are building code violations." The policeman smiled, winked a piercing blue eye at Marina.

"Complaints? From who?" Gabriel inquired, both puzzled and annoyed, getting up, walking toward them.

"We're not required to give out that information," the inspector replied with a pleased sneer. The policeman continued to gaze around the room while avoiding eye contact.

"This is nothing more than harassment!" Skip interjected, yelling from his seat. "You're just here because of the meeting."

"Who told you to come here?" Marina asked. Her attitude was casual, even friendly. Then Marina winked at the policeman, played with a tendril of hair. The policeman flexed his muscles.

"Why don't you go arrest a criminal," Miss Levy said to the policeman, joining the group. She was dressed in a pink sherbert après-ski suit with matching sequined ski cap and puffy pink slippers.

"This building has no certificate of occupancy," the inspector announced with firm finality. "Therefore, no one should be living here. Now, can you all move aside and let us pass."

"I've been living here for longer than you have been alive," Miss Levy said, her voice trembling. She felt herself grow weaker every day. She did not have the strength to fight anymore.

"It's not in our computers," the inspector said. "And if it's not in our computers, it doesn't exist. And if it doesn't exist, people can't live in it. Everyone is going to have to move."

"How can it not exist, if you're standing in it, if we're living in it?" Gabriel asked, folding his arms.

"Listen, buddy. I just do what they tell me," the inspector said, for the first time not wholly in a belligerent tone. "I don't make the rules, I enforce them. Now, can you please show us where your boiler is and the electrical panels?"

"It doesn't exist," Gabriel asked. "How can I show you these things?" Gabriel's tone was almost pleading now, having seen a small break in the hostility.

The inspector scratched his head, not sure how to react to that one.

Then Skip walked up to him. He seemed bent over, like an old man. "What's your name?" he asked, pointing his pen at the inspector. "Who are you?" the inspector asked. He wiped the sweat from his face again. "I don't have to tell you."

"Who am I? Who am I?" Skip asked, wagging his pen. "You don't know who I am?" he sputtered.

"Yeah, that's why I asked," the inspector replied, taking a pen and a pad from his pocket. He breathed heavily. "What is your name?" the inspector repeated. "I'm the person who takes down names, not you." He was angry now.

"You're going to take down my name? You're going to take down my name?" Skip repeated, walking closer to the inspector. He coughed. Spittle flew onto the inspector.

He wiped his face, and then his hand against his pants, wondering if he might have caught something from Skip's spittle. He took a step back.

"I don't think so. I'm going to take down *your* name," Skip said. "I'm going to expose you crooks, how it's part of your master plan to get rid of all the old people and the poor people. That's what the building moratorium south of Fifth Street is about."

The inspector's face got redder and redder. A vein showed on his forehead. He looked over at the policeman for support, but the policeman was staring at Marina, clearly transfixed.

"Are you a model," he asked her, "or do you just look like one?" Marina giggled. "I love men in uniform," she replied, fake-flirting. "I love men of authority." Gabriel understood what Marina was up to, but Skip was oblivious.

Skip pushed toward the inspector again, got in his face. "I'm from the press, the *Wire*," Skip announced, "and I demand your name. Now!" he yelled. His anger made him feel almost strong again.

"Shut up, you little faggot, or you'll be sorry," the inspector shouted, looking like he was ready to pop. He had finally lost it.

"Can he do that? Can he call someone that ugly name?" Marina asked the officer sweetly, touching him on the arm, softly. "Isn't that assault?"

"Sam, you're out of line," the policeman said to the inspector. "Apologize to the good citizen." He fixed his eyes back on Marina.

"That Kraut is right," the inspector said, ignoring the policeman. "This funny farm needs to be torn down."

"What Kraut are you talking about?" Gabriel asked, thinking of Heinz Lerman.

"If you want to knock the Venus de Milo Arms down," Miss Levy yelled, "you're going to have to knock me down with it." Her whole body was trembling now.

"Don't worry," Marina said, walking up to Miss Levy and giving her a long hug. "Nobody's going anywhere."

"That's what my father said when the Nazis came. Then they shot him." Her tone was quiet and distant now, even resigned. The way the code inspector stood reminded her of the SS. "I can't believe Jewish politicians are selling out to Germans, and Jewish developers are evicting their own Jewish people. Their bubbies."

"Please," the inspector said. "Can you shut that senile bag up." He'd had enough. He just wanted to get off this beach and back home to Hialeah where everyone was normal.

"You shut up, Hitler," Miss Levy screamed with all her strength. She wished her old boss, Meyer, was still alive. She could have taken care of this problem with a phone call.

"Hitler! Hitler! Hitler!" everyone started to chant, getting out of their seats and surrounding the inspector. He backed away toward the door.

"If you don't have a search warrant," Gabriel said, "I demand that you leave my property."

"I don't need this shit," the inspector mumbled, and then he wrote something down on his pad. "You all better find a new place to live. I'll be back with a warrant to condemn your Venus de Milo Arms!" He marched out.

The policeman stayed, his attention still focused on Marina. Everyone looked at him, wondering what he was going to do.

"Can I get your number?" the policeman asked Marina.

"I'd rather have yours," she mewed in return, still sweet as can be.

"I can't," he said, shaking his head, embarrassed.

"Married?" she asked.

"How'd you know?" he replied a bit meekly, and slumped slightly, deflated.

"All the best ones are taken." She smiled as sincerely as possible.

"I have to go," the policeman said, leaving reluctantly.

When the door to the Venus de Milo Arms swung shut, Gabriel kissed Marina as everyone started to cheer. They felt like they had won their first battle. But Gabriel felt afraid, knowing they were coming back, knowing that Heinz Lerman wouldn't give up so easily.

Passover

Miss Levy tasted, stirred and fussed with her Passover dinner. Delicious smells emanated through her apartment. She was dressed in a conservative black pantsuit with a black top hat. It was the thought of having a seder with her family that had helped her survive the camps.

Miss Levy placed the plate with the engraved Jewish star in the middle of the table. On it she rested a roasted egg, a nut and apple mixture, a roasted shank bone, horseradish, bitter greens and a boiled potato.

Marina arranged the red roses she brought in a crystal vase. Skip sat on Miss Levy's plastic-covered blue velvet couch wrapped in a multicolored blanket. He coughed and spat up something that looked like egg whites into a tissue.

"Where's Jesus?" Miss Levy asked, taking the tissue from Skip and throwing it in the trash.

"Probably still asleep," Gabriel answered, walking out into the hall and knocking on his door. No answer. He used his golden key to open Jesus' door.

"Jesus," Gabriel called out, walking into his apartment. He heard music emanating from the bedroom. The door was open. Jesus was naked on the bed. His eyes were closed. His mouth was open. He was snoring. A rubber tube was stuck to him, snaking from his left nipple to his collarbone. A spent plastic syringe lay next to his arm on the gaudy, giddily patterned baroque Fabrizio sheets. There was dried blood on the silver needle tip.

"Jesus," Gabriel said, shaking him. His body flopped around. The syringe fell onto the floor.

"Wake up," Gabriel yelled.

Jesus wiped his eyes, squinted. He looked up at the clock. "It's morning?"

"Guess again?" Gabriel said.

"Passover," Jesus uttered, jumping up out of bed. He hadn't seen the sun shine in four days. The rubber tube dropped onto the floor.

Jesus walked to the closet, put on a garish silk shirt covered in Florida maps and Spanish galleons, buttoned it from the bottom to the top—he always dressed opposite to the norm. He looked funny dressed in just a shirt, naked below, like a little boy except for his huge uncircumcised dick.

"What's this?" Gabriel asked, picking the syringe up from off the floor.

Jesus didn't say anything—just stared at the syringe as if he were seeing it for the first time. He smiled like a naughty little boy and pulled on black Fabrizio briefs.

Gabriel didn't smile back. "You're shooting up now?" he asked.

"It feels good," Jesus said, looking away, pulling on a pair of slick black leather pants and Fabrizio velvet loafers with little crowns on them.

Gabriel stepped on the syringe. It cracked beneath his foot.

"Come on, *papo*," Jesus said, shrugging his shoulders. "Don't worry. Let's go."

"You are so lucky," Gabriel said. "You have everything. I can't believe you are doing this shit."

Jesus ignored Gabriel, thinking, *All I have is my looks and I am losing them every day and more and more beauties invade South Beach every day. And Fabrizio is not using me for ads anymore.*

They walked next door. Jesus picked up Miss Levy and kissed her. She laughed. "Like you want to kill me with worry?"

She put a yarmulke on his head. They all sat down at the table:

Gabriel, Miss Levy, Skip, Pandora, Jesus and Marina. She handed them each a booklet, the Haggadah.

Miss Levy's eyes closed and from her trembling lips Hebrew filled the air with ancient mystery. They each took turns reading the Passover story from the booklets. Except for Pandora. They dipped greens in saltwater and ate them. Miss Levy broke the matzo and passed it around and they all ate a piece. Then she brought out a big bowl of matzo ball soup, a huge roasted leg of lamb, chopped liver and onion, gefilte fish, all sorts of vegetables and parsley potatoes.

Miss Levy watched them eat and felt happy. It was not the family or seder she had fantasized about in Auschwitz. But it was a family— her family.

They ate coconut macaroons in the living room. Pandora stood in front of everyone, took a deep breath and turned on her boom box. She made a dramatic curtsy in Miss Levy's direction and started lip-synching along with the song.

"*Hava nagila, hava nagila, hava nagila venis'mecha*" started to flow from her mouth and the boom box at the same time. Then everyone started singing along to the chorus. Jesus rested his cigar in the ashtray, stood, grabbed Miss Levy's hands and pulled her up and started to dance with her. She shut her eyes and remembered dancing on stage at the Latin Quarter, the Beachcomber, Copa City. She heard the thundering applause.

Marina grabbed Gabriel's hand and then Skip's and they all started dancing in a circle around Jesus and Miss Levy. As the music got faster, they danced faster until they felt the room spinning out of control, until the music stopped. Then the five of them fell into each other's arms.

"Will you take me to visit my family? Or as close as I can get?" Miss Levy asked Gabriel. "The Holocaust Memorial," she said. "I go every Passover." She grabbed Gabriel's arm and they walked downstairs and got inside his grandfather's Cadillac convertible.

Gabriel started the car and they drove out of the garage, into the moonlight. They drove up Washington Avenue past three sets of klieg lights searching, washing the sky, attracting people to the clubs, like bugs to light.

"You in the moonlight, dressed in your grandfather's pin-striped suit, driving in this car. It's like I've stepped back into the happiest time of my life." She shut her eyes and inhaled, and the car reeked of Alvin, Gabriel's grandfather.

They drove a couple blocks, past the Miami Beach Convention Center, and then a couple more and they could see the massive green arm and hand of the Holocaust Memorial in the distance. The large green patina bronzed sculpture that served as Miami Beach's memorial to a distant hell stuck out above the palms, getting bigger and bigger as they got closer.

They arrived, and Miss Levy looked up at the giant arm and the horrible starving skeletal figures hanging from it with a look of such sadness frozen on her face that Gabriel wanted to take her away from there. As they got out of the car and walked closer, he could see the detail of the figures—the naked emaciated bodies of men, women and children. There were numbers on the forearm of the gigantic arm. It was a solidified nightmare, a horror movie on still frame, not subtle or abstract. *But this actually happened to Miss Levy,* Gabriel thought, *to the person whose arm I am holding.*

They walked to the black walls covered in rows and rows and rows of names carved into the marble. Miss Levy ran her trembling fingers against the names, as if she were blind and reading Braille.

"Why me?" she asked. "Why was I chosen?" She kept walking slowly. The reflection of the hand in the silvery black pool that surrounded the monument seemed to be following them, as if it wanted to grab them.

Then, Miss Levy stopped, bent down and kissed the wall, kissed the black. Her face reflected back at her in a blur from the marble. It was as if she was kissing herself. Her red lipstick formed a contorted circle in the shape of lips around the names engraved in the wall.

Gabriel leaned forward and read the names: IRA LEVY, GUNDULA LEVY, MAGDA LEVY. His eyes started to burn. Her red lipstick seemed to turn into a smear of blood before his watery eyes, as if the black wall were bleeding.

Miss Levy touched the tear that flowed down Gabriel's cheek. It disappeared. She looked away. They kept strolling hand in hand.

"When I die, I want my ashes scattered here in this pond. I want to be cremated, like my family in the Nazi ovens," she said. A firefly sparked behind her, blinked on and off. "I'm all that's left of the Levy family. I was fourteen when they took us to the ghetto in Warsaw. They killed my father first. He was a professor, a peaceful man, a dreamer. He would let me put the shaving cream on his face before he shaved. During the uprising in the ghetto, he killed a Nazi with his bare hands."

Miss Levy spoke without emotion, as if she were telling a story that had nothing to do with her. Sweat formed on her face.

"After the uprising, we were moved to Auschwitz. When we arrived, there was a sign that said, 'Work will set you free.' Me and my mother and my twin sister, Magda. We were led up a ramp."

She took a deep breath, swallowed, took out a handkerchief and wiped the sweat from her face.

"At that exact moment," she said, "at the exact instant I thought we would survive, an SS guard walked up to us and cried, 'Zwillinge! Zwillinge!'" She coughed, cleared her throat. "See the ZW," she said, pointing to her tattoo. "That stands for 'zwillinge,' for twins."

Gabriel looked at her forearm. They sat together on a bench. He stroked the neat row of blue-black numbers and letters—ZW3898.7—tattooed on her forearm, rubbed them with his thumb. They had now blurred with age, like memories. He noticed that the seven was bisected with a European slash.

"The guard, he told us to come with him. We just held hands, the three of us, my mother in between. We started to follow him. He said, 'Just the girls.' The soldier pulled us apart. My mother screamed, kicked and bit the guard. It was all so fast. He hit my mother over the head with the butt of his rifle. She fell to the ground."

A tacky, purple Lamborghini with super-souped-up tires preened by, a hip-hopped remix of Marley blaring from the radio,

Exodus, movement of jah people.

Gabriel wanted to attack someone, to hurt someone, but there was no enemy. The enemy was a memory.

"They took us to the hospital," she said. "They did experiments on us because we were twins. Toward the end of the war, they moved us. We walked from Auschwitz to Germany. My twin sister Magda died walking. I left her on the side of the road, just like that. That is how I became the only one left in my family."

Miss Levy stopped talking. She felt overcome by anger, fear, pain, shame and powerlessness.

"When I have children," Gabriel said, "I will bring them here and tell them your story."

"When I shut my eyes and I see their faces, the faces of my family," she said, "they have not aged. That's why the first time I saw you, I thought you were your grandfather. He's also there in my head, in permanent youth, in the room with my family."

Miss Levy glanced at Gabriel's face in the moonlight, and saw his grandfather, and moved toward him and hugged him gently. "Your grandfather trained for the army here in Miami Beach, got sand in his shoes, said the only thing that kept him alive during the war was the thought of coming back to Miami Beach. And he brought me back with him. And now he sent you to me." She shut her eyes. She saw the tanks break through the high barbed-wire fence, the electrical fence spark as it shorted out. Then everything was very quiet. The tanks idled.

Gabriel and Miss Levy walked back to the car.

"Your grandfather was with the troops that liberated us. I'll never forget the first time I saw him. He was so tall and blond. So Aryan-looking. The Nazi ideal. Like you. So even though he was beautiful and American, he scared me. I was a human skeleton. I was dirty. Bald. He walked straight up to me and said, "A sweet for a sweet," and I had learned English in school so I understood. He gave me a chocolate wrapped up in silver paper in the shape of a tiny mountain. He said it was a Hershey Kiss, a chocolate Kiss. He smiled at me. Beautiful white teeth. I opened my mouth and he placed the Kiss on my tongue and it was the most perfect taste I had ever tasted. I started to cry and it got worse and I couldn't help it. He hugged me tight, even though I was so ugly and dirty and smelly. He sang:

Ev'rything went wrong,
And the whole day long
I'd feel so blue.
For the longest while
I forgot to smile;
Then I met you.
Now that my blue days have passed,
Now that I've found you at last:

I'll be loving you
Always
With a love that's true
Always.

I felt safe for the first time in a long time."

SUNSTROKER

by Skip Bowling

Well, South Beach has been christened "Pussy Paradise" by none other than the pussy bible *Playboy*. They wrote, "South Beach has a greater concentration of female beauty . . . than has ever occurred in the history of the planet. . . . We are talking about 120 blocks. 1,500 models live in these blocks year-round. The math is simple. There are about thirteen beauties per block."

An odd alphabet soup of fame floated onto our island of multiple pleasures this week. Seen around town: moguls **Andrew Tobias** and **Barry Diller** at **The Raleigh, Eddie Murphy** at the **Butter Club**, Robert De Niro in **Liquid**, **Carmen D'Alessio** from **Studio 54** at **The Spot**, **Timothy Leary** at **Uncle Sam's Music Café**, Johnny Depp at **The Century**, **Lee Radziwell** at **The Strand**, **Joan Collins** at the **Blue Door, Jackie Mason** at **Wolfies, Ima Sumac** at **The Talkhouse, Laurie Anderson** at **The Guzman** and **Brett Easton Ellis** and **General H. Norman Schwarzkopf** promoting their latest opuses at **Books & Books.**

And the biggest boldface of them all, **Madonna**, is working on her literary masterpiece, **SEX.** She was spotted posing butt naked in the hitchhiking position in front of South Beach's **Cheers, Club Deuce.** Some of the lines in Madonna's sex book, according to my unconfirmed sources: "Me and

Ingrid are laying around naked on the sundeck. . . . Her pussy is so wet right now it's dripping." Alert the Pulitzer Prize committee.

Farther up the beach, two more signs of the apocalypse or the future of South Beach. The city fathers, or Silly Hall, in their wisdom decided South Beach needed cars more than a boxer's shrine. They allowed the demolition of the world-renowned **Fifth Street Gym, Angelo Dundee's Harvard.** This is where **Muhammad Ali** trained when he was **Cassius Clay,** where the **Beatles** stopped by to meet the Champ, who rhymed, "When **Sonny Liston** reads about the Beatles visiting me, he'll get so mad I'll knock him out in three."

The second sign of the coming apocalypse was the opening of **The Gap** on Collins Avenue at Eighth Street, a mere block from the famous **News Cafe.** I was given a special Gap wristband so I could enter the VIP room. How un-American. Everyone should be equal in a Gap. Coming soon to a neighborhood near you. South Beach—a dreco, deco Mall.

Then on to red-hot swanky **Bar Room,** the newest addition to the dynamic duo, **Chris Paciello** and **Ingrid Casares'** three-ring nightclub circus. In the VIP, **Tommy Hilfiger** was celebrating his new line with a bevy of super-boldface and superbeautiful creatures. **The Nanny, Fran Drescher,** was chatting with **k.d. lang.** Funny man, **Chris Rock, Ben Stiller, Lenny Kravitz** and the **Red Hot Chili Peppers' Anthony Kiedis** were fighting off the pussy posse. **Ed Norton** was getting down with **Cameron Diaz.** When I thought they couldn't pack in any more fame, the entire cast of *Ally McBeal* arrived. Two of Chris Paciello's rumored paramours vied for attention: MTV's **Daisy Fuentes** and the ultrasizzling **Jennifer Lopez.** Jennifer had been observed in a lip lock with our Chris earlier at the **Pelican Hotel.** Too bad Chris can't bottle whatever it is that drives the ladies wild.

I grabbed a pair of complimentary sunglasses by the door and dragged my ass out into the blinding morning light. There was still a desperate crowd begging to get in. As I said excuse me to a beautiful doe-eyed boy who was blocking my exit, he dropped to the ground, his eyes rolled back till they were completely white, his lips turned blue. I tried to help him as everyone else ignored us, stepped over us, trying to get into Bar Room. By the time the ambulance arrived, he was dead from an overdose. Just another casualty of glamorous SOBE!

Skip Checks into the Roach Motel

Gabriel stared at the door of the Venus de Milo Arms. His heart skipped a beat. He'd been subconsciously waiting for this. He had seen it before, stuck on other buildings in South Beach. Two emergency orange–colored pieces of tape held up the white pieces of paper, scars against the etched glass door, bureaucratic graffiti. On the tape was written in block black letters,

IMPORTANT NOTICE

Gabriel yanked it down from the door, read the papers from the City of Miami Beach Code Compliance Department. As a result of a supposedly mandatory forty-year inspection of the building, it had slapped the Venus de Milo Arms with 378 code violations. The City of Miami Beach declared the building in extremis and said that if the owner did not cure the violations in one month, said owner would have to demolish the building or the city would demolish it for him and charge the expenses to the owner.

Gabriel braced himself, walked straight to Skip's apartment, code violation notice balled up in his front pocket, sticking out like a cancerous tumor. He knocked on Skip's door, opened it and entered.

Skip pulled the sheet over his head. His room smelled of sickness, smelled of medicine.

Gabriel grabbed the sheet and pulled it from over Skip's head.

"Let me sleep, Daddy," Skip murmured weakly. His eyes were dull. His cheeks had sunk into his face.

Skip focused on Gabriel, read the alarm in his expression. He sat up straight. "What's wrong?" he asked.

Gabriel yanked the violation from his pocket, knocking over a plastic vial of red pills, which scattered across the floor. He got down on his hands and knees and put them back into the vial as Skip read the Notice of Violation. A wiry black pubic hair stuck to a pill.

"That fucking Nazi Kraut! This fucking corrupt asswipe city!"

"I don't have the money to fix all this stuff—plumbing, electrical, structural. And even if I had the money, I don't know if I have the time or if it can even be done at all. I'm fucked." Gabriel sat on the bed next to Skip.

"We'll figure something out," Skip said, not too positively. "I'll write about it in 'Sunstroker.' Expose the corruption."

"Oh, Skip. Did I make a huge mistake? Am I going to lose it all no matter what? Should I have taken the four million from Hitler? At least then I could have bought some safe place for us all to live."

"Let me think; give me some time. I know everything about everybody in South Beach. I will save the Venus, I promise." And he was already conceiving of a blackmail plot in his head.

"The Venus de Milo Arms feels more like a real home to me than any other place I ever had." Gabriel's voice cracked, and he looked at Skip.

Skip had turned blank white, and pearls of sweat formed on his forehead. He couldn't seem to catch his breath. He wheezed, choked, spit up a gob of phlegm.

"You OK, Skip?" Gabriel asked, pushing the Venus's plight out of his head.

"I keep having these fucking spells—fever, sweats, can't catch my breath," Skip said. "I feel terrible."

"I know," Gabriel said, thinking that Skip must be in really bad shape because he never complained. "You don't look so good."

"You really know how to make a dying queen feel fabulous," Skip said.

"You're a drama queen, not a dying queen."

"I'm so sick of being sick," Skip coughed. "The worst thing is I still love Dennis, the man who gave me AIDS. I replay the moment he told me over and over in my head. He held me in his arms. I felt protected. I felt like I had a father for the first time in my life." Skip shook his head. "Dennis started to cry. I licked the tears from his cheek. I asked him what was wrong and he said, 'I have AIDS. I'm sorry. I lied to you. I don't want to die alone. I'm so sorry.'"

Gabriel sat next to Skip on the bed, touched his matted hair.

"I took care of Dennis until he died." Skip took a deep breath. "He didn't have to die alone. But I have to. I have no one. . . ."

"You have me, all of us at the Venus," Gabriel told him, and this put everything in perspective, and he no longer felt sorry for himself. He realized the Venus was the people who lived there, his new family, and not the brick and mortar. He realized he had his health and as much of a cliché as that was, his health was everything. Gabriel squared his shoulders and tried to wipe the defeated expression from his face.

"Bring me my computer," Skip said, shaking his head as if trying to shake the thought out, changing the subject. "Tell me about the opening. 'Sunstroker' is due today."

"Another synagogue became a club, called Pork," Gabriel said, as he handed Skip his PowerBook from the desk. Skip struggled to a sitting position, booted up his notebook computer.

"There were some Hasidim out front picketing."

"Now that all the old Jews are dying or being evicted, there's no one left in South Beach to go to the synagogues," Skip said as he typed. His wrists looked so skinny, like his hands were too big for his arms.

"Same old pandemonium at the door. Inside, they had a vignette of a guy dressed like a rabbi tied to a cross, being fed a pork chop by a midget Christ."

"A little person, real class, so cliché," Skip said, as he kept typing, breathing deeply. "Who was there?"

"Gloria Estefan, Donatella Versace, Fabrizio with a bevy of beautiful boys and Sly Stallone."

"What? Sly?" he asked, looking up at Gabriel. "What was he doing? Who was he with?" Skip asked, and there was excitement in his voice. It was the first time in a long time he looked animated, the first time he didn't look sick. Gabriel felt sorry for him, stuck in bed, missing the gigantic party that was South Beach.

"He was with some older has-been model woman, Angie somebody. She is supposedly pregnant by him. Fabrizio was with his entourage. Then Jesus showed up and he was so high. He grabbed me by the hand and took me over to Fabrizio, who ignored him."

Skip started to cough, and it was like he had something deep inside that was stuck, that he couldn't get out. Gabriel wished he could spit for him.

"Fabrizio keeps trying to fuck Jesus," Gabriel said. "He won't use him in any ads, and Jesus is exclusive to him by contract so he can't work for anyone else."

"That sucks, but at least he's getting paid," Skip said, as he kept typing away. Then, with an effort, Skip stood up and groaned, and for Gabriel it was like watching an old man, like Skip was moving in slow motion.

"Thank God that's over with," Skip said, faxing his finished "Sunstroker" to the *Wire*. He sat back on his rolling desk chair, shut his eyes and took deep breaths. He was exhausted. "Can you take me to the hospital now?" he asked, shivering and his teeth clapped together like gag windup teeth. It was as if now that Skip had finished his column, he was no longer fighting the sickness.

Gabriel helped Skip into his car. They drove up Ocean Drive toward Mount Sinai Hospital. The neon was starting to turn on. Day shift turned into night shift, nine to five to five to nine. The music from the cafés changed as they drove, like the sound track to a motion picture. People were headed back from their day on the beach, all tanned and buff and healthy-looking. Gabriel glanced at Skip. He was all white, looked as if all the blood had drained from him. It seemed so unfair. What had Skip ever done to anyone? South Beach was the place to get tanned, high and laid, not a place to get sick. Yet people were getting sick, though you would never see them. They would just disappear, return to their families to die. It was like the land of the body snatchers. God's funny little game of last call.

Gabriel stopped at a red light. A girl being pulled by a pit bull on a sequined leash floated by on Rollerblades. She was wearing a G-string made of holographic material. The setting sun seemed to stick to her bleached blonde hair, which floated down her naked, brown ass cheeks. She smiled at Gabriel. He imagined resting his head against her ass cheeks as if they were a pillow.

They are going to find a cure, Gabriel told himself. *Skip will beat it. He has time*, Gabriel thought as he parked the car at Mount Sinai Hospital on the north end of South Beach. Skip's eyes were shut and he was slumped over, crumpled up. Gabriel stared at the grove of coconut palms, at the spotlit green leaves blowing in the wind.

"You won't let me become a vegetable?" Skip asked, sitting up.

"I'll take care of you," Gabriel said. "Let's go."

"Promise me," Skip said. "You won't let me die alone in this roach motel."

"I promise," Gabriel said. "Everyone loves you. You're famous. You could never die alone."

"The only one at Walter Winchell's funeral was his daughter," Skip said, opening the car door.

They walked slowly to the emergency room. Skip looked at Gabriel with a helpless expression as they entered Mount Sinai. It was freezing and smelled of disinfectant. In the emergency room, a man held his head with a bloody rag. A woman tried desperately to comfort a baby that wouldn't stop screeching.

Gabriel and Skip walked to the front desk and the fine-looking male receptionist smiled and asked, "Skip, what's hanging? I still have that article you wrote on me." Skip forced a dim smile as the man kept talking a mile a minute. "He wrote me up in 'Sunstroker' as one of the hottest people under the sun. Got me laid. Repeatedly," he said, standing, grinding the air.

"Skip's real sick," Gabriel said. "He needs a doctor."

"I'll get you right in, put you at the head of the line. Fill out this form."

"You're so big," Gabriel said, trying to flatter him. "You're even a VIP in the hospital."

Skip sat down, filled out the form. "You see that guy with the spots over there?" Skip said. "He fucked me. He was the most beautiful man who ever fucked me. He was also the dumbest. He was a model. I'm sure he fucked me so I would write him up, give him some publicity. He told me he loved my writing. He used a rubber. But I can't help but think I could have given it to him."

"That's stupid," Gabriel said. "He could have got it anywhere."

"What king of a sadistic God would make a person so beautiful and then take it away?" Skip asked. He shook his head, coughed, rubbed his forehead. "God must hate fags."

"Then why did he make them?" Gabriel asked.

"Maybe God realized he made a mistake," Skip said.

The spotted man turned around, said, "Skip, what's a guy like you doing in a place like this?"

"It's the hippest new club, George," Skip said. "The one you don't want to get into and then can never get out of."

George laughed. "You always make me laugh," he said. "Every week, I look forward to your column. I even had them send it to me when I was in San Francisco."

"What were you doing there?"

"I was there for the glory holes."

"What?" Skip asked.

"They're the only place where I'm still pretty. The only thing I have left, the only thing not spotted. When I stick my dick through the hole, that's all anyone can see and I'm still the prettiest boy in the world."

Then the man at the front desk called Skip. Gabriel followed him. A petite Filipino nurse escorted them to a little curtained-off cubicle. "Doctor will come soon," she said, leaving them alone.

Gabriel felt Skip's forehead. He was burning up.

The doctor arrived, and she was young and beautiful. Her face was fresh-looking and pure and calming. "I'm Dr. Lynette," she said. "I'm here to make you better." She exuded confidence.

"I'll be in the waiting room," Gabriel said, leaving. He sat down and shut his eyes and tried not to think. Then he heard his name being called out. He went up to the front desk. Dr. Lynette came out.

"How is he?" Gabriel asked the beautiful doctor, trying to read the expression on her face, which just seemed tired.

"I want to keep him here. He has pneumonia. Temperature of one hundred and three. We need to start on antibiotics immediately, take some tests. He should have come in earlier. This is very serious, even for a person without a compromised immune system."

Gabriel shook his head.

"He'll be all right," Dr. Lynette said. "I'll take special care of him. I'm too busy so I live vicariously through 'Sunstroker.' Pretend I'm one of the beautiful people."

"Take it from me, you are," Gabriel said.

She smiled, blushed. "Don't worry. Skip's one of my boys now."

"Thank you," Gabriel said, and he went back to Skip's cubicle. He looked so fragile and alone. Gabriel felt it in his heart and he fought the tears, tried to be strong.

"Please, don't cry for me," Skip said. His voice cracked. Gabriel fought to hold himself together. He tried not to think of Skip dying and the Venus de Milo Arms being demolished. But he couldn't.

The White Party

"Welcome to the White Party, Gabriel," a man dressed in a white, sequined sailor suit said, dropping the white velvet rope. Vizcaya looked like a mirage, a fantasy turned to stone, a misplaced, majestic Renaissance palace. White smoke filled the entrance room, floated across the marble floor. Two white-painted twin angels with golden hair and oversized wings played two twin golden harps.

Gabriel walked into another room. The beat hit. He smelled sweat, felt heat from a mass of muscle and white on the dance floor—leather, feathers, tulle and spandex. A man that Gabriel vaguely recognized as a dealer of party favors, wearing a white tuxedo, danced over to him and said, "Gabriel, man, you look so straight, you're bringing me down. Take this." He pushed a little bag with some powder into his hand.

Gabriel shoved the bag into his pocket, went to the bar and bought a double Chivas on the rocks from a man wearing a white rubber nurse's uniform. He thought of Skip in the hospital. He felt so sad. He was only at this party because Skip wanted a report on it for "Sunstroker." He thought of the engineer he'd hired to inspect the Venus de Milo Arms that day who just kept shaking his head and saying, "This is not good, not good," as he scrutinized the building to figure out what it would cost to fix the 378 code violations.

Gabriel couldn't take it, had to escape, went outside and stuck his face into the plastic bag and snorted some powder. It coated his nose, smelled like aspirin. He kept sucking until he tasted it in his mouth. He took deep breaths, looked around. The bay stretched before him like an endless silvery black moving sheet. People strolled by, hand in hand. In the moonlight, dressed in white, they looked like ghosts.

Gabriel sat on a white marble bench, gazed at the row of yachts, all gleaming white fiberglass. He felt stuck, like he couldn't move, like his body was going numb, dissolving into itself. He felt his brain shutting down. He walked to a huge forest green yacht with a Donzi, a Cigarette and a gold and green helicopter perched on top. An old man dressed like the Pope leaned from the boat, his liver-spotted arm stretched out. Gabriel started to laugh, remembering that Skip told him that Vizcaya was the home of a meeting between Ronald Reagan and Pope John Paul II. A beautiful, hairless, shirtless, pantless boy with a white sailor cap and an absurdly big bulge in his bright tighty-whitie 2(x)ist, bent forward and licked the pill from the Pope's palm. Delicate pink tongue lapping thickened yellowed palm.

The boy saw Gabriel staring at him and smiled. Gabriel realized it was Butch, the stripper from the Warsaw Ballroom whom he'd first seen with Fabrizio when he was new to South Beach, who'd helped him rescue Jesus.

"It's good shit," Butch said, walking over to Gabriel. His hands slid all over Gabriel as he talked. "That's like the fourth time I've been on that line," he said, wiping the sweat from his face with his hand. "Troll's been passing E out for hours. Shit," he begged. "Get me on that boat."

"Why do you think they'll let me on the boat?" Gabriel asked.

"You're famous," Butch replied. "And you know Fabrizio."

"So, how's that gonna help?"

"It's his party. I'm good enough to do him but not to go to his party," he said, grabbing Gabriel's hand and pulling him in the direction of the gangway.

A huge black albino guy guarded the entrance to the yacht. He was all white, except for his orange Afro and pink eyes. "Name?" he asked, barely looking at Gabriel, and then down at his clipboard as if it was a big hassle.

"Gabriel Tucker," Butch answered.

"Welcome," he said, ticking Gabriel's name off the list, moving aside.

Gabriel and Butch walked over the gangway onto the boat. A waiter, nude except for his sequined penis, a wife beater and white gloved hands with the fingers cut out, walked over holding a silver tray containing glasses filled with bubbling pink champagne.

"Nice abs," Butch said, glancing at the waiter's washboard stomach, grabbing two glasses and gulping them down. An old man started chanting to Butch, "Billy Budd, Billy Budd!"

"Name's Butch," he said, "but I can be that Billy guy for a price."

Gabriel walked into the main salon. Everywhere he looked, there was sleek teak, gleaming chrome, tartan-patterned carpet. There were beautiful beefy studs, stretched glamazons, pale tattooed androgynous boys and girls, butch dykes, lipstick lesbians, a sprinkling of straight-looking guppie types, a couple of gigantic wigged drag queens and a bunch of Eurotrash. There was Madonna, Sly, Cher, Calvin, Malcolm. A lot of one-named fame. All dressed in white. Much of it designer, all of it tight.

Gabriel watched the party around him and felt totally disconnected, like his brain couldn't control his body. He felt more of whatever he snorted hit his brain. He started walking. He had to lie down for a while. He descended some stairs with clear Plexiglas railings. He passed the engine room, tried the doors of what he thought were cabins. They were locked. He felt himself stumbling. He held himself up by pushing against teak. He stopped, took deep breaths, tried to calm down. On the walls were framed *New York Times* clippings about the sinking of the *Titanic*. They went fuzzy before his eyes. He pushed another door. It opened. It was a bathroom. He sat on the toilet. Everywhere he looked, he saw himself, looking back at himself from mirrored walls and ceiling. He saw himself start to spin. He concentrated on a framed poem, tried to get straight. He read,

At the fete for Malcolm's fifty-eighth.

A bookend of Tisches,
The Bob, the Larry
Also the Browns/Evanses
Tina and Harry

Hugh Auchincloss and George Plimpton
Designer Bill Blass
Elizabeth Taylor, Kitty Carlisle Hart
Barbara Walters for Class.

We toasted to Malcolm the Great
By Plane, Train, Car and Boat, Living Life at Fifty-Eight.

Then he heard something—a voice he recognized—and headed toward it. It was Jesus. He sounded like he needed help. He went through a door on the other side of the bathroom. Everything was green and smoking and hot. He was in a green, granite steam room. He worked his way to the sound of Jesus' moaning, as naked people dissolving into the steam groped at him. His clothes stuck to his body. He choked on the steamed air.

Gabriel was sure now: It was Jesus. He found another door on the other side of the steam room. The doorknob turned in his hand and he fell forward into the room, onto the floor.

Above him, above the gigantic bed on the mirrored ceiling, he saw them. He shut his eyes. Then he opened them to make sure he was seeing what he was seeing. Jesus' eyes were shut. He looked so messed up, but Gabriel didn't know if it was just because he was looking at him through his own messed-up eyes. Jesus was groaning in pain with each thrust, gritting his teeth. His eyes looked so sad, so very far away, as if he was crying without tears.

Fabrizio held a handful of his impossibly thick blue-black hair as he fucked him hard, doggie style.

Gabriel tried to get up, to rescue Jesus, but he couldn't. He couldn't move. He felt like he had fallen into a black hole; it was as if with each thrust by Fabrizio, sand was being thrown over his head. He was being buried alive. Then he couldn't feel his body anymore. He felt tranquilized. He sunk into a K-hole. Reality was snatched out from under him as in a magician's tabletop trick.

Gabriel's last thought wasn't Fabrizio or Jesus or the fucking. It was of the code violation notice and the orange tape, a scar against his beautiful Venus de Milo Arms. Then blankness.

Too Many Pricks

Gabriel rolled up the engineer's report on the Venus de Milo Arms and stuck it in his back pocket, then walked out of the Venus and headed north toward Mount Sinai Hospital. Skip would help him figure out what to do to save the Venus, he told himself, but he didn't really believe it. He was counting on a sick man in the hospital. Gabriel could not get the number out of his head. Eight hundred thousand dollars! According to the engineer's report, it would cost approximately eight hundred thousand dollars to bring the Venus up to present code and cure the 378 violations. *Eight hundred fucking thousand dollars*, he thought. Where was he going to get that much money? He walked faster.

At the same time, back at his apartment in the Venus, Jesus gritted his teeth and stuck the needle into his skin, into his vein. He pushed the plunger, held his breath, felt the sting. He pulled the needle out, wiped the sweat from his face and crawled back into bed and pulled the sheet over his head. He felt so sad all the time, so empty, so lonely. All he had was his looks and his body, and they weren't working anymore. *Fuck Fabrizio*, he thought. He was a whore again. He was Fabrizio's whore. The heroin slipped over him and he started to feel all right.

Across Miami Beach, at Mount Sinai Hospital on the bay, a sleepy-looking nurse with a very round face jabbed a needle into Skip's vein. He gritted his teeth, looked away.

"These vampires can't get enough of my blood," Skip said.

"We take it in the back and make *morcillo*, tasty blood sausage," the short, round nurse said with a heavy Latin accent. The vial filled with deep red blood.

Skip felt grateful for the joke, in fact felt grateful for anything that might stop him from thinking, for even a second, that he was a condemned man.

Skip winced. He felt pain, like a knife cutting across his chest.

"Is it your shingles, *amor?*" the nurse asked.

"Yes," Skip answered, the itching streak of pain driving him crazy. He had to fight the urge not to scratch the blisters off.

The nurse untied his gown. A new flaming line of red blisters spread across his chest. "Let me fix that *bonito*," she said.

Skip concentrated on the nurse's fat brown fingers to try to forget the pain as she painted the red blisters pink with great globs of calamine lotion.

"I'll check on you later, *guapo*," the nurse said to Skip. She rumpled his greasy hair, and there was something so maternal, so caring in her touch. Skip smiled.

All the way on the other coast of Miami Beach, in a dingy apartment on Biscayne Bay, Pandora turned her head away and gritted her teeth as the hairy little man injected her ass with estrogen. *Soon,* she thought, *soon I'll be a real woman.* She needed five thousand dollars more and then she would have saved the twenty-five thousand she needed for the operation. She had been getting the shots for over six months now. She was getting smoother, her breasts fuller and her *it* smaller.

The man pulled the needle out. Pandora gave him a crisp one-hundred-dollar bill, feeling a burst of femininity. She smiled in her mind, imagining her thing was already gone.

Meanwhile, to the west, on Alton Road in Miami Beach, Marina and Miss Levy sat in the veterinarian's operating room as he anesthetized an ugly black cat who had a tail that looked like a squirrel.

"This one makes fifteen strays we have fixed," Miss Levy said, and then she felt exhausted and out of breath. The smell was making her woozy. She went into the hall. Her sneakers squeaked against the yellowed white linoleum.

"You feeling all right?" Marina asked, following her out.

"I'm fine," Miss Levy answered, sitting down.

A man sat across from her with a long-haired German shepherd with one of its front legs in a cast. There was a little girl with a parrot in a cage sitting with her mother. "Polly can't talk," she said.

Miss Levy felt a numbness slowly crawling up the left side of her body. It reached her head, and then she felt dizzy.

"Miss Levy," Marina said.

"Yes," she slurred. Her tongue was very heavy. Her vision fogged. It hurt to speak. Half her face wasn't working. She shut her eyes. Her head started to pound. She felt panic.

"You OK?"

All the color drained from her face. She tried to answer but couldn't. Her brain couldn't make her mouth work. She fell over sideways.

"Miss Levy," Marina cried.

Miss Levy tried to open her eyes. They felt glued shut. Her right eyelid quivered and then opened for an instant.

"Somebody call an ambulance," Marina yelled.

"Can you hear me, Miss Levy?" the vet implored, putting his finger on her wrist, checking her pulse. "Speak to me, Miss Levy!" the vet demanded, grabbing her hands. Her fingers were dead weight. "If you can hear me, squeeze my hand!"

Miss Levy heard the vet, but he seemed very far away. She was sinking back into time, sticking at that smell, that rank smell of body odor, rot, smoldering fire, sickness and death. She saw dull gray and dark blue stripes. I'm going to hell, back to hell, she thought. She started to pray.

"The ambulance is coming," the nurse said as the German shepherd in the waiting room started to bark.

"Squeeze my hand," the vet repeated, bringing her back for a second. The vet turned into the handsome doctor. She saw his immaculate uniform, shiny boots, the riding crop in his right hand.

She knew that Dr. Mengele was the reason she and her sister survived. She also knew he was the one hurting her sister. He patted them on the head, whistled Wagner. His white kid gloves felt so soft. He smelled of lavender.

"Miss Levy!" Marina yelled. "Stay with me! Please!"

Miss Levy saw her twin sister, Magda. She smiled. She was so happy she was alive. Every time they took Magda away, she was sure she wasn't coming back.

"What did they do to you?" she asked her sister.

"They gave me five injections," Magda said, holding up her left arm. "Took some blood," she said, holding up her right. "They didn't hurt me. Just the pricks, a little."

"I have a surprise for you," Magda said. "Dr. Münch gave it to me this morning."

"What?" Miss Levy asked.

Her sister smiled. "Guess which hand?" she asked, holding out her cupped hands.

Miss Levy guessed the left one.

Magda opened her hand. There was a red drop on her small white palm. It was a strawberry.

"For you. I carried it all day. I was so afraid I would lose it."

"You eat it," Miss Levy said. And her dream faded again, as it had a thousand times before.

Then, back in the real world, at South Beach Animal Hospital, the scream of a siren got louder as the ambulance pulled up to the front of the building. Red lights blinked through the window. Then the paramedics ran inside with a stretcher. They carried Miss Levy out, still as a corpse.

Marina jumped into the back of the ambulance. They screeched off. It was another blinding Miami day. The paramedics continued working on Miss Levy.

"Can you hear me, lady?"

"Her name is Miss Levy," Marina said.

Miss Levy was in Auschwitz, far away. She opened her hand and looked at the tiny strawberry.

The ambulance arrived at Mount Sinai Hospital and the attendants carried Miss Levy into the emergency room. Marina was left by herself, feeling very alone.

"Miss," a nurse said. "We need you to fill out these forms." Marina looked up at the nurse just as Gabriel walked into the lobby. He had come to visit Skip.

"What happened? What's wrong?" Gabriel asked Marina.

"Miss Levy," Marina murmured, and she could no longer speak. She fell into Gabriel's arms and started to cry softly.

In the emergency room, Miss Levy bit into the half of the strawberry her sister Magda had given her, and she tasted love.

Jesus Becomes a Confection

Jesus arrived at Fabrizio's palazzo, rang the buzzer on the intricate golden wrought iron gate. The security camera scanned and then stopped.

"It's Jesus," he said.

"Please go to the service entrance," the butler replied.

Jesus walked to the back of the house. He had never been told to go to the service entrance before. The windows from the second-floor ballroom above glowed. Lacy curtains were being sucked in and out by the breeze, as if the whole building were breathing. Chatting interrupted by whinnies of laughter and chamber music drifted into the dark night. Jesus knocked on a door marked "*Service*."

The butler led him on a path of polished river stones through Fabrizio's massive kitchen, past a dozen chefs in white hats and about a dozen hard-bodied, tan, shirtless waiters with bow ties and tight black tuxedo pants. Jesus smelled a trail of garlic sautéing in butter, melted chocolate and a cake baking.

Then they stopped at a pantry with a gigantic silver tray on a Formica-topped table. The walls were covered in white ceramic tiles. The one window was frosted.

"Wait here," the butler said, curtly, leaving.

Jesus sat on the table, swung his legs back and forth, bit his nails.

Then the salon doors swung open and Butch sauntered into the room.

"Fabrizio hired me to help him with the shoot," Butch said, reaching into his pocket, pulling out a baggy. "You want some?" he asked.

"What?"

"I have ecstasy and a little coke."

"X," Jesus answered, thinking, *I need to calm down.*

Butch gave him two white pills with tiny Buddhas on them. "This is primo," he said.

Jesus squished some saliva around his mouth and swallowed the pills. "What the shoot about?" Jesus asked.

"I don't know," Butch answered. "Fabrizio told me he wants to keep it a surprise."

Then the doors swung open again and a chef rolled in a cart with a huge pot full of melted chocolate. He left.

Jesus looked from the pot to Butch.

"You are supposed to take off your clothes and lie on the tray," Butch said, pointing at the table. "I'm supposed to coat you in chocolate."

"*Que?*" Jesus asked. "You suppose to what? Chocolate?"

"That's what Fabrizio told me."

"*Que?*" Jesus repeated. It wasn't making any sense. Where was the makeup artist, the stylist, the photographer? Why Butch? The ecstasy was confusing him. *Rafter Chic, Brutal Chic, Heroin Chic,* he thought; *maybe Chocolate-Covered Chic is next?*

"It's for the job," Butch said. "Fabrizio told me."

"OK," Jesus said, thinking he'd do anything to get back in magazines, to keep making money, to keep being famous, before it was too late. He stripped naked. It was easier than trying to figure out what was happening.

Butch's eyes grazed over his tight hard body. "You're hot. I'll do you for free anytime, and I'm not even gay," he said. "I'm just gay for pay."

Jesus climbed up on the huge silver tray. The ecstasy was making him hot, so the cool silver tray felt good against his skin.

"Fabrizio said you are supposed to get in a seductive position," Butch said.

Jesus stretched out, rested his head on his arm and glanced at Butch.

Butch half-smiled at him. He rolled the huge pot of chocolate sauce over to the table. He grabbed a handful of chocolate and slopped it on Jesus' feet.

Jesus shut his eyes, tried not to think, felt the drug make his fear synthetically dissolve. The chocolate was cooler than room temperature. It felt good, smelled good.

Butch slathered the melted chocolate up his legs. Jesus imagined he was getting a second skin, one that would not let any more hurt inside. Butch pushed the trolley with the chocolate around to Jesus' back, finished up the spots on his legs. Then he coated his hard ass.

"You look good enough to eat," Butch said.

Jesus opened his eyes, looked down. The chocolate accentuated his perfect body, made his abs gleam brown. The photos and the ad were going to be great, he thought.

"I have to do your face now," Butch said, and then he slathered melted chocolate on Jesus' hair and forehead.

"Stay still. I don't want to get any chocolate in your eyes." Butch finished, delicately covering Jesus' face.

Butch stepped back. "You look cool," he said, and then left the room.

What now, Jesus thought as the chefs entered and surrounded him with fruit and cake and candy and nuts. They continued until they'd filled up the entire platter. Then ten shirtless waiters picked up the tray and carried him out of the kitchen.

Jesus felt really high. He had a flash of himself at his funeral, with these guys as his pallbearers. The marble mosaics, ornate gilded oil paintings, Venetian mirrors and crystal chandeliers of Fabrizio's palazzo were all running together, a rich swirl before his eyes. Colors seemed to be crawling together, too, as they carried him through the room.

The waiters brought Jesus to a dark room and then put him down. He squinted. He heard shuffling, breathing—a giggle. Then, there was a drumroll and the room was flooded with bright light. Jesus was blinded. His eyes darted around once the spots disappeared. He was on the dining room table, surrounded by guests in evening gowns and tuxedos.

Then he heard the tinkling of metal against glass. He looked in the direction of the sound. Fabrizio held his glass in the air, cleared his throat and said, "Ladies and gentlemen, dessert is served."

Jesus heard gasps, and someone clapped. Dessert, he thought, wondering what was for dessert. Something was happening but he didn't know what. He was so high.

Fabrizio grabbed a strawberry off the platter, dipped it into the chocolate covering Jesus' chest. "The icing on the cake." He laughed.

Jesus twisted, sat up. The strawberry touched the spot right over his pounding heart. The thought, the fact, finally cut through the ecstasy. There was no shoot. He was just dessert.

"Everyone," Fabrizio announced. "Don't be shy. Eat!"

Jesus froze. He felt like he was back on the raft, floating in the middle of nowhere, covered in a crust of salt. He looked at Fabrizio, looked into his brown eyes, searching for something, he didn't know what. He wanted to leave, but he couldn't. It was like the chocolate had stuck him to the plate. Then he started to cry. Salty tears mixed with sweet liquid chocolate on his cheeks.

Fabrizio froze, the strawberry in his hand. He looked away. *This isn't working*, he thought. He started to tremble. He felt Jesus' tears. Instead of pushing him away, he connected with him, with his sadness. He wanted to get him out of his system, despoil him, turn him into an inanimate object and make him finite, a possession. He wanted to turn him into food, something he could swallow, something that could turn to shit inside himself, something he could excrete. He wanted to erase the feelings he had for him. But it was not working.

Jesus couldn't stop himself from crying. The sadness was convulsing from deep inside. He tried to get up off the table. He wanted to go far away and never come back, but he couldn't. He was Xing out of his mind. He hugged himself into the fetal position. He shivered.

Fabrizio looked away. Embarrassing Jesus had made him feel worse instead of better. He felt even more for him. And it was a strange kind of feeling—not the kind of feeling that made him want to fuck him but one that made him want to take care of him. He had been fighting it ever since he met Jesus. It was something he had never experienced before and he finally surrendered to it, took off his tuxedo jacket and wrapped it around Jesus.

SUNSTROKER

by Skip Bowling

This week, on the cultural circuit, the launch of Renaissance man **Mickey Wolfson's** world, the **Wolfsonian Foundation Gallery** on Washington Avenue, at the old **Washington Storage Building,** where Miami Beach's pampered elite used to store their expensive accoutrements, in its last period of glamour (furs, Rollses et al). My date for the evening, performance artist **Marina Russell.** Among the beautiful objects were **Princess Mimi Romanoff** of Russia, **Baron Paolo Von Wedel** of Italy, **Lady Hennessey Brown,** who just returned from photographing the royal circumcision of **Prince Sergio Von Slong** of Estonia. Seen chatting out in front of a rescued stainless steel art deco bridge tender's house that once hung over the **Miami River** was famed architect of exuberance **Morris Lapidus** and America's queen of the socialites, the ever-chic **Beth Rudin DeWoody.**

On the walk home, on **Washington Avenue,** from my night of culture, I noticed that **Jessie's Doll House; Torah Treasures; the Cancer League thrift store; Tony and Nina Alterations,** where they "mend everything but a broken heart"; the **Thrifty Market,** with the poster of the old lady being arrested and the warning "Beware of Kleptomania Disease, It Can Be Caught"; and the **Dentures While You Wait** store had all closed down. Then an old lady yelled, "We old

people built this town and now you want to get rid of us!"
from the terrace of the **Astor Hotel.** I couldn't help but think
how the old South Beach was slipping away right before my
eyes.

And it is beyond me how the corrupt silly hall that runs
this city does not understand after seeing the renaissance of
South Beach that we have to preserve every deco building,
every piece of history we have left. **Heinz Lerman** has
greased the powers that be into getting my deco home, the
Venus de Milo Arms, declared unsafe so he can knock it
down and build a high-rise condo hotel. I warn you to back off
or I will unleash the power of the bard on you. I am everywhere. I know all. I will hang your dirty laundry out to dry.

Then, the next day, a Laundromat full of dirty laundry
exploded on South Beach, aka Club Land. Fresh from getting
the key to the city from **Mayor Kasdin,** club king **Chris
Paciello** was arrested for murder. Miami's deco **Federal
Courthouse** was transformed into a V-VIP room during Mr.
Paciello's bail hearing. Inside it was standing room only, like
one of Chris's clubs—the beautiful, the rich and the crème de
la crème of South Beach nightclub society. Is nightclub
society an oxymoron? How could Chris be a murderer?

Sexy **Ingrid Casares,** Chris's partner, stood by her man.
"Chris is innocent and everyone who is here today knows it!"
she proclaimed. Chris's girlfriend, sizzling calendar girl/
Univision TV hostess **Sofia Vergara** (former love of **Enrique
Iglesias**), arrived in low-cut top showing off her breasts. No
wonder her web site has had over twenty million hits.
Seventy other citizens were there to testify to Chris's good
character. When cock-of-the walk Chris was led into the
courtroom, there was an audible gasp. He looked deflated
(prison food or no steroids). His pump was gone. The courtroom of Miami's elite learned that his nickname back in
Staten Island was **"the Binger"** 'cause he liked to binge on
crimes. One Versace-clad matron in front of me whispered to
her companion, "Oh my God, I let him in my home."

Who is Chris? Dr. Jekyll or Mr. Hyde? He had two names, three birth dates, two social security numbers, thirteen addresses and two driver's licenses. Undercover Miami police officer **Andrew Dohler** had Chris on tape asking him to frame **Gerry Kelly, Level's** much-loved club impresario, on drug charges because he quit working at **Liquid.** "We got to get his head fuckin' broken in," Paciello said. "I feel like putting on my costume—going trick or treatin'. . . . I gotta come out of fucking retirement. I've become a big pussy down here. A big sucka."

Was South Beach a bigger sucka? Was our golden boy the goon over Miami? Or did the police frame him? Is he the new Gen X **Meyer Lansky?**"

Bail was set at $3 million. As Mr. Paciello was led from the courtroom, the crowd cheered and yelled, "We love you!"

I Will Not Be a Whore

Jesus' back stuck to the seat of Marina's van as they cruised up Collins Avenue, past the magnificent succession of minihotels topped by heraldic spires: the Kent, the Marlin, the Tudor, the Essex House, the Palmer House. The day was steamy tropical—hot, with streams of tantalizing breeze. *It's a Cuban kind of day*, Jesus thought. *The perfect day for a new start.*

"I feel like a load has been lifted," Jesus said to Marina as they drove past the 11th Street Diner and into the alley behind Fabrizio's palazzo. They parked and rang the service bell. Fabrizio's butler answered the door again. This was the second load of gifts that Fabrizio had given Jesus that he was returning. He had already returned a painting, chairs, a TV and a stereo.

"Please," the butler begged. "Senor Fabrizio ordered me to give you back your things. I called him in Milano." The butler picked up a box of Fabrizio couture that Jesus had just returned and handed it to him. "No, I am not allowed to take them. Please, I will lose my job," the butler said.

"I will just leave them," Jesus said, putting the boxes by the door.

Then the butler's cell phone rang. "*Sí, sí, sí*, he's here," the butler answered. "It's Senor Fabrizio. He needs to talk to you." He held out the phone to Jesus.

"I have nothing to say," Jesus replied, pushing the phone away.

"Fabrizio say he's sorry," the butler said to Jesus.

Jesus just shook his head and kept unloading more stuff that Fabrizio had given him.

"Mr. Fabrizio says these are your things and he will not allow me to take them."

"But I don't want them," Jesus said.

"I'm sorry," the butler said, shutting the door of the mansion. Jesus looked at Marina. She shook her head. "Let's give it to charity. Donate it to Beth Jacob. That's Miss Levy's synagogue."

They loaded the boxes back into the van and headed across town past the parade of small deco apartment buildings as construction noise boomed: the whine of drills and the pounding of hammers. Rotten, forgotten deco apartments were in the process of being fixed up. It was like the giant nursing home that was South Beach had morphed into an international youth camp. South Beach was like a college town at the beginning of a semester. There were U-Hauls parked all over the place. The old people were all exiting, stage left. South Beach had become a town of newlyweds and nearly deads.

They passed Flamingo Park, once the sight of Polo Fields, then shuffleboard courts and homeless encampment and now a yuppie playground by day and cruising spot by night. They arrived at the Beth Jacob Synagogue, the only synagogue that hadn't been turned into a club, the last stronghold of seniors. They parked, walked past a mosaic Star of David into the community center in the back. A dapper old man in a striped suit and bow tie played the piano. A group of women were dancing the polka together. They had either all outlived their husbands or their husbands didn't dance anymore.

Tears formed in Marina's eyes as she thought of Miss Levy, half frozen in the hospital. The music stopped. One of the old ladies, with particularly beautiful wrinkles and shining eyes, smiled a toothless grin and hugged Marina.

"Miss Levy will be fine. She will be back dancing with us soon." All the women surrounded them.

"This is Mrs. Klein. She leads the dance class," Marina said to Jesus. "And this is Jesus."

"Nice to meet you," Jesus said as the group started to murmur. "So this is Jesus," one said. "The star from the magazines."

Jesus tried to hide his sadness with a smile, tried to forget that Miss Levy was sick. That Miss Levy and Skip were in the hospital had been a wake-up call for him. He realized that he had to get his life together before it was too late. He realized that he had to stop spending his time in a drugged, drunken stupor. He was young. He was healthy. He was in America. He had everything.

"How is her other boy, Skip?" Mrs. Klein asked.

"He's getting better. He's in the same room in the hospital as Miss Levy," Marina said. "They're taking care of each other."

"They will be fine," Mrs. Klein said, and the other women shook their heads. They were not convincing. They had seen a lot of death. Miami Beach to them was a place where people came to die.

"Jesus has brought some things to donate," Marina said.

"How nice," Mrs. Klein said. "Tell Mera we're saving her place in the dance line."

Marina and Jesus said good-bye and the pianist started to play and the women started to dance again in a line. They followed Mrs. Klein's movements, feebly stretching and reaching their arthritic hands to the ceiling along with the music, remembering days past when their bodies weren't rebelling, when they deftly danced a particular fox-trot or waltz or rumba or cha-cha with a love.

Marina and Jesus returned to the car and carried back the boxes of Fabrizio stuff, filling up a cart marked "Donations."

"I wonder what Fabrizio will think when he sees some old man in his tufted leather pants and chain link shirt," Marina said, laughing.

"I feel good," Jesus said, as they drove off. "Like the chocolate that Fabrizo put on me finally come off."

"That is one of the things South Beach taught me. When I got sick and my husband dumped me. When I wanted to die. I started driving and I found this place, found the Venus de Milo Arms, found the answer."

"*Que?*" Jesus asked. "What answer?"

"To feel good about yourself, help others. Giving fixes you."

"That is why you always helping peoples," Jesus said as they pulled into the Venus. "Maybe I try." He kissed Marina good-bye and walked into his near-empty apartment. He looked out at the sheet of blue ocean through the porthole window, looked all the way to Cuba in his mind, and he remembered his life there and realized how lucky he was to be here in Miami, to have found a family in the Venus de Milo Arms, and for the first time in a long time he felt like a very rich man.

He searched the bathroom, under the bed, combed his little studio apartment and found all his drugs and liquor and threw them into the toilet and flushed.

Then he heard a knock on his door. He opened it. It was Gabriel.

"Read this," he said, handing Jesus the letter he'd just received in the mail.

Jesus looked at it, did not understand. "What this is?"

"A letter from the Juelle Brothers Demolition Company," Gabriel replied. "Offering us a special deal to knock down the Venus de Milo Arms."

"We have to do it," Jesus said.

"What?" Gabriel asked.

"Skip's plan," Jesus said.

"I know," Gabriel said. "We have a right, a moral duty. It's even in the Constitution. No illegal seizures."

"I spend my whole life in Cuba fighting. I am a soldier. You are a soldier."

"OK. Let's do it."

Jesus shook his hand. "Me and you. They can't beat us!"

"No one is knocking the Venus de Milo Arms down," Gabriel said, shaking Jesus' hand. "So help me God." And he wished he believed it.

Skip's Blackmail Plot

Pandora checked her makeup, blotted her excess lipstick with a piece of tissue, spritzed perfume. She felt nervous, like she was about to star in a play. If everything went well, she would save the Venus de Milo Arms.

She fluffed the rose-shaped pillows on her overstuffed faux–leopard skin couch. Her apartment was crammed with flea market finds. It was a sort of Kmart version of Fabrizio's style, a sort of transvesticized illusion of elegance, culture and affluence. There was an extravagant mirror with a gilded fiberglass frame over a reproduction red velvet–covered Louis XV chair and an extravagant Home Depot crystal chandelier.

I will not be a victim, Pandora told herself. *Never again.* The upholstered buttons on her couch reminded her of the black buttons flying, bouncing off the floor. She remembered Heinz Lerman saying, "You help me, I pay you good. You are my spy."

I'll show you, Pandora thought. *I won't be your spy.* Heinz Lerman had sent her roses and candy and kept calling her, begging to see her again, apologizing over and over. In some perverted way, he cared about her.

She checked her watch, stood up and fumbled with the lights, dimming them and then turning them a little brighter. Then her doorbell rang.

Pandora opened the door and air-kissed Jesus and then Gabriel on both cheeks. Gabriel had a small video camera in his hand.

"You sure you want to do this?" Gabriel asked.

"Yes," Pandora mouthed, nodding her head. She paced.

"That *hijo de puta* won't hurt not one hair on your *bonita* head," Jesus said. "I got this to make sure." He pulled out a switch-blade and clicked it, and an eight-inch blade flicked out. It gleamed.

"Put that away, *bandito*," Gabriel said. "The camera is our weapon."

"This knife is our amigo, in case," Jesus said, folding the blade back into the holder.

Pandora led them into her pink, cocoonlike bedroom. Pink flock wallpaper covered the walls. A pink satin bedspread with an embroidered heart covered her bed. Pink light from the neon Venus de Milo sign flowed through her window.

Pandora grabbed Gabriel's hand and led him to the closet. He opened the door and went inside. Jesus followed. Gabriel cracked the door.

"Sit on the bed, Pandora," he said.

Pandora sat down. Gabriel started filming. Pandora blew him a kiss.

"Cut," Gabriel said. "Perfect."

Gabriel rewound the film, played it for Jesus and Pandora. Then the doorbell rang and she froze, felt a pain in her tongue, the tongue that wasn't there, like a phantom limb: the pain that was a sign of danger.

Gabriel caught the look on her face. "We don't have to do this," he said, even though Skip's plan was the only thing he could think of to save the Venus, his home. But he wasn't sure if anything was worth crossing this line, especially since he had to ask Pandora to cross it with him, to put her in danger.

Pandora forced a nervous smile, made an "OK" sign with her fingers.

Jesus had no such qualms. As was true for Gabriel, this was not just about a building; this was also about his home and his only family. It wasn't even a close call for him. He also knew the price

Pandora was willing to pay and felt it was a fair price. Jesus went back in the closet, pulled the door shut.

Pandora gulped air, then shook her head, transformed her look from fear to control. She had to save the Venus. She opened the door. Her body tensed.

Heinz Lerman was dressed in an Armani tuxedo, had a cool bottle of Dom Pérignon in his hand. Pandora forced a fake smile.

"Let me open it for you," he said, walking into her apartment. He popped the cork, took a swig from the champagne bottle and handed it to Pandora. She went into the kitchen and got two glasses. She returned and poured them each a glassful. They sat together on her couch.

"To me getting the Venus With No Arms, so I can build my condo," he toasted. "It will be Pandora's Bohemian Towers. I will set you up in a penthouse. You won't have to live in this slum."

Pandora shook her head. *Concentrate*, she told herself. Get him into the bedroom and get him out of here. They finished the champagne. Then Heinz lunged at her, locking his mouth over hers. Teeth clacked.

No, she thought, *this is not how it's going to be*. She would control him. She had what he wanted. She had the power. She pulled his head back by his hair, stood up in one quick motion and brought his face against her crotch. His eyes lifted, stared up at her.

Pandora stared back defiantly, directly into his eyes. She dominated him with her look. Because she couldn't talk with her mouth, she was an expert at talking with her eyes. He capitulated. His eyes went fuzzy and then he closed them and moaned. He got down on the floor and his head dropped to her feet, licking her stilettos.

"I'm sorry, Pandora. I am a bad boy. Punish me," he begged.

Pandora lifted up her foot. Heinz licked the sole. She brought it down on his head, pinning him to the floor: Needle black stilettos pierced haylike blond hair. He moaned again. He gave in because that's what he really wanted, to give up control. She went into her bedroom. He followed her on all fours.

Pandora picked up a pad of paper from the bed.

Strip! Now!!!!!

"Yes, Mistress," he obeyed, standing before her naked and pink, light blond hair covering his entire soft body. He shuffled nervously. She shoved him onto his knees roughly. He moaned.

Gabriel filmed the action from the closet. He concentrated so hard he forgot to breathe.

Heinz knelt down before her. She kicked off her high heels. He kissed her feet and shrimped her toes. His hands, fingertips traveled up her legs. She slapped them, took a step back and pulled her dress over her head.

She stood there naked except for her white bra and panties. Heinz looked up at her from his knees, his eyes glazed over with lust. She was his fantasy. She was everything that was forbidden to him: a black woman, a dick.

Then, Pandora reached under her bed and pulled out a very detailed, obscenely large, lifelike, chocolate brown dildo. It had rubber veins running up it. Heinz stared at it. His dick twitched. She pointed. He flung himself on the bed, on all fours, legs spread apart. His plump pink ass stared at the camera, like an albino pumpkin with a pink eye.

She grabbed a tube of K-Y Jelly and held it up to his ass and squirted it. Then she started to work the big brown thing in. First there was resistance. He squirmed. She grabbed his balls and squeezed, holding him down. He choked, gulped. The dildo slipped in with a squish. She moved it in and out.

The German felt so much pleasure, he could not hold it in. He started moaning, the sound going from human to animal the more and faster she fucked him with the rubber dick. It was a sound of half pleasure, half pain. Heinz had never felt so good in his whole life. He twisted around and looked back at her over his shoulder. He gazed into her eyes and felt for her something beyond lust, something that was soft and confusing. Then he turned around quickly. The dildo slipped from Pandora's hand and stayed in his ass, sticking out obscenely, a dismembered dick. He couldn't control himself. He grabbed her panties, pulling them down roughly.

Pandora's mouth opened, a silent scream. In the closet, Jesus' body tensed as he unlocked his switchblade. Gabriel put his hand on Jesus' shoulder, stopping him.

At the same time Pandora's dick was released from her panties, Heinz shot snotty white, groaning. Pandora covered her genitals with her hands, then ran into the bathroom. Heinz fell forward onto the bed, lay there for a while, recovering. Then he yanked the dildo from his ass, pulled on his clothes, took out an envelope full of money and left it on the bedside table. He walked back to the bathroom door.

"I'm putting your present next to the bed," he said, clearing his throat. "I had a great time. Please let me come back. Thank you."

She didn't answer. She pictured her body without her *it*.

The German sighed and walked out. He hated himself for wanting her. Then he pushed what had just happened out of his head and pictured the wrecking ball smashing the Venus de Milo Arms to bits, pictured Pandora's Bohemian Towers rising up proudly. He smiled to himself.

Love Sprouts from Ash

Skip got up from his hospital bed in the room he shared with Miss Levy and sat on the red vinyl chair near the window. He stared at the blue-blue bay, at the carpet of waterfront mansions along North Bay Road, at downtown Miami, the Town That Cocaine Built, poking up in the distance. A speedboat zoomed toward the hospital. A tanned teenager in a pink bikini cut back and forth across the boat's wake, carving a momentary zigzag pattern on the sea. *I'm on another planet*, Skip thought. *I'm floating in this timeless frozen prison they call Mount Sinai Hospital and life continues on the other side of the glass.*

Miss Levy was asleep in the hospital bed across from him. She opened her eyes. She looked at Skip sitting in the chair by the window. His face was so thin she could see his skull beneath, like the people in Auschwitz. Then, she shut her eyes and drifted back to the past. She saw Erwin Schimitzek, the nice man with the *Rosa winkel,* the pink triangle. She remembered waking up after the operation on her privates and Erwin being there, sitting on a chair, waiting for her. "Thank God you are back, my beautiful child," he said, then dissolved into tears. She had heard Erwin Schimitzek crying, another time. She had snuck up and looked through the window. They ordered him to dance, those men in their crisp SS uniforms with the shiny buttons. He was naked. He danced, like a girl. The men clapped, passed around a bottle, took swigs. The more they clapped, the more they laughed, the more he cried.

Then they brought in a naked girl. She was so skinny and bald that she looked fragile, like she could break in half at any moment. She stood shivering, her hands covering her genitals, her eyes shut. They pushed her down on the floor. Her head looked like an egg. Two men held her legs apart, open. They pushed Erwin Schimitzek down on top of her. Miss Levy didn't understand what it was the soldiers wanted her friend with the pink triangle to do.

"Fuck her! Fuck her!" they yelled.

"No!" he yelled. This fuck must be a terrible thing, she thought.

Then the SS men stuck the bottle they were drinking up Erwin's ass.

Back in the real world, Skip heard Miss Levy groan from the hospital bed. He got up from the chair and walked over to her bedside. Her forehead was covered in sweat drops, like dew. He mopped them up with a tissue. He was out of breath from the short trip from the chair to the bed. Skip felt his strength slipping a little every day. He was staying alive for Miss Levy. He didn't want her to be alone in the hospital.

Miss Levy coughed and then opened her eyes. She stretched clumsily with one half of her body, fighting the sheets. She looked drab and old and emaciated in her blue hospital gown. She stared at Skip as if she was searching for something. He wiped the dribble from the side of her mouth and the tears dripping out of her right eye.

Miss Levy squinted and saw Skip and then the man with the pink triangle and then Skip. The two flicked back and forth like an alternating sign. She rubbed her eyes. And she came back.

"Skip," she mumbled out of the side of her mouth. Only half her face worked.

"Miss Levy," he cried, surprised. "You're in the hospital," he said as calmly as possible. "You had a stroke." He rang for the nurse.

"Skip," she slurred again, realizing where she was.

"You're going to be fine," he said, as he heard squeaking and looked toward the door. He expected to see a nurse, but it was his doctor, Dr. Lynette, the beautiful one.

"Miss Levy spoke. She recognized me," Skip said to Dr. Lynette.

Dr. Lynette grabbed Miss Levy's arm, felt her pulse. "Do you know your name?" The doctor asked.

"Mera," she answered. "Mera Levy." Her words were all garbled, like a skipping tape. Her lips were stiff. She felt like half her body was missing.

"Try to get some sleep now," Dr. Lynette said, and her voice sounded sweet and professional at the same time.

Miss Levy shut her eyes. Waking up had exhausted her. She drifted back to sleep.

Then Jesus walked into the room. His thick black hair was wet, hanging down into his face, a lock slipping over his left eye. His plump red lips glistened. He had just come from a Fabrizio shoot.

"Miss Levy woke up and recognized me," Skip said to Jesus. "She knew her name."

"Great," Jesus said, walking up to her bed, peering at her tenderly.

Dr. Lynette saw the way Jesus looked at Miss Levy, and she thought he was the most beautiful thing she had ever seen.

"How are you, Skip?" Jesus asked.

"Fine," he answered, "now that you and the sexy Florence Nightingale are here."

Dr. Lynette smiled. "Just come from swimming?" she asked Jesus. She felt stupid, like a schoolgirl with a crush. People had crushes on her, not the other way around. It was a new feeling that she did not like.

"A photo shoot," Jesus answered.

"You're a model," she said. "How glamorous."

Jesus flicked his hair back. "If bouncing naked on a horse in the ocean for eight hours is glamorous. My butt is killing me."

"Now I understand why my patients get so excited when you come to the hospital. I thought it was just how you look. But it's because you're famous."

"How do I look?" he asked, flirting now.

"Easy on the eyes." She smiled.

"Excuse me, there are sick people in this room," Skip interjected, smiling. "We need some attention, too."

"Oh, that's what I came to tell you," Dr. Lynette said to Skip.

"Tell me what?" Skip asked.

"That your T cells are up. It's time for you to go home."

Skip smiled, pictured himself back in his little apartment in the Venus, back with his beloved books and his novel. Then he caught himself. "I still feel too weak," he lied. He had to stay with Miss Levy.

"Aw, do not be a baby," Jesus teased, walking over to Skip, hugging him. "Dr. Lynette won't let you go if you not ready. I come and help you to leave *mañana*."

"We'll see," Skip said, relaxing into Jesus' heat as Jesus massaged his shoulders.

Dr. Lynette watched Jesus and Skip, watched the way Jesus' touch seemed to make Skip feel better. "I need your help," Dr. Lynette said to Jesus.

"What?"

"I would like you to visit my patients. Come on rounds with me, cheer them up."

"When?" Jesus asked.

"Right now," Dr. Lynette said. "Help me finish my rounds now."

"Who needs *General Hospital* when you got this," Skip said. Dr. Lynette laughed.

"I come and help you move home tomorrow," Jesus said, kissing Skip on the cheek.

Dr. Lynette and Jesus walked out of the room together.

Trying to Stop the Tide

The hot, humid air outside pushed against the cool, air-conditioned air inside, frosting the sliding glass door of Gabriel's apartment. The sheet of glass struggled to separate the two climates, fake winter and true summer. Gabriel walked out onto his balcony. He sat down on the golden aluminum lounge chair with teal and white plastic straps and gazed at the sea. It twinkled idly. He breathed in salty-sweet ocean air and baked in the heat. Sweat zigzagged down his abs and pooled in his belly button. "I saved the Venus de Milo for you, Grandpa," Gabriel said to the pelican. He remembered his grandfather pointing at a pelican and saying, "The most wonderful bird is the pelican. His beak can hold more than his belly. His beak can hold enough food for a week. And I'll be damned if I can tell how the hell he can."

The bird winked at Gabriel, took off and flew over the beach, soaring just inches above the water. It was a sign. He felt good. What he was about to do was worth it.

He wrote on the yellow pad:

Dear Mr. Heinz Lerman,
If any attempt is made to harm the Venus
de Milo Arms or any of the residents of the

*Venus de Milo Arms—the enclosed videotape
will be sent to the press and your wife.*
Sincerely,
Old South Beach

Skip had found out that all of Mr. Lerman's money came from
his wife. She was in Germany controlling his purse strings.

He went back inside, pulled on a shirt and flip-flops. He picked
up the videotape and inserted it in an envelope, saw a clip of the
video behind his eyes, saw Pandora insert the huge brown dildo in
the German. He wrote on the envelope:

*Personal and Confidential. To be opened
only by Mr. Heinz Lerman*

Gabriel licked the envelope shut. Now you, Marina, he thought.
Now you have to save me from myself. Then he put his video camera and film and an extra battery in his backpack and went to Jesus'
apartment and knocked.

The door opened. At first, Gabriel didn't recognize her. He had
seen her only in her doctor's uniform. Her hair had always been
tied into an efficient bun. Now liberated tendrils formed a halo, the
color of eggplants.

"How are you, Dr. Lynette?" Gabriel asked, taking in her incredible figure. She had on a flowered sarong and a matching bikini
top. Her breasts were high and round.

"Great," she replied, kissing him on the cheek, and he smelled
the slightest scent of hospital mixed with oranges. Jesus walked out
of the bathroom, looking incredibly happy.

"Wow," Gabriel said, gazing around the apartment, placing the
manila envelope and his backpack on the new apothecary table;
Jesus had bought new furniture to replace the Fabrizio furniture
he had given away. "The apartment looks great."

"Lynn, she help me," Jesus said. "She has great taste."

"I really like it," Gabriel said. "I hated all that Fabrizio crap."

"Marina, she will be mad," Jesus said. "I buy all the things at those stores she don't like. You know, Pottery Horn and Piers One. The chains that she say are ruining South Beach. I like them."

"Tell her you bought it all at thrift shops."

Dr. Lynette's cell phone rang. Her face tightened as she listened and shook her head. "I'll be right there," she said, clicking her phone shut.

"Sorry, guys, but I have to go to the hospital," she said gloomily, pulling on a blouse over her bikini top. She pecked Gabriel on the cheek again and then kissed Jesus on the lips. "I'll call you later," she said, and left.

"So tell me all about it, stud," Gabriel demanded as soon as the door shut.

"What?" Jesus teased.

"Don't play with me."

"What you mean?" Jesus repeated. "You have the film?" he asked, changing the subject.

"Yep," Gabriel answered, holding up the envelope.

"How it turns out?"

"We might win an Oscar," Gabriel said. "Come with me to drop it off at Heinz's office?"

"Sure," Jesus said, pulling his new Gap ribbed T-shirt and khaki shorts over his Speedo.

They walked out of the Venus and cut across to Lincoln Road. All the old stores had morphed into chains. The discount shoe shops, the electronics dealers, the dollar stores, the kitschy souvenir shops, the mental health and social security office had all gone. Diamonds and Chicken Soup had been replaced by Banana Republic. Merle's Closet was now a Victoria's Secret. The only original stores left were Moseley's, where Princess Grace had her linens designed, and a gigantic Woolworth's. Even the artists had been displaced: Carlos Alves's studio has become a Pottery Barn. Lincoln Road had not only morphed into a mall overnight but had been invaded by yuppies.

"So are you going to tell me about you and the good doctor?" Gabriel asked Jesus.

Jesus smiled faintly. "What to say? We are friends."

"Come on, stud, you can do better than that."

"No stud. Not me. Not with Lynn. She make me scared. She is great."

"And?" Gabriel asked.

"No," Jesus answered. "No, I have not sleep with her. Three weeks. That's a record. Three weeks we been together every spare time she have."

"Sounds like love to me," Gabriel said. "Jesus has a girlfriend."

"Quit funning me," Jesus said, laughing, punching him on the shoulder.

They reached the Van Dyke Building, once the offices of Carl Fisher, one of the beach's earliest developers and now the headquarters of Lerman's Miami Beach Realty Preservation, Inc. They took the elevator to the top floor and gave the envelope with the tape to Heinz Lerman's secretary. Gabriel felt a moment of guilt, but with the thought of losing the Venus, the guilt passed quickly.

Then Gabriel noticed the time. "I got to go," he told Jesus. "To help Marina with an art project."

"OK, *papo*," Jesus said. "*Hasta luego.*"

"Bye," Gabriel said, and he walked ten blocks down Ocean Drive to South Pointe Park. He passed through the mangroves and over a small pine bridge until he reached the high crown of palms and the huge casurina, the spot that Skip had christened Paradise. Then the smell of swamp was replaced by the smell of salted sea. He stood on the gigantic flat stone and searched for Marina. He spotted her on the beach. She was pacing, all dressed in black.

Gabriel climbed off the rock and worked his way through the sea oats to her. Sweetheart seeds stuck to his socks. He kissed her. She was in art mode, half present, half in her head.

"I need you to videotape me," she said. "It's going to take a long time."

"I have a long time."

"I'm going to stop the tide," she said. "Things are changing too fast. I have to stop the tide."

"Whatever you say."

"I want you to tape me for ten minutes, every hour."

"No problem."

"You ready?" She took off her Adidas.

Gabriel checked the camera, looked at his watch. It was one o'clock. "Ready and waiting."

"Let's begin," Marina said. She looked tense, like a runner at the start of a race. Gabriel started filming.

Marina took a deep breath and gingerly walked down to where the waves were drawing a crooked white froth line on the golden beach. She stood where the hissing bubbles touched the tips of her baby pink–painted toenails. She took a deep breath, shut her eyes and raised her arms horizontally out in front of her. She spread her fingers open.

Gabriel kept filming for ten minutes. She just stood there, directing the water, directing the waves to stop. They refused.

Gabriel sat down on the beach and watched Marina stand there as the water slowly crept forward, covering her toes and then her feet and then her ankles. He watched her motionless arms start to tremble. He thought, *How futile, how beautiful, how ridiculous, how stubborn, how poetic.* He watched her hour after hour, watched as her stretched arms started to sink down. Every hour he would tape her for ten minutes. He watched the sun set, an impossibly beautiful brilliant orange ball. He watched until she slowly slumped forward under a glittering starry starry sky, until her body gave out and she fell forward, onto the sand and into a persistent rising tide. She had a flash of Gabriel holding his hands over her face, sheltering her, protecting her from the sun so her face wouldn't burn. Gabriel wrapped his arms around her and carried her out of the knee-deep breaking sea.

Gabriel Pops the Question

The sweat dripped down Gabriel's body as he wrote on the beach in South Pointe Park, in Paradise. He had to take the relationship to the next step. He wanted to spend the rest of his life with Marina.

He would try to make her understand in a gesture and language she would appreciate. He had been writing on the sand with a stick for hours. He wrote the question over and over, thousands and thousands of times. His back ached. His arms shook. His fingers cramped. He had covered the entire cove with the question. He was finished. He looked at his watch. It was a quarter to six in the evening. He had only fifteen minutes to spare. He stretched, walked on the foam of the breaking waves so as not to disturb the questions. He wiped the sweat off his body with a towel. He unhooked the garment bag from the sea grape tree, unzipped it and took out his grandfather's tuxedo. He pulled off the dry-cleaning tag, put on the black pants with the black satin trim running up the legs. His hands shook as he inserted the gold studs through the buttonholes of the crisp white shirt. He put on the bow tie. The collar scratched his neck. He tucked his shirt into his pants. He put on his grandfather's cream tuxedo jacket.

Calm down, he told himself, checking his watch. *Only seven minutes,* he thought. He looked into his travel mirror, combed his hair and then recombed it. *Stop,* he told himself.

He took the bottle of champagne from the Igloo and put it in the sterling silver ice bucket engraved with his grandfather's initials. He filled it up with the melting ice. He grabbed the plastic bag filled with dozens of multicolored hibiscuses that he had picked earlier form the Venus de Milo Arm's garden. He walked carefully back to the center of the cove, the center of the mile of questions.

He placed the dripping silver bucket with the chilling champagne next to him on the sand. Then he plucked the hibiscus petals, thinking: *She loves me; she loves me not; she loves me. . . .* Yellow pollen stuck to the blond hair on the back of his hands. He spread the petals around him until he was circled by a multicolored sprinkling of pink, yellow, white, orange and red.

It was one minute before seven-thirty. One minute before sunset. He took deep breaths and stared at the break in the trees, watching for Marina. His stomach hurt. He wished he could turn back, but it was already arranged. *This will finally make her open up all the way,* he told himself. She would realize he was here to stay.

The setting sun made the sky look as if it was about to burst into flames. Then he saw Marina.

Marina saw the sunset first, and then Gabriel. She walked onto the beach, reading the question over and over again. Panic shot through her. She glanced from the questions to Gabriel to the questions. She felt more and more afraid as she walked toward him.

Gabriel's heart jumped. He reached into his pocket and pulled out the engagement ring and put it in his open palm. He knelt down on one knee and held the ring out to her. It captured and reflected the sunset back at her.

Marina looked down—everywhere the question, over and over and over. She reached Gabriel, stared at the ring.

"I took the diamond off the key Miss Levy gave my grandfather and had it set it in this ring," he said, his voice cracking. He forced himself not to think of the Venus, still in grave danger, as they had heard nothing since he had dropped off the Lerman video. He felt sweat under his arms, tried to smile.

Marina froze, started to tremble. She stared at the ring. The silence screamed.

"I know it's quick," Gabriel said. "But now that both Skip and Miss Levy are in the hospital, it doesn't seem like there's that much time."

Marina forced herself to look at Gabriel. She wrapped her hand around the ring, squeezed it.

"I love you," Gabriel said. "I want to marry you. I want to make babies with you."

She tried to hold it but a sob broke through. "I'm sorry," Marina cried, turning around and running, the ring clasped in her hand so hard that the diamond cut into her palm, trampling the question, over and over:

MARINA, WILL YOU MARRY ME?

Gabriel remained on one knee. The sea devoured the sun.

Miss Levy Finally Finds Love

Gabriel looked at the clock. It was one in the afternoon. He pulled the sheet over his head, curled up into the fetal position. He wanted to stay in bed forever.

He forced himself up, out of bed. His head ached—the aftermath of coke, crystal, rum and whatever else he did last night. At least there's no one in my bed, he thought as he walked naked to the kitchen to get some water. He heard a noise outside. Footsteps. They stopped. An air mail envelope slid out from under his front door. His name was printed on it. He had an urge to slide it back out into the hall. He knew it was trouble. But instead he sat on his couch and opened it. *How much worse can things get?* he thought as he read:

> *To Whom It May Concern:*
> *Any attempt to contact my wife or show her the manufactured tape will result in the turning over to the Miami Beach Police the evidence that my private investigators have compiled about a Miss Mera Levy who lives at the Venus de Milo Arms. I have proof that she was an associate of Meyer Lansky and is presently operating as a bookie and money courier. It would be a pity if she had*

to spend her final years behind bars. Sell the Venus and make yourself enough money to live happily ever after.

Your Developer Pal

Gabriel felt his heart pounding in his chest. He remembered all the phone calls and conversations he'd overheard Miss Levy have about the greyhounds and horses and jai alai. He knew she was a bookie and had been a showgirl when she was young. But a Meyer Lansky associate? A mob girl? He felt totally defeated. Instead of Marina's opening up when he'd asked her to marry him, she had slammed shut, taken the ring and run away. He would now have no wife, maybe no girlfriend. And now that the blackmail plan hadn't worked, he would have no Venus. He couldn't risk Miss Levy's going to jail. And with Skip and Miss Levy in the hospital, he did not know how much longer he would have them. Soon, there would be nothing left to take. He decided to go to the hospital to talk with Skip. If he didn't talk to someone about Marina and Miss Levy, the Venus and his fears, he would go crazy.

He walked up Collins Avenue past the Delano Hotel's winged top, which rose up like an overgrown Aztec headdress. Wispy white curtains fluttered in the wind around the entrance porch. This made Gabriel think of a wedding veil, which made him even sadder.

Farther up the beach, at Mount Sinai Hospital, Skip sat on a chair across from Miss Levy's bed. Neon green Jell-O jiggled on Skip's spoon. Miss Levy strained to open her mouth. Only one side moved. Skip slipped in the spoon carefully. She sucked some Jell-O off the spoon. More slithered down her cheek, like a brilliant green slug.

Miss Levy swallowed. She felt her body disconnecting from itself. It hurt her to be out of control. Skip wiped the green Jell-O off her face with a blue napkin.

"No more," Miss Levy slurred out of the side of her mouth. *I don't want to live anymore*, she thought.

"Have some milk shake," Skip said, picking up the plastic cup with the bendable straw, holding it to her mouth. She placed her lips on the straw and pretended to swallow a mouthful as a tear dripped from her frozen eye.

"You're getting back at me for making you eat? Right, Skippy?"

"How do you expect to get better if you don't eat?" He repeated the question she'd asked him over and over when she was taking care of him. He smiled.

"I'm the mother," Miss Levy said. "You're the child. And I am not going to get better."

"Don't talk rubbish," he said, laughing. "You are strong. You are young." He repeated her words back at her again. Their roles had reversed. Instead of Miss Levy's taking care of him, he was taking care of her. He would not leave until she was well enough to come home with him to the Venus de Milo Arms.

"No," Miss Levy ordered. "Listen to me!"

"Sure," Skip said, and there was something in her voice that frightened him.

"Under the bed. My purse. Inside. My will. I want to be cremated. I want my ashes scattered in the pond around the Holocaust Memorial. I want to join my family there. All the instructions are in my purse. My purse. Under the bed."

"I will," Skip said. "I will make sure to do it." And his voice cracked and he thought, *This is not supposed to be happening. I'm the one who was supposed to die first.* He couldn't stand her pain. She patted him on the head with her right hand, her good hand.

"This is the way," Miss Levy said. "The old have to die before the young. I have to get heaven ready for you."

"I love you," Skip said.

"I love you, too, my beautiful boy," Miss Levy said. She shut her eyes.

Skip held her till she fell asleep in his arms. He thought of his first love, thought how Miss Levy had just repeated the last words Dennis had ever said to him: I love you, my beautiful boy. He shut his eyes, synchronized his breathing with hers, felt her warmth and dissolved into her Vicks smell.

Then, Skip heard a noise. He looked up. It was Marina. He got off the bed gently, careful not to wake Miss Levy.

"What's wrong with you?" Skip asked Marina. She looked terrible, had dark circles under her eyes. He could tell she'd been crying. They walked over to the window and sat facing one another.

Marina's forced smile fractured into a grimace. Tears started to well up in her eyes. She felt so selfish. She was healthy. He and Miss Levy were sick, stuck in the hospital. *She* should be comforting *them.*

"I'm sorry," Marina said. "How are you feeling?"

"Please," Skip begged. "Don't treat me like a sick person. Tell me what's wrong."

"Gabriel asked me to marry him."

"Oh, how terrible," Skip said, smiling, looking at her, puzzled. She shrugged.

"So what's wrong?" Skip asked gently. "He loves you. You love him. Right?"

"Yes," she answered. She brought her legs to her chest and hugged them. "He asked me and I ran. I got so scared."

"Scared of what?"

"I was married before," she said, drawing tighter into herself. "I got successful. My husband was an artist, too. He got jealous. I got sick. He deserted me."

"What does that have to do with Gabriel? He didn't leave you."

"I know . . . it doesn't make sense."

"Grab love when you can," Skip said. "It's very simple, but it seems like the hardest lesson to learn."

"I was sick. I had cancer."

"I know," Skip said. "I read about it when I researched you."

"I can't have children."

"So what?"

"Gabriel is always talking about having kids. I'm afraid to tell him. I might lose him."

Skip sat upright, moving toward her. "You don't know Gabriel at all, do you?"

She turned her head away from him.

"God," he said, "you are so lucky." He took a deep breath. "I will never have that again, what you have. Take it from a dying man: Don't give it up. Fight for it. It's the only thing worth fighting for."

They heard a rustling sound from Miss Levy's bed. She coughed, rubbed her eyes as if waking up. She had heard everything.

"Marina," she slurred.

"Miss Levy," Marina answered, walking over to her bed.

"Will you do me a favor, dear?" Miss Levy asked. "Will you get my bag from under the bed?"

Marina grabbed Miss Levy's parsley-colored paisley purse. Tangled up in the strap was a matching cap.

"Can you open it?"

Marina opened the clasp on the bag and handed the purse to Miss Levy.

Miss Levy used her good hand to take the chain with the diamond-encrusted key from her neck. She fumbled around until she found the envelope she was looking for, marked "Marina," and opened it. She placed the key in the envelope, sealed it and put it back into her purse, and then held all of it on her lap.

Skip picked up her parsley-colored paisley cap and put it on Miss Levy's head. "Now you match. Now you will get better," Skip said.

Pandora walked into the hospital room. She was carrying her boom box and a gigantic arrangement of roses. She put the flowers next to Miss Levy's bed, kissed her on the cheek. Then Jesus walked in with Dr. Lynette. Going on rounds with her, helping her help others had made him feel good about himself. He no longer needed the drugs or the nightlife or the fame or the money or the casual sex. All he needed was Dr. Lynette.

Miss Levy looked around the room and smiled. She felt so lucky to have them all, and said a silent prayer for their happiness.

Pandora flipped on her boom box, started to lip-synch to Miss Levy:

> *Everything went wrong*
> *And the whole day long*
> *I'd feel so blue*
> *For the longest while*
> *I forgot to smile*
> *Then I met you*

Now that my blue days have passed
Now that I've found you at last

I'll be loving you, always
With a love that's true, always

They all gathered around Miss Levy's bed and started singing along with Pandora. Then Gabriel entered the room. He walked up to Miss Levy's bed, stood next to Marina and started singing with them.

Miss Levy saw that Gabriel was dressed in one of his grandfather's vintage shirts, patterned in strawberries. He moved to the head of the bed and kissed her. She closed her eyes and took a deep breath, and smelled him, and something inside her slipped and he changed into his grandfather. She saw Alvin. She was sure. Her eyes shined. She allowed herself to slip away, to let go. She embraced Malakh ha-Mavet, the Angel of Death, South Beach's most powerful citizen.

"Alvin," she uttered—her last word, with her last breath.

"I'm here," Gabriel said, loudly. "I've missed you. I love you," pretending to be his grandfather.

Miss Levy let go, felt free and so light. She grabbed Alvin's hand and slipped away to her twin sister, to her mother and her father. They were still young. All these years and they had not aged.

Free at Last

Skip peeled back the white sheet covering Miss Levy's face. He couldn't stop staring at her. She looked so calm and relaxed, as if the pain had been released. He wished she could tell him what it was like to be dead. He knew he would be there soon. He lay in the bed next to her.

Two Haitian orderlies with very black skin pushed a stretcher into their room.

"I'm sorry," one said, as he made the sign of the cross and pulled the sheet back over her face.

"Wait," Skip said, removing the sheet from her face and kissing her on the cheeks. She felt ice cold. He placed the sheet back.

"Your grandmother?" the other orderly asked, concerned.

"Yes," Skip lied, as they moved her to the stretcher.

Tears flowed down Skip's cheeks as they rolled her away. The wheels of the stretcher squeaked. He waved.

He sat down on the chair by the window. He stared at Miss Levy's empty bed. He felt very alone. He wiped his eyes. Then, he took a deep breath, stood up, stripped off his hospital gown and dressed in his street clothes—a Madonna T-shirt and 501s. He was so emaciated that his once tight clothes hung from his body. He grabbed Miss Levy's paisley purse from under her bed.

He strolled out of the room, snuck past the extraordinarily tarted-up nurse at the reception desk. He walked past row after row of ugly portraits of hospital donors. Skip shivered, wondering why they had to turn up the air conditioner so high. He walked to the maternity ward and looked through the glass at the babies. This always made him happy: new life. Then he walked out of the hospital into the setting sun. A pane of glass no longer separated him from the real world. He could feel the warmth and taste the fresh air. He squinted into the orange-streaked, burning sky.

He hailed a cab and rode through the pastel-painted buildings of South Beach. He could not believe how much had changed in the months that he'd been in the hospital. More buildings had been fixed up. There were cranes everywhere, marking the spots of future high-rises. He drove past a corner where the Sands, an incredible deco hotel, had once stood.

COMING SOON

Artist Colony Lofts and Hotel
Luxury Residences
$500,000 to $5,000,000

The cab arrived at the Venus. He walked inside and felt like he was stepping into a security blanket and then he thought how the Venus might soon be demolished and felt a moment of sadness. He went up to his apartment, grabbed a Diet Coke and a cigarette. He sat on his bed and opened Miss Levy's paisley purse. Inside were a bunch of different-size, different-colored envelopes. They were marked:

Pandora, Marina, Jesus, Gabriel, Skip

Skip put all the envelopes back in Miss Levy's purse except the one with his name on it. He lit a cigarette, took a puff, coughed. He chugged some Diet Coke. It tasted so delicious. He burped. Then he sat down at his desk and opened his large manila envelope.

There was a card and a black bound book with gold embossed letters marked "MY DIARY." On the cover of the card was a Tom of Finland drawing of a naked muscle hunk, bound and gagged. Skip smiled to himself.

He opened the card, and printed inside was:

I AM A PRISONER OF YOUR LOVE

Below she wrote,

My Dearest Skip,
My brilliant son,
Enclosed please find my diary. I hope you can use it to help finish your novel. I know it will be a great success! You are a very talented writer.
Thank you for taking such good care of me.

Love forever,
Miss Levy

Skip lay back in bed and opened her diary and started reading. Miss Levy's life unfolded before him. As he read, the ending to his novel, *The Venus de Milo Arms*, came to him, slowly and delicately. Then, he reached a section that made everything make sense. He couldn't believe it. His heart beat fast. He reread the pages again and again, not knowing what to do. But then he figured it out. He ripped out the pages, put them into a white envelope and wrote:

To be read by Gabriel to Marina on the beach in front of the Venus de Milo Arms after my funeral.

He placed the envelope back in Miss Levy's bag. The diary was the missing piece of the puzzle, not only for his novel but for Marina and Gabriel's relationship. It would stop history from repeating itself.

Skip sat at his desk, turned on his computer. It was as if Miss Levy's diary had melted his writer's block and had unleashed something magical. He now understood Miss Levy, now understood how to write the character based on her. The words just seemed to flow out of him, on automatic. He wrote page after page, and it was flowing so fast that his fingers could not keep up with the words coming from his head. He felt Miss Levy's presence, felt her cheering him on, giving him confidence. Finally, he took a deep breath and typed:

The End

Offing It

Skip woke up. He rubbed his eyes, looked around. He was not in the hospital. He was in his apartment at the Venus de Milo Arms. It was dark — nighttime. He glanced at the clock. It was three. He remembered the calm, relaxed expression on Miss Levy's face when she died. He sat up, lit a cigarette. He grabbed the phone, speed-dialed the number. *Make him be home,* Skip thought. Miss Levy had not only finished his book for him, she had taught him to not be afraid of death.

"Yep," Butch answered the phone. He sounded wide awake.

"Butch, it's Skip."

"Hey, Skippy," Butch said, relieved to hear from him. "I heard you were sick."

"I'm better. Ready," Skip said firmly. "Ready to do what we talked about." He took a deep drag on his cigarette.

"You sure?" Butch asked.

"Very," Skip answered. "Can we hook up now?"

"Yes," Butch replied.

"If you come, you have to do it. I'll pay you five hundred dollars."

"OK," Butch agreed.

"Meet me by the barbecue stand in South Pointe Park."

"Give me fifteen," Butch replied. He finished off the last few bites of his Velveeta and fried SPAM on Wonder bread and washed it down with some Nestlé's Quik. He hated the rough stuff. He preferred the sex. He understood the pleasure of sex, had felt it. He didn't understand the pleasure of pain. Pain is why he'd ended up selling his ass on South Beach. It was the pain of his drunken father's beatings that had made him run away. He had to remind himself that pain made the client feel good. He knew Skip was very sick, that his blood was full of AIDS. He wished he didn't have to hurt him. He wished he could tell Skip no, but his rent was due tomorrow and if he didn't get some crystal, he would go nuts.

Back in the Venus, Skip brushed his teeth, splashed his face with cold water, sprayed Right Guard under his arms. Then he realized the absurdity of his actions. He wrote on a yellow legal pad:

> Dear Gabriel,
> I have finished my novel. Please try to get it published. You will find it in the file marked "Venus de Milo Arms." I appoint you my literary executor. Please throw my ashes along with Miss Levy's in the pond surrounding the Holocaust Memorial. That is what she wanted and this is what I want. She left some stuff for you and the others in her bag.
> You can find me at Paradise. I know you love me too much to kill me. Thanks for being such a good friend and for helping write "Sunstroker."
> Tell Jesus and Marina and Pandora I'll be waiting for them at the velvet ropes in the sky!
>   Love,
>   Skip

Skip folded down the screen on his laptop. He placed it in front of his bedroom door and set Miss Levy's envelope-filled bag on top of it. Then he placed his note for Gabriel on the straps on her paisley purse.

Skip put on a T-shirt marked "South Beach—America's Riviera," a pair of Hawaiian-patterned shorts and a Mickey Mouse cap. He grabbed a roll of duct tape and two sharp, serrated knives. He yanked the white cotton sheet off his bed, wrapped the knives in the sheet and put them and the tape into a Burdines department store bag. He grabbed his wallet and left.

Skip walked out of the Venus de Milo Arms, past the Warsaw Ballroom, the club that made South Beach, the club where New York boys discovered Cuban boys and vice versa. It was closed. A sign on the building said, "The future home of Jerry's Deli." He shook his head. *It's all over,* he thought. *Already.*

He went to the ATM at the Bank of America, stuck in his card and punched in his code. The machine spit out twenty-five crisp twenty-dollar bills. Now, he had only twenty dollars left in his account. He had used all his savings to pay hustlers. He didn't feel close to any of them but Butch. Butch was the only one he still liked after the session was over. He pretended he was just going on a stroll, tried not to think about what he was doing, afraid he would chicken out.

In South Pointe Park, on the very tip of Miami Beach, Butch paced around the barbecue pit. *Where the hell is Skip?* He just wanted to get his money and get it over with. He wanted to hurt Skip as little as he had to in order to earn his money. He bit the cuticle of his nail. He wanted to get the money and score some Tina.

Skip saw Butch in the moonlight, by the barbecue. He sauntered up to him. They shook hands, stiffly, like businessmen. Skip smelled of Old Spice, the cologne Butch's father would wear.

"Nice to see you," Butch said, sincerely. "I'm glad you got better."

"I feel great," Skip lied. He felt so tired from the walk that he had to sit down.

"You sure?" Butch asked, concerned. "You look so thin."

"I'm on the South Beach Diet," Skip grinned, sitting down. "Wanna smoke?"

"Thanks," Butch replied, and Skip put two cigarettes in his mouth, lit them and then handed one to him. Butch sucked in the smoke and pursed his lips and blew out smoke rings that got bigger and bigger and then disappeared in the night air. And it was not until that moment in the moonlight that Skip understood the intensity of his attraction. The realization took his breath away. Butch looked like Dennis, the only man he'd ever loved, the man who gave him AIDS. Physically he was Dennis's replica, only beefier and shorter.

Skip inhaled and peered out over the ocean. A full moon painted the black waves silver; stars twinkled. They smoked next to one another in silence. Their shoulders touched. Skip took the last puff of his cigarette and then ground the butt into the sand.

"You ready to do this?" Skip asked, his voice cracking.

"Yes," Butch answered. He was tired of Skip's death fixation. "You got the bucks?"

Skip pulled out the roll of twenties and showed them to Butch.

Butch eyed the cash, thinking, *There's my rent and drug money. Thank God.*

Skip shoved the roll back into his pocket. He opened his bag and pulled out the sheet, and the two knives fell to the ground. He picked them up. "I want you to tape my arms and legs together with duct tape. Then stab me in the back and the chest. Then wrap me in the white sheet. Exactly like we talked about."

"Can't I just do it with my belt?" Butch asked. He thought of the last time, strangling Skip till he almost lost consciousness, and then releasing him.

"No. You have to do it my way."

"But I hate blood."

"Do it how I say or I'll find someone else."

"OK," Butch lied.

Skip handed him the money. Butch tucked the roll into his back pocket.

"You took the cash. There's no going back."

"Right."

"You're like Dr. Kevorkian. This is a mercy killing. I'm dying. I feel the AIDS in my brain. I don't want to go back to the hospital. I don't want to end up a vegetable. All I ever had was my brain. You are giving me a great gift."

"Right," Butch repeated, "whatever." He fingered the cash bulge in his pocket.

"Follow me," Skip said, handing Butch the Burdines bag.

They picked their way through sea grapes. A ghost white crab scampered into a hole. Moonlight peeked through the thicket. It smelled fertile, of salted decay.

When they passed over a small bridge, Butch reached into the bag and dropped the knives into the brackish tar-colored water. There was no way he was going to stab Skip. He figured he would take his money and rough him up a bit and then strangle him a little with his belt like the last time. He could not kill anyone, he thought, especially not a nice guy like Skip.

Then they passed the gigantic flat stone and worked their way down to the shore. The froth of the breaking waves formed a squiggly white line on the beach. Skip couldn't believe he was finally doing this. He no longer felt tired. He no longer felt sick. He had played this scene over in his head so many times that he couldn't believe it was really happening. He sat on the sand, started to tremble.

Skip was so nervous he was making Butch nervous. Butch pulled down his pants and cupped his genitals and held them out to Skip like an offering. He smiled. "Wouldn't you rather just blow me like everyone?" he begged. "Please."

Skip shook his head. He looked at Butch's beautiful innocent face, his dimples, and he looked like an angel to him. My angel of death, he thought.

"I'm sorry, that will not do it for me, Butch," he said. "That will only take the pain away for a little while." He felt sorry for Butch for a second and pushed the thought out of his mind.

Butch shrugged, pulled up his pants.

"You understand what I want you to do?"

"Yes," Butch answered mechanically, "duct-tape you, hit you, stab you and wrap you in the sheet."

"Lots of stab wounds, on my back and chest. Make sure I have on my Mickey Mouse ears cap. I want to die with it on my head. I want to highlight the absurdity of life."

"OK," Butch said, listening to the words but ignoring them.

"Lots of blood. I want it dramatic. I want to die a drama queen."

Butch reached into the Burdines bag, took out the tape.

"Wait," Skip said.

"Yes," Butch said, hoping that he had changed his mind.

"Let's smoke another cigarette," Skip said, and his fingers shook as he grabbed the packet from his pants and pulled one out and lit it. *Am I doing the right thing?* he wondered. He sucked in the smoke and it calmed him. *The fantastic feeling of finally satisfying the craving—that's what it will feel like when Butch kills me, like that times a million,* he told himself. He stubbed the cigarette out.

"Let's do it," Skip demanded. "Now!"

Butch stood up. He grabbed Skip's hair, yanked it hard, pulling him into a standing position. His arm bulged, veins stood up.

"OK, fuck-face, fag, piece of shit," Butch scowled, slapping Skip with his open hand—two, three, four times. "Fucking cocksucking worthless asshole."

Skip flinched with each slap. His face turned red—scarlet. Red hand slap prints formed on his sunken cheeks. He wanted more, to kill the deeper pain. He bit his tongue, felt the sting on his cheeks, tasted blood. It tasted good.

Butch punched him hard in the stomach. Skip felt the wind knocked from him as he fell forward onto the beach. Butch slammed his foot on Skip's head, shoving his face into the sand as he unrolled the duct tape. He wrapped the tape around Skip's ankles and up to his chest, then around his arms behind his back. "Worthless, cunt, pussy boy." He let the rest of the roll hang off Skip. He turned him over. Skip's face was powdered with sand. He was wheezing and gasping for air.

Then Butch took a step back, erased Skip in his mind and turned him into everyone who ever hurt him: his father who beat him and threw him out of the house, his mother who let his father hurt him, the policeman who raped him at gunpoint. He punched Skip in the chest, harder and harder, each time yelling "Fag," over and over. Then he punched him in the face.

Skip moaned. The punches made him feel excited, giddy, almost drugged, as he walked the tightrope between pleasure and pain. He was dazed. A trickle of blood scrawled from his nose and puddled on his chin. Soon, he knew, all the pain would go away.

A mosquito bit Butch on the cheek. "Fuck," he yelled, smacking it.

Skip looked up at Butch. Moonlight glinted in his beautiful blue eyes. Dew stuck to his eyelashes. Skip saw Dennis, the love of his life.

Butch caught Skip's expression, the love. He felt sick. The sight of blood always made him feel sick. He could smell the blood in his nose when he breathed. He gagged. He couldn't take it anymore. He yanked off his new GAP brown leather belt. He had to get this over with before he puked. He threw the belt around Skip's throat. *I'll choke him a little until he almost passes out, like the last time,* he thought. He hated hurting Skip. He reminded himself over and over that he was giving Skip pleasure, doing a job, doing what he'd been paid to do.

"No!" Skip yelled, as loud as he could, pulling the belt from around his neck. "The knives. Stab me. Not the belt," Skip sputtered. Blood gurgled in his throat.

"I dropped them. In the water."

"Fuck you. You stupid. Idiot. Moron," Skip screamed. "You're the fucking fag!"

Butch heard his father's voice, smelt his Old Spice smell. "Shut the fuck up!"

"Forget it!" Skip yelled. He spit a mouthful of spit mixed with blood at Butch.

It stuck to Butch's cheek. He wiped it. It felt like snot. He looked at his fingers, covered in blood and spit. He vomited.

"Forget it! Pussy!" Skip screamed.

Butch grabbed the belt, pulled it tight, yanking Skip off the ground, thinking Skip meant forget the knives. Butch choked him, counted to thirty, wanting to give the little fucker his money's worth. *I'm no fag,* he thought. He imagined he was strangling his father.

Skip struggled. He grasped the belt around his neck, tried to loosen it. His face turned purple. Then his hands dropped to his sides and he relaxed: A peaceful expression formed on his face.

Butch released the belt. Skip fell to the ground. Butch wiped his hands in the sand, waited for Skip to come to.

But instead, Skip started to convulse, as if there was something in his body trying to escape. He rattled. Butch panicked, got down on his knees, wiped the blood and spit from inside Skip's mouth, gasped air, put his lips on Skip's lips, forcing his air into Skip, like blowing up a balloon. He'd learned mouth-to-mouth when he was a lifeguard.

He tasted blood, coppery like sucking a quarter, but sweeter. He knew that Skip had AIDS, knew that trying to save Skip could ultimately kill him. He blew air into Skip's mouth over and over, thinking, *Please don't die. Please don't die.*

Skip fought not to come back, felt the air in his mouth in some distant place and refused to accept it.

Butch spat, red-tinged spit. He realized he had strangled Skip for too long, realized that if he came back now, he would really be messed up. He remembered Skip saying: "I don't want to end up a vegetable." Butch couldn't let that happen, couldn't do that to him. He grabbed the belt and pulled as tight as he could as he sobbed, "I'm sorry, Skippy. I'm so sorry!"

Butch pulled till he could pull no more, till his arm cramped. Then he let go and ran as fast as he could up the beach.

The Day South Beach Died

Gabriel banged on Skip's door at the Venus. He had just come from Mount Sinai Hospital, where the nurse had told him that Skip had disappeared sometime during the night. "Skip," he yelled, as he stuck his golden master key into Skip's lock. He opened the door and entered the apartment. He saw the note with "Gabriel" written on it, resting on the handles of Miss Levy's paisley purse. He rushed into the bedroom. No Skip.

He hurried back and opened his note, knowing exactly what type of note it was, but hoping against hope.

You can find me in Paradise.

Gabriel shoved the paper into his pocket and ran out of Skip's apartment, rushed down the stairs to Ocean Drive. He crossed the road and jogged on the sidewalk that ran along the beach toward South Pointe Park. *Not now,* Gabriel thought. He couldn't deal with more death. More sadness. Not after Miss Levy. Please. He started to pray, the first time in a very long time. *Oh God, please no.* What else could he lose? His love, Marina; his home, the Venus; his friend, Skip. Would it never end?

He peered across the street as he ran up Ocean Drive, passing a fanciful lifeguard stand that looked like a rocket ship. He kept jogging, seeing the Fabrizio mansion in the distance. Then he saw

Fabrizio himself, dressed in gray and black. He was carrying a newspaper. Fabrizio smiled at Gabriel and waved.

Then a young man in a T-shirt and baggy shorts, the band of his Fabrizio underwear sticking out, darted across the road in front of Gabriel. He wore a black baseball cap pulled down over his eyes. He dashed up the coral steps of the Fabrizio mansion as Fabrizio bent forward and placed his key into the lock of his wrought iron gate.

Gabriel thought the guy was going to ask for an autograph until he saw a flash of silver in the sunlight, saw the barrel of the gun. Then a shot blasted and echoed back. The bullet flew through Fabrizio's neck and hit the tip of the metal railing of the gate, split apart, a fragment piercing the eye of a pigeon and killing it instantly. Then another shot blasted through Fabrizio's head as his body dropped to the steps. South Beach, Fabrizio's dream, had become his grave.

"You fucking bastard," Gabriel yelled at the same time as he thought, *This is not real.* They're making a movie. The killer dashed away as the door of the mansion flew open. Gabriel chased the man with the gun up Ocean Drive.

Jesus ran down the steps of the Fabrizio mansion. Blood flowed from Fabrizio's head, pooled and trickled down the steps.

"No! No!" Jesus screamed, opening the gate.

Gabriel was on automatic. He kept running after the killer. The man veered into an alley behind Twelfth Street. Gabriel followed, not even thinking about the gun until the man turned, smiled and pointed it at him. Gabriel ducked behind a Dumpster. The man with the gun scurried into a parking garage.

Back in front of the mansion, Jesus got down on the ground and cradled Fabrizio on his lap. Tears streamed down his face as Fabrizio's blood soaked his clothes.

Gabriel got out from behind the Dumpster. *I have to find Skip,* he thought. *Before it's too late.* He heard police sirens blaring from every direction as he ran to South Pointe Park. Gabriel worked his way through the thicket until he arrived at the gigantic flat rock, Skip's favorite spot, Paradise.

Gabriel searched for Skip. He scanned the beach, looked at the blue waves breaking white, looked at the little sandpipers chasing and then fleeing from the foam. He remembered Marina trying to stop the tide and himself writing over and over: Will you marry me?

Thank you, God, Gabriel thought. He's not here. I'm going to go back to the Venus and find him working on his computer, writing a new "Sunstroker." Then he looked up and saw buzzards circling. His heart sank.

He saw a Mickey Mouse ears cap sticking out from some sea oats, kept walking forward, in slow motion, in a daze, afraid of what he would find.

Then Gabriel saw Skip. His face was white, covered in dried brown blood. Flies buzzed around wildly. Ants crawled in his open eyes. He was curled up in the fetal position. Gabriel removed the Gap belt from around his neck and put the Mickey Mouse cap on his head.

Farther up the beach at the Fabrizio mansion, a crazed fan ripped out the Fabrizio ad of Jesus naked on a raft from an old *Vogue* magazine. She dipped it in the designer's blood to keep as a souvenir.

Miss Levy Becomes
the Wizard of Oz

Gabriel yawned, rested his head on the steering wheel and shut his eyes. The traffic on Ocean Drive had stopped. He had been at the police station for the last four hours, answering questions and scanning mug shots. After that, he'd gone to the Nieberg Midwood funeral home to pick up Miss Levy and Skip. The two twin urns sat side by side on the Cadillac seat next to him, Miss Levy in a golden urn and Skip in a silver one.

The cars started to crawl forward, one inch at a time. A mob stood gawking at the bloodstained coral steps in front of the Fabrizio mansion. Media trucks lined both sides of Ocean Drive. Antennas and satellite dishes stuck up into the cloudless blue sky. Reporters milled around with microphones and cameras. An emaciated model wannabe in a purple leather G-string and pink Fabrizio stilettos cried hysterically on cue for the cameras. A leather daddy held up a sign: "Good-bye Mr. Fabulous." "Get your Fabrizio souvenir here!" a teenage hip-hop boy yelled, holding up a T-shirt with Fabrizio's picture and "R.I.P." printed on it. A guy dressed as a SoBe soda bottle was passing out free samples. "Take a sip of the hippest place on earth," the man in the bottle cried.

Then the limo in front of Gabriel stopped. A blonde woman in a black Fabrizio suit, carrying a dozen red roses, stepped out. The crowd gasped, parted, moaned: "Madonna."

She walked up the steps, knelt and placed the roses on the red-brown bloodstains. She made the sign of the cross as a cluster of rabid reporters rushed her and knocked her over. Her wig flew off. She gasped, yanked the wig back on her head. It was a drag Madonna impersonator. She got up and said, "I'll be performing tonight at Score, a special tribute to Fabrizio." Her wig was crooked.

Gabriel turned away, stared across the street at the twinkling ocean. *Fame is like having no walls*, he thought, finally inching past the mansion and making it back to the Venus. A horde of reporters was camped out on the front steps so he drove around to the alley and into the garage. He grabbed the two urns from the car seat, hugging them to his body. They were warm and slick. "We're home now," he said to them, walking to his apartment, wondering suddenly how long the Venus de Milo Arms would be anyone's home. He was on the verge of hysteria, or numb, not sure which. He just wanted to get in bed and curl up in the fetal position and escape through sleep.

Suddenly he heard the click, click, click of a camera, the flash blinding him. He blinked. Spots floated before his eyes and then disappeared.

"Mr. Tucker, Gabriel," the man with the camera cried, holding out a wad of hundreds. "I'm from the *Enquirer*."

"Leave me alone," Gabriel demanded, and kept walking.

"Who killed Fabrizio?" the reporter pestered, following him. "Did he receive threats from the mafia?"

Gabriel ignored him, rested the urns on the floor, opened his apartment door.

"What about Skip Bowling?" he pleaded. "Is it true they're going to knock down the Venus de Milo Arms? Was he depressed?"

"Nothing," Gabriel said, grabbing the urns and slamming the door in his face. He smiled, thinking Skip had become famous by the timing of his death. He had become one of the people he wrote about. He was sure that somewhere, Skip was getting a great laugh out of it.

Gabriel put the two urns on his coffee table, next to the envelopes Miss Levy had left and the last letter from his attorney advising him that the Venus de Milo code violation hearing was in two weeks and that if he couldn't show how he was going to fix the problems, the Venus would be demolished. He picked up the envelope with his name, flopped down on his couch, stared at Miss Levy's weak handwriting. He didn't know why but he couldn't open it. He shut his eyes and fell into a deep, dreamless sleep.

Gabriel was awakened by a knock on his door. It was four o'clock. "Who is it?" he asked.

"Me," Jesus answered, and Gabriel let him in. "I'm glad to see a friendly face, *papo.*"

"Me, too," Gabriel replied.

"I am trap in my apartment by the reporters," Jesus said.

"One took my picture in the hall," Gabriel said, sitting down on the couch.

"They like rats," Jesus said, sitting across from Gabriel.

"Those police asked you questions over and over?" Gabriel asked Jesus.

"For hours. They ask me about the mafia, the mob, and to launder money," Jesus said. "What they talking about? How you put money in the laundry?"

Gabriel smiled. "You don't actually wash it. You make it clean so it can't be traced."

"They think Skip and Fabrizio murderer are the same person."

"They have Skip's computer," Gabriel replied. "They saw the Internet messages he posted to hire someone to kill him."

"Poor little guy," Jesus said.

"I feel terrible, because he asked me to do it, to help him commit suicide when the time came."

"He want to die," Jesus said. "We must to respect his choice."

"I tell myself he would have suffered worse if he didn't die."

They heard footsteps by the door, and the doorbell rang. "Who is it?" Gabriel asked.

"Marina and Pandora," Marina answered. Gabriel opened the door.

Gabriel looked at Marina and felt his heart beating. She hugged him and relaxed into his arms, into his warmth. Gabriel shut his eyes and saw the question written all over Paradise: Will you marry me? Then he saw Skip's dead body. He pushed it out of his head, hugged her harder.

Pandora stared at Marina and Gabriel. *Someday, someone will love me like that. That's all I want,* she thought. *I will do whatever it takes.*

Jesus caught the look on Pandora's face. He got up and grabbed her hand and led her to the couch. They all stared at the envelopes with their names written on them resting on the table.

"They know who killed Fabrizio," Marina said, breaking the silence.

"They caught him?" Gabriel asked.

"No," Marina said, "but they know who did it. Turn on the TV."

Gabriel flipped on the TV, went to CNN. The rabid reporter prattled on about a spree killer and a trail of bodies, kinky tastes, the gay mafia, the circuit, South Beach, a hedonistic fantasyland where no one cares. They flashed a picture of a slight young man, and prattled on about his being a high-class prostitute.

"That's the guy," Gabriel said. "I recognize him."

"A high-class prostitute? That guy?" Jesus said. "He could not give it for free in South Beach!"

Skip's face came on the screen, a photo of him in his Mickey Mouse ears cap.

"It is possible that the alleged murderer of Fabrizio may have struck earlier in South Beach. Skip Bowling, gossip columnist and chronicler of the giddy South Beach scene, was found strangled to death in nearby South Pointe Park. He was known to frequent S&M bars and to engage male prostitutes."

Gabriel stared at Skip's face staring back at him blankly from the screen. He looked from his face to the silver urn. Marina flicked off the TV.

"So which one is Skip and which is Miss Levy?" Marina asked.

"Skip is in silver and Miss Levy is in gold," Gabriel answered as Jesus reached for the envelope with his name on it.

Gabriel picked up the other envelopes and handed them out. They opened them together.

On Pandora's card, there were two ruby slippers covered in red glitter. Inside was printed:

You are already in Kansas

Miss Levy wrote:

To my dearest Pandora,
To the loveliest woman I have ever known.
Use this little gift of money for the surgery,
so you can be who you already are. Also, I
want you to have all my outfits and jewelry
and glasses. I could think of no one who
would look more beautiful in them.
I love you always,
Miss Levy

Pandora stared at the check enclosed with the card. It was for twenty-five thousand dollars—the exact amount of money she needed to get the sexual reassignment surgery. She was shocked. She had not even known that Miss Levy knew she wanted the operation.

Jesus looked at his card. On the cover was a photograph of a group of students in graduation robes throwing their caps into the air. Inside there was a check for twenty thousand dollars and the words:

Gold and silver may tarnish away but a
good education is here to stay.

Underneath she wrote:

To Jesus,
Please use this money to go to school. You
are more than just a pretty face. You are
very smart. You and I are very similar. We
both were tortured and came to this coun-
try as refugees. We are survivors. You can do

whatever you put your mind to. Thank you for bringing so much joy into an old woman's life.

> *Te Amo,*
> *Your Miami Abuela*
> *Miss Levy*

Jesus smiled to himself. He shut his eyes and thought of Miss Levy and his mother and his grandmother and Skip and Fabrizio. He imagined he had not lost them but that they were looking after him from somewhere above.

Marina's card had a picture of a log cabin on the front, with a family playing and smoke coming out of the chimney.

Inside was printed:

Home Is Where the Heart Is.

Underneath this Miss Levy wrote:

Marina,
Don't be afraid of love. Don't make the mistake I made. Thank you for taking care of me. I know you will take good care of the others. This gives me great comfort. You and I are the same. Jews and artists are chosen people.

> *With love and respect,*
> *Miss Mera Levy*

P.S. A goldener shlisl efent ale tirn. A golden key opens all doors.

Marina shook her head, trying to understand Miss Levy's message. She reached in and pulled out the chain with the golden key with the diamond on it, the one that matched Gabriel's, the one that he had placed on the engagement ring. She cupped her hand around the key and put it in her pocket. She stared at Gabriel. She tried to imagine her life without him. She couldn't. She understood.

Gabriel studied his card, a drawing of a big heart with a smiley face. Inside Miss Levy had written:

My Dearest Gabriel,
I am so happy you came into my life. You are a tribute to your grandfather.

Go into my apartment, in my closet, and lift up the heart-shaped rug. Underneath you will find a safe. The combination is 39 to the right, 82 to the left, 74 to the right and finally 49 to the left. Everything in the box is yours—the letters from your grandfather, the hundred thousand in cash, and the stocks I bought over the years from the money I made from my job and from skimming a little bit of the action. I have signed them over to you on the back. I have saved all this money for years, not knowing what I was waiting for. I never spent anything because after Auschwitz I was afraid of losing everything. Then you came along and I realized I was saving it for you to save the Venus de Milo Arms, your grandfather's legacy, our home. Use the money to fix the violations. The shares are worth about five million dollars. Don't let them take the Venus away from us. I lost everything before. Don't let it happen again. Tell your children about my family and me.

You are now rich in money and I want you also to be rich in love. Don't give up on Marina. She loves you.

Always follow your heart.
Miss Levy

Gabriel took a deep breath. He couldn't believe it. He was rich again, very rich. He felt so happy and relieved. This meant he could save the Venus, save his home, save a part of his new world, no matter what Heinz Lerman or the city of Miami Beach did. He hadn't realized until this moment how desperately he needed the Venus—his anchor, his home. So much had happened in the last few days that he had no idea how to process it. He put the card back into the envelope and looked up at the others. They seemed lost in their own worlds, in their own thoughts. Marina caught Gabriel's eye and took his hand into her own. She stuck the other hand into her pocket and grasped the golden key.

Dust to Dust

Gabriel, Marina, Pandora and Jesus stood in the setting sun at the Holocaust Memorial. The giant green hand towered above them. Jesus held two helium balloons. The two urns rested in front of them on the edge of the black pond that reflected the giant hand. Purple water lilies dotted the water. Mottled orange koi swam, rippling the mirror.

Jesus knelt down and tied the pink balloon to Skip's silver urn and the blue balloon to Miss Levy's golden urn.

The sun, a gigantic orange globe in the sky, slowly slipped downward. Marina walked to the edge of the pond. She reached into her pocket and pulled out a vial containing a clear liquid. She turned to the others. "In this bottle are my tears. Some of the tears I have cried for Skip and Miss Levy. I am going to release these tears into the water. I want you all to release your sadness with me." She knelt down and opened the bottle. "Thank you for the gift that is Skip and Miss Levy," she said, as she poured her tears into the pond water.

Tears filled Gabriel's eyes. They overflowed, slipped out, swam down his cheeks. He wiped his face with the sleeves of his grandfather's army uniform, which he had found hanging in his closet. Pandora sobbed silently, wearing Miss Levy's matching paisley purse, dress and cap. Marina hugged her. Jesus looked straight ahead.

"Come with me," Gabriel said. He led them to the black marble wall with the engraved names of Holocaust victims, guiding them to the spot that said: Ira Levy, Gundula Levy, Magda Levy. He pulled a lipstick tube from his pocket, one of the many lipsticks he'd found in Miss Levy's apartment, and wrote on the black marble wall:

MERA LEVY   SKIP BOWLING

In pink lipstick. After Skip's name, he drew a pink triangle.

Pandora leaned forward and kissed the triangle, leaving a shadow of red lipstick on the pink triangle. The black wall with endless names reflected their images back at them, distorted like shadows of themselves. Pandora opened her bag and pulled out three of Miss Levy's caps, put one on each of them.

Then, they all walked down to the edge of the pond and glanced at their reflections on the transparent tar black water and couldn't help but smile.

Pandora flipped on her boom box, started to lip-synch,

> *I'll be loving you*
> *Always,*
> *With a love that's true*
> *Always . . .*

> *Days may not be fair always,*
> *That's when I'll be there always.*
> *Not for just an hour,*
> *Not for just a day,*
> *Not for just a year,*
> *But always.*

> *I'll be loving you*
> *Always,*
> *With a love that's true*
> *Always.*

Marina, Gabriel and Jesus wrapped their arms around one another and swayed together to the music. The sun had now slid farther down the sky. Jesus untied the balloons from the urns, tied them to his wrist. He took off his shirt and pants and waded across the pond in his Fabrizio briefs. He climbed up the giant green arm and sat in the gigantic green hand. Gabriel took the top off the golden urn and held it up in his hands. Marina took the top off the silver urn and held it up in her hands. Pandora grabbed a handful of pink hibiscus petals from her bag. They looked up, watching the setting sun. The sky streaked orange and pink. Jesus looked golden.

When the sun reached the point where the giant hand was grasping the ball of fire, Jesus started to count. "Ten, nine, eight, seven, six, five, four, three, two, one."

Jesus released the balloons as Marina and Gabriel turned over the urns and scattered the ashes into the pond. Pandora threw the pink petals into the sky. The cloud of dust billowed down, white like powdered sugar, and spread as pink hibiscus petals stuck to the flat black water. Then the ashes sank, as the balloons floated up.

Venus Grows Arms

Jesus sat in Fabrizio's lawyer's office in the SunTrust building. He felt as if he were floating in a mahogany box ten stories in the air. The walls were lined with thick leather-bound legal books. He looked down at the island of Miami Beach spread below him through the glass window wall. He wondered what the lawyer wanted from him.

The lawyer entered his office. He was pear-shaped, with a weathered face and a few strands of hair combed over his scalp. The strands looked stiff and glued down.

"Tom Gliberman," the lawyer said, shaking Jesus' hand.

"Jesus. Nice to meet you," he said, standing up.

"Please be seated," Mr. Gliberman said, sitting at his desk. He shuffled through some papers and then handed Jesus a document. "This is the last will and testimony of Mr. Salvatore Fabrizio."

Jesus looked surprised. He wondered what this had to do with him.

"On page five,"—the lawyer cleared his throat—"the will reads: 'I, Salvatore Fabrizio, leave to my friend, Jesus Mas Canosa, the sum of ten million dollars and my property located on Ocean Drive known as the House of Fabrizio and all the furniture and fixtures and personal effects within said property.'"

"*Que?* What?" Jesus asked, shocked. "What you mean?"

The lawyer shook his head and smiled. "What I am saying is that you are a very rich young man."

Jesus shut his eyes, thought he was dreaming.

"There is a caveat."

"A what?" Jesus asked.

"A condition."

Here it comes, Jesus thought. He knew it was too good to be true.

"The only condition I put on this gift is that a portion of this gift be used for charity. I leave this up to the discretion of Mr. Jesus Mas Canosa."

Jesus exhaled. *This America,* he thought. *I was right — the streets are paved in gold.* But he'd learned that the gold was the people. He thought of Fabrizio and Skip and Miss Levy. And the idea hit him. He would turn Fabrizio's house into a hospice for the elderly and people with AIDS. They could help each other. He would call it the "Salvatore Fabrizio, Skip Bowling, Mera Levy Arms." He smiled to himself.

Pandora Exorcises Her *It*

Farther down on Miami Beach, Pandora sat in the waiting room of Mount Sinai Hospital. She thought she would be scared, but she felt excited, elated. Soon her body would be right. Soon she would look like who she really was.

She put on her earphones, switched on her CD player, "I will survive." She leaned back in the chair and shut her eyes and lip-synched to the song.

Then a nurse tapped her on the shoulder. She had a beautiful smile. Pandora removed the earphones.

"They're ready for you now, dear."

Pandora followed the nurse up to the fifth floor. "You are beautiful," the nurse said. "You are the most beautiful woman who has ever come in for transformation."

Pandora smiled, took off her yellow sundress and bra and panties, looked at her *It* for the last time and then changed into a hospital gown. Two orderlies arrived and helped Pandora climb onto a cold metal hospital gurney. The wheels squeaked as they pushed her down the corridor to the operating room.

The nurse helped her transfer to the operating table. An anesthesiologist put on a blood pressure cuff, a cardiac monitor and an oxygen saturation monitor. The nurse shaved her pubic hair and put some tight stockings on her legs and then put her feet in stirrups.

The surgeon entered the room. His mouth and nose were covered with a mask. He had kindly eyes.

The anesthesiologist said, "You are going to feel a prick," and he injected the anesthesia.

She felt stinging, like a mosquito bite. She imagined the doctor was her lover and she was giving her body over to him.

Then the doctor started prepping her with antiseptic. It felt cold, smelled strong.

She smiled, imagined her body without her *It*. She felt really happy for the first time in her life, and drifted away.

Butch Plays with His Grand Slam Breakfast

At the Denny's on Lincoln Road, Butch sat playing with his Grand Slam breakfast. He had dark circles under his eyes. His hair was greasy. The eggs tasted like sawdust, the pancakes like straw. Every time he shut his eyes, he saw Skip lying on the beach, convulsing. Every time he fell asleep, he had nightmares about Skip searching for him, going from bar to bar, zombielike, in his Mickey Mouse ears cap, looking for him so he could finish off the job. Butch told himself over and over that he'd done Skip a favor, done what Skip had paid him to do. But that didn't seem to help. He couldn't eat. He couldn't fuck. He was afraid to sleep.

Happily Ever After

Farther up the beach, in front of the Venus de Milo Arms, Marina and Gabriel sat on a towel with a map of Florida printed on it. The waves broke gently and frothed onto the beach. A white ibis fished in the broken blue waves.

Gabriel looked up from Skip's manuscript, *The Venus de Milo Arms*. "The end," he said, passing Marina the last page. They had been reading it together ever since Skip died.

Marina saw the tears falling beneath Gabriel's mirrored shades. She rested his head tenderly on her lap. She patted his hair. He closed his eyes and inhaled her smell, and it was like a sleeping potion. He drifted off to sleep.

She stuck her hand in her pocket, felt the engagement ring made from the diamond off the golden key he'd inherited from his grandfather. She carried it around wherever she went. Yet she could not bring herself to put it on. In her other pocket was the chain with the key with the other identical diamond, the one that Miss Levy had left her in the envelope. She could not put this on either.

Marina's tears rained down onto Gabriel, asleep on her lap. His blond hair absorbed them, erased them. The sun was bouncing off Gabriel's cheek. She was afraid his face would burn so she held up her hands to shield his face from the sun, remembering when he'd done this for her, remembering that that was the moment she'd fallen in love.

Gabriel opened his eyes and saw her hands. This gave him the confidence he needed.

"Skip left me another envelope," he said, pulling it out of his pocket.

To be read by Gabriel to Marina on the beach in front of the Venus de Milo Arms

"I'm afraid to read it," Gabriel said. "I don't know why."

"It is kind of weird."

Gabriel opened the envelope. He felt like Skip was there. He pulled out the page. It was old and yellowed. He cleared his throat and read:

August 20, 1946
Dear Diary,
I cannot stand the pain. Today, on the beach in front of the Venus de Milo Arms, Alvin asked me to marry him. He gave me a golden key that he said was the key to his heart. He repeated my favorite Yiddish expression: A golden key opens all doors. A goldener shlisl efent ale tirn.
I love him but I am so afraid. I can't say yes. I am damaged goods. They destroyed me in the camps. I am afraid to be touched by anyone down there. I cannot have children. The doctor told me I am full of scars from the experiments at Auschwitz. I love Alvin too much to agree to marry him. He talks about having children all the time. I cannot give him what he wants. I am so sad. I can't stop crying. I am doing this for him.

Gabriel shook his head. Marina looked like she was in a trance. He read the other page of Miss Levy's diary that Skip had put into the envelope.

January 1, 1947
Dear Diary,
My heart is dead. I went to see Alvin. I set one of the diamonds that I had been saving ever since the camp on the golden key Alvin gave me, and set the other one, my sister's diamond, on an identical key that I had made for him. I wanted him to have my most prized possession. I went to see Alvin in his new home in New York City. I went to give him the key to my heart. I went to tell him everything, to see if he would still have me. That I drove him away because I loved him too much to saddle him with a broken girl. I arrived at his apartment. He was not home. The maid told me he was in the hospital. His wife was having a baby. I left the key with the diamond for him. My heart is dead.

Gabriel had always wondered what happened between Miss Levy and his grandfather. He wondered now why Skip wanted him to read these pages from Miss Levy's diary to Marina. He wondered what Skip was trying to tell them. "It's so sad. I'm sure my grandfather wouldn't have cared that Miss Levy couldn't have children," Gabriel said.

"Me, too," Marina blurted. "I can't have children. I had breast cancer. The chemo stopped my period. It never came back. My first husband left me in the middle of my treatment. Today is the five-year anniversary of the end of my treatment. They call it a cure after five years."

"Why didn't you tell me?" Gabriel asked.

"I'm broken also. I was afraid you wouldn't want me if you knew."

Gabriel smiled. "I don't care. I love you."

She reached into her pocket, pulled out the chain with the golden key with the diamond that Miss Levy had left her and hung it around her neck. Then she took the ring that Gabriel had made for her with the diamond from his key and put it on her finger.

Gabriel leaned forward and kissed her. The golden key around his neck touched the golden key around her neck.

SUNSTROKER

by Gabriel Tucker

I can't believe **South Beach** has gone from slum to brand name. Where are the street people, the beautiful gay boys, the gorgeous old people, the drag queens, the trendoids, the artists, the bohemians, the Hasidim? When did South Beach turn into Anywhere, U.S.A.? Where did the yuppies come from? Stepford? The club that put South Beach on the map, **Warsaw,** has become **Jerry's Deli.** Ecstasy and steroids have been replaced by pickles and sauerkraut. The Gay Club **Salvation** has become an **Office Depot.**

This month three great South Beach originals went to the VIP room in the sky: **Skip Bowling; Mera Levy,** the **Queen of South Beach;** and **Salvatore Fabrizio.** R.I.P. my good friends.

Jesus Mas Canosa (the face of **Fabrizio**) cut the ribbon to mark the opening of the **Salvatore Fabrizio, Skip Bowling, Mera Levy Arms.** It will be an AIDS hospice and senior care facility, housed in Salvatore Fabrizio's old home. Now, some of the last refuges of Old South Beach will have a comfortable place to spend their final years.

The late **Skip Bowling,** who used to write this column, has had his novel, *The Venus de Milo Arms,* bought posthumously by **Grove.** Meanwhile, the S&M boys at **The Meatlocker** on Alton Road have set up a defense fund for hustler/go-go boy **Butch** (whose real name is **Henry Jones,** from **Onawa, Iowa**). He has been charged with first degree murder in the killing of Skip Bowling.

The demolition derby continued when **Heinz Lerman** demolished two deco hotels, **The Futuro** and **The Americana**. These buildings were built in 1950, which was one year too late to be declared historic and afforded deco protection. He has broken ground for a forty-story convention center/hotel condominium project on **Ocean Drive** and **18th Street**. Rumor has it, the hotel is going to be leased to the **Loews Hotel** chain.

Marina Russell, the **Venus de Milo's** artist in residence, has been chosen to be in this year's **Whitney Biennial. Pandora Catherine Williams,** local legend and another member of the Venus family, was married this week to **Maxwell Beaverbrook III** in the **Battell Chapel** at **Yale University.** Pandora was resplendent in a shimmering white beaded **Vera Wang** gown with a full-length handmade veil of French point lace by **Esteban Cortizar.** After honeymooning in her hubby's house in **East Hampton,** she will be moving to his stud farm in **Louisville, Kentucky.**

Back in Clubland, South Beach continues to frenzy about the disappearance of **Chris Paciello.** After pleading guilty to murder, robbery and racketeering, he dropped off the face of the earth. Rumor has it he has entered the federal witness protection program.

Like rats abandoning a sinking ship, our original one-named boldfaces have scampered from South Beach: **Madonna** and **Sly.** Madonna's mansion on the bay has been bought by the world's richest dog and she is rumored to be moving to London to write children's books. I kid you not. Sly's home is set to become a housing development and he is moving to L.A. to make another hundred **Rocky's.** Much of our star-studded sandbox has turned into a drunken bridge and tunnel frat house. The **Hare Krishnas** are chanting all over, a sign from above that South Beach may be over.

But the ghosts of South Beach's last boom—**Frank Sinatra, Jerry Lewis, Dean Martin, Liberace, Tom Jones, Ed Sullivan** and **Arthur Godfrey**—are hanging with the new IT crowd: **Lenny Kravitz, Gwyneth Paltrow, Lil' Kim, Jon Bon Jovi, Britney Spears, Will Smith, Christina Aguilera, Leonardo DiCaprio, Toby Maguire** and the ever-present **Diddy.** South Beach continues to be a fame catwalk. Since I have been here it has gone from a place where neon goes to die to the place where **Paris Hilton** goes to puke.

J-Lo and hubby **Marc** have bought a multimillion-dollar love shack on North Bay Road. **Art Basel's** coming to Miami Beach has turned South Beach into an art world Price Club for billionaires.

South Beach is like a cockroach—no matter what you do, you can't kill it. It will survive! Well, that's it for this week, my pretties. Over and out from your new "Sunstroker" columnist, **Gabriel Tucker.**

This book is dedicated to the pioneers, dreamers, developers, drag queens, artists, celebrities, hustlers, grifters, models, promoters, characters, confidence men, snake oil salesmen and extraordinary people who came together at a very special time and together created South Beach, the last great new city of the last millennium, circa 1986–2000 **Luis Canales, Craig Robins, Debbie Ohanian, Patrick McMullan, Lynn & Daniel Gelfman, Mette Tommerup, Juliet Passati, Tom Austin, Susan Ainsworth, Sarah & George Plimpton, Francesca, Robert Chambers, Nick D'Annunzio, Tara Solomon, Emilio & Gloria Estefan, Nick Neuharth, Lupe, Dara Friedman, Mark Handforth, Jud Laird, Jeremy Jackson, Steph Lallouz, Elsa, Gundula Friedman, Christina Palesi, Starr Hagenbring, Denny Kaplan, Maida Heatter, Matti Bower, Nancy Liebman, Barbara Capitman, Diane Iannucci, Allison Blackwell, Tomara Hendershot, Daisy Olivera, Steve Hlavac, Richard Hoberman, Charles Schreiner, Cher, Bone Boys, Kitty Meow-Shawn Palacious, Calvin Klein, Roberto Juarez, Dana Keith, Juan Carlos Arcila-Duque, Christopher Ciccone, Diane Siquier, Mick Hucknall, Kenny Zarrilli, Abel Holtz, Barbara Hulanicki, Susan & Kenny Lyons, Oribe, Kasha, Martha Stewart, Prince, Pat Booth, Lady Hennessey Brown, Ingrid Casares, Jacquelynn D. Powers, Sarah Churchville, Pamela Brandt, John Hood, Jose Ortiz,**

Chrispy Soloperto, Norma Jean Abraham, Elizabeth Beracasa, George Lindemann, Esteban Londono, Allison Spear, Patricia Romero, Scott Price, Manny Hernandez, Star Lady, Anne Rice, Robert Miller, David Geffen, Judy Drucker, Bobby Radical, André Balazs, Cubby, Carl Zablotny, Michael W. Sasser, Jeffery Sanker, Edison Farrow, Patricia Field, Peter McGuire, Iggy Pop, Conni Cabral, David Dermer, Tomata du Plenty, Irene Marie, Ted from Ted's Hideway, Luis Diaz, Skull Sisters, Jeff Lyon, Cameron Diaz, Lou from Lou's Tattoos, Silvio Fittipaldi, Patrick Kennedy, Wendy Doherty, Ora, Eva, Carmel & Doron Ophir, Mark Haygood, Sandra Shulman, Christopher Makos, Andy Tobias, Barry Diller, Thomas Heidemann, Tony Mellilo, Neisen Kasdin, Chef Johnny Vinczencz, Danny Tenaglia, Todd Oldham, Susanne Bartsch, David Barton, Tony Goldman, Judy Cantor, William Kerry, Susan Brustman, Mike Mazer, Tommy Pucci, Napoleon, Nicola Siervo, Chris Paciello, Gillbert Stafford, Arel Ramos, Kent Karlock, Michael Musto, the Bee Gees, Karen Schacter, Donald Trump, Lesley Abravanel, Lydia Martin, Larry Edwards, Ricky Martin, Leah Kleman, Nam June Paik, David Kelsey, Gustavo Novoa, Larry Vicker, Doris Feinberg, Paul Arthaud, Ernie Levy, Connor Lumpkin, Patrick Riley, Debbie Harry, Mark Buonoconti, Anthony Addison, Pablo Cano, Fran Clougherty, Greg Aunapu, Ruben Pagan, Jorge Larios, Senufa, Jody McDonald, Manny Vallee, Fabien Ceijas, Harry Martinez, Pepe Botella, Andre Boudou, George Pelletier, Pat Booth, Andrea D'Ammigo, John Sex & the Bodacious Tatas, Jimmy Sadler, Pedro Almodovar, Tina Borso, Jaunty Jomolka, Kevens Celestial, Jenny Pickens, Becky Brownel, Jimmy Nickerson, Victor Farinas, Willy Moore, Jane Pittman, Teddy Gunther, Les Garland, Bill Booth & Annie Conners, Debra Ordway, Anna Williams, Becky De Los Santos, Irene Williams, Kiki & Unik, Mark Soyka, Dan Osteria, Edward Charles Visitacion, Tananarive Due, Dee Spence, Mike Skull, Amir Amor, Grace Jones, Suzanne Pallot, Richard Pullman, Mai Lai, Scott Hankes, Jennie Yip, Roberto Jose Burnett, Desiree Reyes, Phillipe Stark, William Lane, Michael Dorian,

Pilar, Michael & Mary Dreiling, Ronnie Ramirez, Horatio Ledon, Alan Roth, Alan Randoloph, Daisy Fuentes, Jennifer Lopez, Antonio Sabata Jr., Traci Lords, Ron Wood, Michael McManus, Jack Penrod, Susan Magrino, Iris Linares, Jordan Levin, Bambi La Fleur, Chris Falcon, Dah Len, Jett Kain, Sean Penn, Ramon Perez Dorrbecker, Tico Torres, Barbarella, Willy Charino, Elsa Benitez, Carlos Castellar, Miguel Delgado, Michael Kadosh, Oliver Stone, Anthony Salriver, Ester Percal, Scott Carey, Lourdes Castellon, Yves Dilena, Roman Jones, Bogart, Jon Jon Bubblegum, Leslie Doyle, Pinky, Michael Capponi, Merle & Danny Weiss, John Wright, Richard Perez Feria, Patrick Kahn, Oscar & Tina Perez, Sandre Rotofsky, Marlena Ess, Maryel Epps, Sam Notobartolo, Kenny Bernstein, Randy Underwood, Jerry & Sandi Powers, Walib & Suzy Wahab, Ralffy Boy, Cindy Carr, Frederick Rochas, Carlos Bentancourt, Ernie Harrell, David Keith, Arianne Brown, Jarel, Gilian Sacco, Carter Smith, Denise Gonzalez, Rod Hagwood, Ugo Colombo, Dennis & Debra Scholl, Samantha Stein, Gary Farmer, Dan Bowman, Bronzino, Whitney Donati, Jacques & Pascal, Michael Stevens, Phil Spector, Steven Tyler, Joan London, Gary Hart, Johnny Depp, Craig Coleman/Varla, Shaun Leibowitz, Dan Sehres, Tony C., Dave Thomas, Jon Secada, Omar Martinez, Morris Lapidus, Ty Basset, Valery Petterson, Marci Chariff, Yvette Saavedra, Woody Graber, Sara Lavine, Margarena Fernandez, Robert Ziehm, Victor Calderone, Sam Sahali, Rick Waldock, Helen M. Z. Ceverne, Steven Bawz, Lance Burnstein, Tatiana Packer, Ian Appel, Todd Saunders, Buck Lunch, Jimmy Page, Dr. Shine, Richie Rich, Carolyn Rahming, Lola Fuln, Mac & Mary Klien, Brian Mehmel, Todd Green, Robert Vandal, John Krohl, Jennifer Rubell, Regine, Jason & Michelle Rubell, Mera & Don Rubell, Johanna Stella, Joanne Benggio, Steven Schnitzer, David Sarner, Joanne Benggio, Stephanie Sayfie-Aagaard, Daniel Bates, Elaine Kellog, Brenda Dempsey, Claudia Bogen, Fred Fox, Judd from Picture Perfect, Jimmy & Lisa, Lee Brian Schrager, Lisa Ellis, Joey Bernal, Pilar Gato-Casero, Mickey Wolfson Jr., Ilio Ulivi Zingo, Marc Jacobs, Ross

Powers, Lenley, Dean Edward Smith, Mey Lynn Pellegrino, Robin Hass, Jim Mullin, Newton Paris, Michael Gruber, Tracy Phillips, Kennan & Betsy Seigal, Carlos Alfonso, Rolly Chang, Suzanne Lipschutz, J. P. Faber, Montse Guillen, Miralda, Mark Needle & Carol Jackque, Jaime Cardona, Michael Kinerk, Dennis Wilhelm, Sandy Gallen, Helen Reece, August Cook, Enrique Iglesias, Ivan Bernstein, Carolina Garcia-Aguilera, Michael Reece, Shelly Novak-Tommy, Buck Winthrop, Noah Lazes, Wilt Chamberlain, David Lee Roth, Raul Aguila, Christian De La Huerta, A. C. Weinstein, Prince Egon Von Furstenberg, Ashton Hawkins, David Naranjo, Thierry Mugler, Carla Romanoff, Mary Russell, Anthony & Alina Shriver, Joe Allen, Didi Allen, Michael Tilson Thomas, Shawn Lewis,Tyson Beckford, Amy Cappellazzo, Nat Rew, Jeffery Thrasher, Tommy Decker, Mother Kibble, Deeana Thomas, Valeri Donati, Lisa Cox, Eden Roundtree, Emmerson Fittipaldi, Alian Berrebi, Nicki Studs, Dan Crithchett, Gene Martinez, Julio Iglesias, Sonia Meneghetti, Troy Parsons, Kelly Blevins, Donald & Lisa Pliner, Mickey Grendene, Gilles Boulliard, Woddy Vondracker, Pierre Zon Zon, Stephan Johanson, Vanessa Nigro, Edna Buchanan, Jeff Donnelly, Beth Donlop, Frank Ricigliano, Tom Healy, Fred Hochberg, Judy Robertson, Claire Austin, Brette Sokol, Raul Suarez, Leslie Diver, John Lantigua, Nil Lara, Larry Edwards, Gorgina Bianchi, Michele Addison, Cladia Schiffer, Richard Johnson, Suzy Buckley, Laura Paresky, Leslie Wolfson, Richard Santelises, Susan Abrams, Lana F. Bernstein, Paul Crockket, Cookie Kinkead, George Whitehead, Mark Balzli, Nicky Von Tcharner, Massimo Furlan, Steven Dorf, Pamella Canellas, Diddy, D. J. Lippy, Carmen Electra, Bart Hoover, Anita, Nicodemus, Jeffery Chodorow, Howard Goldman, Sean Penn, Jonathan Weiss, Larry Calender, Ignacio Zavalia, Henrietta Robinson, Rick Carino, George Wayne, Jimmy Sadler, Lawrence Levy, Eugene Rodriguez, J. P. Parlavecchio, Anita Parks, Arturo Padron, Nicky Von Tschnarner, Patrick Kennedy, Ruth Beers, Chyna Bleu, Diana Yanez, Nelson Benedico,

Brette St. Claire, Evan Bernstein, Tim Hogel, Roy Hanson, Pascal Frattelini, Osmond, Norman Bedford, Stephany Lobado, Vanessa Brewster, Sofia Vergara, Peppe Cavalieri, Roxanne Scella, Scot Ferree, Ron Dietrich, Lisa Cole, Tony Sanchez, Yamir Perez, Sam Zaoui, Jeorge Napolean, Jenny Laboriel, David Resnick, Saul Gross, George Falcon, Jaime Ferrano, Bobby Drummond, Lilly Zanardi, Jose Ramon Diaz, Tommy Tune, Marco Norma, Howard Davis, Gilles Bouilliard, Keyes Hardin, Michel Theuws, Jack Gavelin, Rupert Everett, Martin Cis, Nathan Browning, Roy Azmir, Todd Nelberg, Robert & Ramiro Ramirez, Scott Ellis, Marcia Walkenstein, Robert Burman, Gail Meadows, Olga Solomina, Tara Gilani, John Herman, Simon Cruz, Mark Bosco, Zori Herman, Peter Bill, Philippe Protin, Marilyn Gottlieb Roberts, Cambell & Liz McGrath, Kevin Crawford, Ted MacLoughlin, Bobby Guilmartin, Gian Franco & Marina Meza, Dee Dee, Stephen & Melissa Horowitz, Holly Leventhal, George Tamsitt, Art Lavine, Damien Rojo, George Mangrum, Eva Pereira, Antonio Arevalo, Joan Fleischmann, Philip Nash, David Lombardi, Robet Ziehm, Cesar Balbin, Reynoso, Billy Labbee, Jan Canales, Bruce Weber, Marco Bertini, Jose Ivanes, Kyle Plyer, Mike Riflessi, Kenny Scharf, Joe Weiner, G. Jack Donahue, Maguy Le Coze, Nelson Fox, Jane Woolridge, Luis Landis, Jim & Laura Quinlan, Pietro Pagano, Luca Giussani, Nea Rodriquez, Bill Spring, Jay Carter, J. C. Carroll, Marcy Lefton, Kerry Simon, Michelle King, Alex Kellington, Claudia & Jaques Auger, Brian Crusoe, Didier Milon, Dick & Merrie Thomas, Steve Menendez, Heather Davis, Brigette Grosjean, Arthur Baron, Dana Ross, Efraim Rodriguez, Michael Miconne, Malcom Kelso, Klime Kovaceski, Jeffery Barrone, Renee Delaplaine, Mauritizio, Maria Contessa, Joe-Bon, Rocky Aoki, Janice Dickinson, Angie Everhart, Randee Gerber, James Daigle, James Raight, Steven Bauer, Joy Moos, Cindy Crawford, David Flower, Edwige, Sabastian Vilgrain, Carol Rollo, Peter Page, Ugo Columbo, Sandra Noriega, Mary Keating, Rebecca Walton, Jose Ramirez, Mike Mazar, Janet Jorgulesco, Lester

Kerrstetter, Paul Gabay, Donna Cyrus, Hubert Boukobska, J. P. Bonsale, Lenny Kravitz, Ashley Montana, David Vance, Gregory & Vanessa Petin, Alex Daoud, Fernando Garcia, Abe Hirschfeld, Cesare Bruni, Francis Milon, Cami Bonsignore, Donna Zemo, Matt & Klynt, Joe Mesa, Randy Sender, Neil Eisenberg, Skip Taylor, Lary Callender, Steve Rhodes, Lasez Hardin, Nelson & Romana, Steve Holloway, Lee Zolman, Sy Shardroff, Danny Emmerman, Valentino Cortizar, Tian, Barry Fritz, Simon Salter, Joseph Abrams—The Hat Man, Nelli Santamarina, Dina & Jeffrey Knapp, Slade Smith, Kirk Semple, Cathy Tuccio, Ellen Sugarman, Zuzu Linley, Terri Lynn, Susan Whitelaw, Lourdes Bennardo, Juan Sohecloz, Kevin Crawford, J. P. Parlevecchio, Michael Caine, Shareef Malnik, David Bracha, Mitchell Kaplan, Seth Browarnik, Marty Cyber Evans, Richard Duncan, Leo Nuñez, Jerry Bruckheimer, Bruce Braxton, Jaime Golb, Carla Fidel, Angelino, Patrick Reilly, Michael Tronn, Danny Santiago, Robin Byrd, Harold Vizethan, David Giles, Bridget Duval-Kennedy, Bill Spector, Sushi, Charif Saya Jeloul, Allison Kostas, Jimmy Rowan, Carlota Casas, Ernesto Arambatzis, Niki Taylor, Stephen Rosenthal, Nancy Leibowitz, Paco De Onis, Joey Carias, Olga Guilot, Susan Garfinkle, Fabrizio Brienza, Mohamid Kashogi, Mick Jagger, Steven Pericone, Johanna Wittgenstein, Rene Rosso, Scott Weinstein, Felix Gray, Felix Gonzales Torres, Joey Arias, Steven Zee, John Jacobus, Dan Sheres, Nancy Chariff, Christopher Siragusa, George Nunez, Alonzo & Tracy Mourning, Jason Barrata, Howard Austin Field, Barbara Cavauto, Gary James, Katie Maginley, Carlos Prio, Leslie Berckmans, Prince Fallah, Tom Belushi, Tito Puente, Tony Guerra, Micha Murakousky, Cedric De Pasquale, Joel M. Pierre, Stephen Keyser, Jose Gardia, Ted Taylor, Marcos De Olivera, Helen Clarke, Geoffrey Murray, Chef Jon, David Resnick, Peggy Bremmer, Sara Hamilton, David S., Nikki Mallon, Garry Fienberg, Greg & Nicolle Bilu Brier, Freddy & Carole La Grassa, Danna & Cheryl Dowd, Lenny Ruedner, Julian Bain, Fabio Moscoloni, Dominique Tordion, Tony Bird, Issa

Nevelson, Lori Capullo, Ana Claudia Choufany, Amanda
Johnson, Mary Luft, Roxana & Robert Rosenthal, Silvana,
Rocco Ancarola, Massimo Baracca, Michael Merlo, Michael
Gitter, Tonino Donino, Massimo Miceli, John Casablancas,
Rebecca Romjin Stamos, Shelly Abramovitz, Annie Acevedo,
Scott Robins, Scott Kasdin, Morgan Craft, Dean Kelly, Bobby
Brandt, Dr. Fred Brandt, Alex Delate, Tag Purvis, Keith
Paciello, Jared Margolis, Oscar Simon, Lino Ponton, Crystal,
Maria Cabrera, Nayib Estefan, Claudia La Branca, Adora, Mary
D., Nancy Ochoa, Cathy Leff, Rhoda Levitt, Ton Luyk, Rachel
Hirschfeld, World Famous Jay Johnny, Marisa Tomei, Michael
Gongora, Karim Masri, Hank Mayer, Michele Oka Doner, Eric
Newill, Bruce Orosz, Melanie Morningstar, John Veal, Sam
Robin, Dennis, Ross Goliwe Sawitz, Marc Cohen, Toni Sushi,
Wallace Tutt, Mel McFarlane, Nisi Berryman, Efrain Veiga,
Carlos Cisneros, Lin & Tied Arison, Norman Van Aken, Arthur
Forgette, Michael Harvey, Steve B. Hamron, Kimberly
Estheridge, Diego Ascaciear, Bob Macleod, Steve Byckjewicy,
Sara Hamilton Bailey, Xavier Maranon, Peggy Bremner, David
Seidner, Karina Restvepo, Sergio Silberheer, Mark Lehmkul,
Andrew Kostas, Andrew Roosevelt, Derick Daniels, Patricia
Borton, Shawn M. Santorufo, Neil Raven, Ingrid Hoffman, Bob
Lisicky, Jerry Statahos, Julie Fettin, Ken Strythers, Nestor
Torres, Nester Lao, RuPaul, Marlene Schmidt, Gigi Honey,
Craig Trentacosta, Roxy Bunny, Michael Baloo, Nicky Narcis,
Eva Diaz, Paloma Villaverde, Denise Di Prima, Damian Dee-
vine, Chayanne, Tara Russo, Uncle Dave, David Colby, Jimmy
Fishman, Thomas Kramer, Lauren Gallo, Gary Pini, Tommy
Pooch, David Herskovitz, Jamiyla, Robert Wennett, Mario
Cader-Frech, Steven Guttenberg, Gay Levine, Scarlet Aguilar,
Elaine Lancaster-James Davis, Mariana Mezza, Sean Saldino,
Steven Giles, Tom Laroc, Michele Pommier, Danny Cardosa,
Ricky Elias, Gianni Versace, Mike Mathers, Ruth Wastie,
Sergio & Melissa Sardina, Mark & Audrey Bench, Gary Santis,
Karon Pitchon, Bruce Bradley, Eric Milon, James Murphy, Don
Maginley, Jimmy Franzo, Anastasia, David Colby, Clayton

Townsend, Alex Campili, Eric Levin, Carl B. Dread, Mark Reid, Claudia Choufanay, Ian & Rita Schrager, Vincenzo Di Grazia, Valentine Andrews, Jean-Luc Brunnel, Pat McIsak, Stephanie Kerlin, Michelle Branka, Vanessa De Paredes, Hernan Chammah, Christian De Massy, Charlie Cinnamon, Michele Pomier, Heather Paga, James St James, David Padillo, Amy Creekmur, John Arango, Linda Bedell, Bob Koske, George Acosta, Jason Binn, Bill Wisser, Cynthia Clift, Anne Day & Spencer Reis, Dade Sokoloff, Paulo Zampolli, Paul Montana, Ish (Wings of Steele), Mickey Rourke, Al Guerrera, Guillermo Gonzales, Dennis Leyva, Amy Compton, Gerry Kelly, Andrew Sasson, Dora Puig, Laurent Bougade, Don Busweiler, Marcella Acosta, Dennis Rodman, Alex Rosado, Kim Starke, Israel Sands, Peter Erlich, Carlos Perez, Jeannie Echemendia, Ginger Beltran, Michael Heiden, Gregory Minelli, Buzzy Skylar, Kevin Arrow, Sophie Delaplaine, David Knapp, Dana Hotchkiss, Ian Maley, Peter Cohen, Janet Duncan, James Hyde, Anwar Zaden, Andrian & Sandrine, Deena and Stewart Stewart, Francis Smith, Ellen Jacoby, Louis Aguirre, Belkys Nerey, Craig Stevens, Megan Guip, Eric Vatel, Joey Delaney, Joey & Jessica Goldman, Suzanne Lambert, Chris Mayer, Rick Delgado, David Granov, Leonard Horowitz, Tara Riordan, Ilona Weiss, Conrad & Natasja Baker, Victor Azria, Marty Kreloff, Dennis Doheny, Don Russakoff, Lynn Howard, Nikki Novak, Tony Miros, Rony Seikley, Coco Lindao, Julie Jewels, Campion Platt, Desmond Child, Steve "Love" Menendez, Elizabeth Zotos, Auturo Sandsvei, Beth Studdinger, Sherry Harper, Anna Isabel Alvarado, Steve Sawitz, Marc Romero, Aubrey Easterlin, Ken Minahan, Bili Case, Carlos Alves, Barbie Krettinger, Todd Glaser, Adolfo Donati, Irene Giersing, Heidi Lane, Vincent Serpa, Al David, Anthony Missonaco, Eric Omores, Romero Brito, ViAnn Henderson, Casey Hardin, Marilyn Manson, Michael Arama, Antilla Laktoush, Willy Littman, Antonio Martucci, Maylene Gonzales, Michael Ault, Carlos LaForest, Nestor Iao, Chicco Secci, Pablo Alfaro, Maria Conchita Alonso,

Brett Masters, Stephen Saban, Gerick Edwards, Roberto Kahn, Raphael Theler, Dennis Britt, Geo Darder, Greg Calejo, Tina Malavé, Dimitrius, Inga Luzka, Eileen Ford, Janet Aptaker, Don Knaver, Teddy Segal, Willy Moser, Danny Garcia, Kal Ruttenstein, Mario Leyon, Alferdo Viloria, Peter Estrada, Basil Racuck, Violeta Stamenic, Frank Wagner, Dotty Larson, Dorothy Combs, Andrea D'Arrigo, Homeless lady that lived in front of the Amoco Station and painted, Lincoln Road Laurie, Rafael Theler, Shana Robins, Christian Hermant, Cher's Angels, Johnny & Tommy Turchin, Steve Nash, Jocelyn Kayz, Jimmy Pepe, Parnell Delcham, Natalie Thomas, Michael Bay, Dr. Ron Roskin, Dominique Galas, Diego Ratchets, Rene Rodriguez, the La Troya Guys, Mark Jacobs, Heather Davis, Lionel Reynard, Erinn Cosby, Dann Gais, Howard Miller, Victor Hugo, Corrado, Cole Haynes, Bill Hyatt, Andrew Delaplaine, Andy Avello, Natalie Fernandez-Roque, Mark Leventhal, Pierre Hector, Kristy Hume, John Demari, Roman, Seymour Gelber, Tracy Young, Jimmy Resnick, J. P. Kilpatrick, Tony Garcia, Henry Auvil, Ernie Serrano, Stanley Levine, Jude of Sempers, Kevin Aviance, Arthur Page, Alex Channing, Michael Aller, Sabino, Kyle Duval, Iran Issa Kahn, Joe Zamore, Kevin Gray, Sly Stallone, Toby Ansin, Rebecca Weinberg, Dianne Camber, Barbara Gillman, Katrina Ranks, Gus Remmy, Tim & Yolanda Hardaway, Fiona Bray, Alex Omes, Mark Benk, Cici, Peggy Loar, Cindy King, Ashley Scott, Steven Polisar, Lincoln O'Barry, Al Malnik, Noel, Bret Taylor, Tanino D., Cyn Zarco, Carlos Menendez, Tim Schnellenberger, Paulette X, Alvina Corado, Dirk Larsen, Mayra Gonzales, Tony Copian, Don Shearer, Joey Steffano, Michelle Vzasic, Franco Pizzorni, Cory King, Gigi & Roxy, Leo Casino, Linda Fanuff, James Butler, Kenny Nix, Bobby Stark, Terry Scott, Oribe, Hannah Lasky, Manuel Noriega, Dr. Aranow, Ellie Schneiderman, Mark Blanford, Max Warsaw, Jack Benggio, Steven Hurwitz, Ramon Guerrero, Ed Granda, Will Smith, Philippe Fatien, Michael Reece, Caren Rabinno, Hal Rubenstein, Robert

Reboso, Heidi Klum, Mel Schlesser, the guy who walks up and down the Venetian Causeway ("The Walker"), David Shannon, Bernie Teeple, Nels Fidel, Capucine, D. L., Esteban Cortizar, Brigitte Andrade, Sarah & Austin Harrelson, David Leddick, Janet Reno, Alexander Stuart, Charong Chow, Richard Jay-Alexander, Elizabeth Saltzman, Michele Addison, Claudia Schiffer, Skip Van Cell, the guy who drives a taxi and dances disco on Lincoln Road, Woody Vondracek, Lynn Bernstein, Margaret Doyle, Linda Polansky, Mel Mendelson, Rosine Smith, Paul Silverthorne, Sandra Bernhard, Emanuel Reiss, Sam Drucker, Richard Hoberman, Isaac Bashevis Singer, Christo Javacheff, Marty Ergas, Neil Berman, Jeanette Joya, Joseph Moseley, Ellie Schneiderman, Marcy Lefton, Dorothy Kohn, Chris & Angelo Dundee, David Paul, Tony & Kent Kay, Selma Bushinsky, Mona Cohen, Steven Ambrose, Robert Holland, the guy who lived under the Miami Beach welcome sign, Susan Gottlieb, Edward Villella, Susan & Dennis Richards, Laurie Bell, Jeffery Deitch, David La Chappelle, Adora, Sexcilla, Tag Purvis, Lorie Mertes, Richard Needham, Anthony Saulnier, Roberta Morgan, Rick Brochetti, Rosario Marquardt, Roberto Behar, Jauretsi, Andrew Reid, Brian Rochlin, Lynda Carver, Laura Sheridan, Stephen M. Cohen, Mary D., Pamela Jones, Connie Ploesser, Favio Behar, Joanne Rosen, Martica Trueba, Silvia Alvarez, Robert Levy, Jerry & Eva Capps, Cesar Sotomayor, Charles Recher, Les Garland, "Captain" Michael Faircloth, Robert Ricciardelli, Ellen Kanner, Morgan Crafts, Sebastian Vilfrain, Pandora Peaks, Stacy Robins, D. J. Shannon, Donatella Versace, Conor Lumpkin, Myles Chefetz, Cliff Finn, Anitra, Dan Paul, Tui Pranich, William Valdez-Zuazou, Jim & Bonnie Clearwater, Manuel Gonzalez, Sheila Elias, Susan Grant Lewin, Raul H. Piombo, Paul Levine, Linda Robinson, Liz Balmaseda, Nancy Moore, Nicky Kardaras, Efraim Conte, Alan Schulman, Alexei Labou II, Diane Siquier, Gigi Meoli, Stephan Dupoux, Sam Boulton, Kareen Johnson, Danilo De la Torre, Charlie Brown, Aaron Watty, Mark

Randazzo, Hunter Reno, Alex Rodriquez, Eric Smith, Cameron Diaz, Theresa Scharf, John & Susan Rothchild, Eugene Patron, David Hart Lynch, Roy & Lea Black, Lisa Cortez, Richard Bronson, Jerry & Victoria Moore, Beth DeWoody, Jose De Cordova, Richard & Valerie Beaubien, Jane Bussey, Rich Osona, Ian Schrager, Madonna.

I truly regret any omissions and misspellings.

Acknowledgments

I would especially like to thank my parents: Dr. Robert and Lynette Tucker-Antoni; my sister, Janine Antoni; my brother, Bob Antoni; my brother-in-law, Paul Ramirez Jonas; Michael Curry; Morgan Entrekin; Andrew Robinton; Gary Cohen, Lewis Oliver III; Tom Austin; Susan Ainsworth; Debbie Ohanian; Don and Mera Rubell; Jennifer Rubell; April Krassner; Glenn Albin; Milo Bell; William Wright; David Wolkowsky; and George and Sarah Plimpton for helping make my dream of this novel come true.